WICKED AGAIN

KATHLEEN AYERS

1

The Peak District, Summer

Marissa stretched her body out across the bed, discreetly pulling the sheet up over her naked body. She was sore. Deliciously so.

A large palm, fingers splayed possessively, rested just below her navel. The owner of the hand watched her, eyes shining like quicksilver in the faint, pink mist of morning light filtering across the bed from the windows. A shock of hair hung over his forehead, delightfully tousled from the previous night's activities.

Heat touched her cheeks just remembering what those activities had included. When was the last time a man had spent the entire night in her bed?

Years. A decade at least. That she had allowed Lord Haddon to do so while they were both guests at a tedious house party hosted by Viscount Pendleton and his mother was nothing short of shocking.

At least for Marissa.

She was no longer the reckless girl of her youth, but Haddon had been very persuasive.

Simon, Lord Pendleton, and his mother, Lydia, had arranged this little house party to not only remind everyone in Derbyshire of their wealth and importance, but also to announce the news of Simon's betrothal to Lady Petra Grantly. Lydia had spared no expense in her efforts to cement herself as the grandest lady in the Peak District. The food thus far had been exquisite. The musicians for the dancing the evening before had been brought all the way from London for the special occasion. Lydia had fairly glowed, moving about to boast of Simon's accomplishments in Parliament and imply with a wink that her son might well be Prime Minister one day.

Despite Lydia's best efforts, and that of Petra's mother, Lady Marsh, Marissa thought both women would find themselves disappointed. Marissa doubted very much that Petra would be marrying Simon.

"You should go," she murmured, admiring Haddon's beauty in the early morning light. It wouldn't do for anyone to see him leaving her room. At the age of forty-nine, Marissa prided herself on a lifetime of discretion in regard to her enjoyment of male companionship. She had first-hand knowledge of what it was like to be the object of gossip. Her family's notoriety had long ago assured Marissa rumor would always follow her. She'd no inclination to add to it.

Especially at her age.

A low growl was Haddon's reply. His fingers, large and blunt, tightened over the top of the sheet, searing her skin through the thin layer of linen. "Not yet, my lady."

A widower with four daughters, Haddon was handsome, charming and several years her junior. Marissa didn't take lovers often, but when she did, the gentlemen in question didn't look a thing like Haddon. No, her lovers were her own age or older. Distinguished. Balding. Perhaps sporting a paunch. Haddon, in contrast, possessed a body hewn from stone, not an ounce of fat on him. The thick mane of hair framing his finely sculpted features was the color of freshly turned earth in the spring, with no hint of a receding hairline.

Haddon tugged at the sheet covering her breasts, clearly determined to expose her body to the morning light.

Marissa was *firmly* against such a thing. True, her waist was still slim and she'd only a bit of gray in her hair, but she *was* the mother to two grown sons and thrice widowed to boot. Portions of her body were no longer the perfection they'd been in her youth. She'd noticed, much to her horror, that her bosom, once a wonder to behold, *sagged*. The previous evening, she'd been fortunate to have wine and the cloak of darkness to boost her bravado. Not so, this morning.

She clasped the linen more securely in her fists.

"Why do you insist on hiding from me? I humored you by dousing the lamp last night, but I find I'm not so tolerant this morning." Haddon lay on his stomach, entirely naked, a tiny smile tugging at his lips.

Marissa started to reply, but then a streak of sunlight fell across the expanse of Haddon's back, drawing her attention to the hard curves of his buttocks and thighs.

It was very difficult to look away, let alone answer him.

A trail of dark hair shadowed his chiseled jawline, giving Haddon a slightly disreputable look. He possessed high cheekbones that demanded attention but only until one caught sight of the silver in his eyes. A most unusual color, like the underside of the moon in the night sky. His eyes were slightly tipped at the corners and framed by lashes most women would envy. Haddon was incredibly attractive and much more exotic looking than any gentleman born and bred in Derbyshire should be.

"I'm no longer a young girl," she reminded him needlessly, acutely aware of her age in comparison to his. Marissa decided she was a novelty to him—a thrice widowed older woman from a notorious family conveniently trapped, as he was, at a boring house party. Still, she found it strange to feel so insecure. Marissa Tremaine—she still thought of herself as such and not as Lady Cupps-Foster—was the daughter of a powerful duke. She was rarely intimidated by anything or anyone.

"No. You aren't." Another sharp pull of the sheet revealed the tops of her nipples. "I find you to be well-aged. Like a giant wheel of cheese. Cheddar, perhaps. My favorite, as it happens."

Marissa giggled. "You equate me to a fine cheddar? I think I'd rather be compared to French wine or brandy. Even a good cider would be preferable."

"Ah, yes, you do possess a delicious aroma now that I think of it." He nuzzled the side of her hip. "I wonder if you taste as good as you smell?" The dark head disappeared beneath the sheet. A moment later the heat of his mouth traveled down one thigh, nibbling at the hollow of her knee as he moved between her legs.

Dear Lord.

Haddon made her forget *everything* but him, which was why she'd awoken this morning with a large, naked male snoring next to her. He was a rake, or at least he had been before he was widowed. She suspected that behind the veneer of doting father to his rambunctious girls, Haddon *still* was.

His teeth nibbled the sensitive skin of her inner thigh and Marissa's body jumped in response.

A wicked laugh came from beneath the sheet.

On principle, she avoided rakes, even reformed ones. Having wed two of them, she knew how much trouble they could be. Haddon might well be worth the difficulty though Marissa had no intention of finding out. A brief dalliance during a tedious house party to alleviate their mutual boredom was acceptable, but Marissa *knew* she couldn't see him again. Even if he hadn't been significantly younger, Haddon possessed the ability to make Marissa feel things she'd rather *not*. There was a reason she kept her relationships limited to gentlemen who would not stir a lick of emotion in her.

Not so with Haddon.

As he nipped his way up the inside of her thigh, Marissa arched back, feeling the response of her body, when she should have been pushing him out the door. Haddon was demanding in bed, taking control of Marissa and her pleasure with breathtaking intensity. Her past lovers were not so robust in their attentions, only mildly satisfying her before taking their leave.

Haddon *insisted* on Marissa's response. Devouring her until she was limp and draped over his chest. He'd done so at least three times last night. She could grow used to such treatment.

And Haddon.

Her mind rebelled instantly at the thought.

As soon as he'd taken her in his arms to dance last night, Marissa's entire being had seemed to fold around Haddon, the sense of belonging to him and *with him* so terrifying, she had almost refused when he insisted on sneaking into her room.

I haven't felt such a thing since Reggie.

Reggie, the father of her youngest son, had been the only one of her three husbands Marissa had actually loved. His loss had been devastating, leaving her adrift and grieving for years. Recovering from his disappearance and restoring her independence had taken great effort.

I can't go through such a thing again.

Her fingers twisted in the sheets of the bed as Haddon's ministrations sent small pricks of bliss rippling across her body. The pressure built slowly from the teasing pressure of his tongue until Marissa found herself rocking her hips into his waiting mouth.

Dear Lord, but he was skilled.

Haddon reached up with one large hand and palmed her breast, the callouses on his fingers adding to the sensation. Seeking out her nipple, he rolled the peak between his thumb and forefinger as his mouth moved against her. Haddon carefully drew out her response until a tortured moan escaped her lips.

An insistent rap sounded at the door. The doorknob twisted.

No. No.

Haddon flung one of her legs over his shoulder, spreading her wider, unconcerned that someone clearly sought entrance to her room.

A fist banged against the wood.

"I don't need my fire lit," she said in a strained voice, cursing the efficiency of the servants at Brushbriar and their determination to perform their duties.

Haddon's chuckle was a low hum against her skin.

"Mother." An annoyed baritone sounded from the other side of the door. "I need to speak to you. *Now*. Open the door."

Marissa sat up in surprise, her body crying out in frustration. Swatting at Haddon's shoulders, she wiggled to get away from him. "Stop," she hissed in a whisper. "Brendan is at the door." What was her son doing demanding entry at this hour in the morning?

Haddon pulled away the sheet until his face was exposed, deliberately flicking his tongue against Marissa while she watched, smiling at her the entire time.

"Stop," she begged. Haddon was *incredibly* wicked. "You've got to hide."

"Marissa," he replied calmly, tossing aside the sheet and setting his chin atop her stomach. "I am *not* going to hide."

"But you must," she said, pulling a pillow over her exposed breasts. "Brendan cannot find you here." She glanced at the window. Her room overlooked Brushbriar's gardens. "Perhaps—"

"Nor am I going to jump out the window to crawl down a trellis. You're not a twittering virgin I've seduced." Haddon didn't seem the least distressed her grown son was demanding entry and he was—

Haddon blew a stream of air between her legs.

"Stop this instant." She kicked until he finally rolled out of bed with a grunt, silver glinting from his eyes.

"Maybe it's best if Brendan knows I'm here." Haddon's eyes flashed with determination, turning them the color of old pewter. "Last night—"

"Are you out of your bloody mind?" Marissa stopped him before he could say more.

"I don't think I am. I've never felt more sane. Don't be stubborn."

"Mother, please open the door." A pause. "*Jesus*, is Haddon in there with you?"

Haddon shot her a triumphant look.

This was, beyond a shadow of a doubt, the most embarrassing and shameful moment of her life. Her son was about to open the door and see Marissa with her lover.

No. Not her lover. Such a moniker proclaimed a relationship. An understanding. This was a *dalliance*. She wrinkled her nose. The entire room smelled of sex. There would be no doubt as to what had taken place last night.

Repeatedly. Just the thought sent a flood of arousal through her.

And Brendan would *know*. She wouldn't be able to make an outlandish excuse about Haddon merely stopping by to take her for an early morning walk or something else equally unbelievable. She shot a pointed look at her lover, who was still naked.

Dalliance.

Haddon's beautiful, *skilled* mouth twisted into a mischievous smile.

"This isn't the least bit amusing," she snapped at him, grabbing the robe flung over the back of a nearby chair. Careful to keep her body hidden behind the pillow, she put her arms through the sleeves, only releasing the pillow once she was assured she was covered.

"You're being ridiculous. I've explored every magnificent inch of you, Marissa." His voice softened. "I find you beautiful. Doesn't that matter?"

Belting the robe, she shot him a pleading look. It was a lovely, thrilling thing for him to say, and Marissa's heart would have swooned had her very large grown son not been demanding entry.

Haddon shook his head at her before walking around the bed, unmindful—or at least uncaring—that his own body was so exposed.

And why should he?

Even in her mounting anxiety and mortification, Marissa couldn't look away. He was such a gorgeous male animal, all sleek lines and elegant strength, dusted with dark hair. Gentlemen she had . . . *dalliances* with weren't even the same species as Haddon.

He reached down and pulled on his trousers, taking his time to do so while Marissa gritted her teeth, resisting the urge to hurry him along. Throwing on his shirt, he picked up his boots and regarded her again, brow raised.

Oh God. He was going to walk out of here in his bare feet. Why not just announce to the entire house party he's been in my room? Perhaps mention it to everyone over breakfast?

"Brendan *can't* see you," she whispered, wondering if she would expire on the spot from embarrassment. "Please hide," Marissa implored again. "Under the bed, perhaps?" She gestured helplessly. "I think you'll fit."

"He already knows I'm here, Marissa." Haddon stalked toward her. His fingers brushed against her skin as he pushed aside the top of the robe with his free hand. Teeth nipped at the exposed length of flesh between her shoulder and neck. She gasped at the sudden stinging sensation before Haddon pressed an open-mouthed kiss to the spot.

A bolt of pure lust shot down between her legs, further stoking the frustration of her body still clamoring for Haddon's mouth. His hands. *Anything.*

"We aren't done, Marissa." The words were deceptively calm.

"But you have to hide," she whispered.

He looked down at her intently before his eyes widened slightly. "Are you *ashamed* of *me*?"

"It isn't shame, *exactly*," she started, hating the way his face clouded at her words. More like mortification. Or horror. Marissa wasn't completely comfortable with her children knowing she sought male companionship on occasion. The current situation was made worse by the fact that Brendan and Haddon were friends. *And* he was so much younger. "I only—"

The line of his jaw hardened. Pink stained the very tops of the magnificent cheekbones. Apparently, she'd flung the worst possible insult at his exotically handsome head.

Haddon's eyes never left hers as he walked to the door with purpose, stood to one side and very *deliberately* flicked the lock.

Marissa's mouth gaped open in astonishment, rendered speechless. She pulled the robe tighter. One hand went to the tangled nest of her hair. Could she fluff the pillows to dispel the shape of Haddon's head and pull up the sheets before Brendan glanced at the bed?

The younger of her two sons flung open the door within seconds and stomped into the room. Brendan was a big man and looked larger still in the space of her guest room. Scowling at Haddon, his fingers curled into fists at his thighs. Brendan liked to brawl and, given his stance, seemed about to throw a punch at Haddon.

"Brendan," Marissa stuttered hoping to avoid bloodshed. "How unexpected to see you so early."

"Apparently," Brendan growled, shooting another murderous look in Haddon's direction.

Haddon stared back, seemingly unconcerned that he may be beaten to death at any moment.

"Did something happen to Petra?" Marissa shouldn't have said such a thing in front of Haddon, but she was flustered. And Petra was the only thing she could think of which would bring Brendan to her room at such an hour.

"No. She's fine. Sleeping," Brendan said, wincing as he realized what he'd given away.

Marissa's eyebrows shot up, and a knowing half-smile tugged at Haddon's lips.

Brendan flexed his hands, his gaze shifting from his mother to Haddon. "I'll thank you to be discreet."

"Morning, Morwick." Haddon crossed his arms in no hurry to exit the room despite Brendan's obvious desire to pummel him. "Did you sleep well? You look tired. As if you were up most of the night. I didn't get much rest last night either, as it turns out."

Marissa blinked. *Must he be so blatant?*

Brendan made a guttural sound and took a menacing step in Haddon's direction. "Get the f—"

"*Good morning*, Lord Haddon," Marissa said sharply, cutting off Brendan's string of vulgarities.

If the two men came to blows in her room, everyone would wonder why Haddon was here, defeating the purpose of her dismissing him. Besides, there was a much larger scandal brewing, one which would rescind her welcome at Brushbriar. Unless she was very much mistaken, Brendan had just admitted to ruining Petra.

Haddon didn't move, the grip on his boots so tight his knuckles whitened. He didn't care to be dismissed—Marissa could tell. In fact, he was bloody furious about it. "We will talk later."

"Please excuse yourself, Lord Haddon." She tipped her chin toward the door, commanding Haddon with her eyes to leave. Didn't he understand the situation?

From the absolutely *chilling* look he gave her, Haddon did *not* understand Marissa's plea for him to leave. He seemed about to comment but must have thought better of it. Instead his lean form bent smoothly into a mocking bow. "Good day, Lady Cupps-Foster."

Marissa held her ground. She hadn't wanted them to

part in such a way, but maybe it was for the best. There was nothing to be gained by continuing their association beyond this house party. Even so, she took hold of the bedpost in an effort to keep herself from running to him.

He was only a dalliance.

He had to be.

Haddon shot her another frosty look.

She lowered her eyes. Marissa told herself he was only annoyed at being dismissed, his ego bruised at having been asked to leave a woman's bed. She doubted it had ever happened to him before.

Marissa didn't look up again until she heard the door close.

Brendan stared at the door for a moment before turning to face her. She expected a barrage of questions or even an angry rant from her son, but his pained expression immediately put her on guard.

"What is it?" A slow spill of dread crawled up her spine.

"You've got to pack and leave for Somerton immediately, Mother. I've ruined Petra."

Marissa wasn't shocked by her son's confession. Brendan and Petra belonged together. Anyone could see it. You'd have to be blind not to. "I assumed as much, but—"

"Mother, I've found Reggie."

"Reggie?" Marissa's knees buckled at the unexpected news. *Her* Reggie? Brendan's father, the previous Earl of Morwick had disappeared so long ago, leaving no trace, she'd finally come to terms with the possibility that he would never be found. There were even rumors, *horrible* ones, that Reggie had run off with another woman, but Marissa had never believed such a thing. He'd loved her. Reggie had left one day to hike and collect the fossils he loved and never returned. "But, how?"

"His remains were found in a cave, less than an hour's walk from Brushbriar."

"That isn't possible." She shook her head. "He wasn't headed toward Brushbriar that day, but up toward the tree line. And John led dozens of men to look for him." Indeed, the entire countryside had searched for days as John, the current Viscount Pendleton's father, had become increasingly distraught looking for his friend. Lydia had sat with Marissa for hours waiting for news of Reggie. But he'd never been found. Things had soured with her neighbors soon after. Pendleton had found a large vein of Blue John on his property and Lydia, absorbed with her newfound wealth, had had little time or inclination to tend to Marissa in her grief. The house party was the first time Marissa had been to Brushbriar in years.

"There's more, Mother." Brendan gently took her fingers, guiding her to sit on the bed. A stricken look had come over his features as if he couldn't bear to impart anything further.

"It's all right, Brendan. I won't fall to pieces. I'm only surprised." The news had taken her unawares, but just knowing that finally her beloved Reggie had been found would give Marissa some closure to that chapter of her life. She'd worried for years he hadn't had a proper burial, his soul trapped forever in limbo. "Did you find him?" Her voice caught. "At the bottom of a ravine? Lodged in a crevice? I was always afraid he'd fall and break his neck. He did so love to roam about and—"

"He was *murdered*, Mother." Brendan's voice shook. "Father was shot."

"But—" *Murdered?* Reggie had no enemies. *None.* He'd been kind. Loving. Absentminded. It was why she'd always thought he'd simply tripped into one of the holes in the limestone while out walking. Flashes and bits of her life with Reggie flew before her eyes in such a fury, she became dizzy.

I loved him so much.

"Are you sure?" she asked, even knowing as she voiced the question that Brendan wasn't the sort to speculate. He had to be sure, or he wouldn't have told her. "Why would anyone do such a thing?"

"For Blue John, Mother. An entire mine full of it."

"What? No!" She shook her head. "It can't be true." Ice seeped up her arms in a cold embrace, the shock threatening to overwhelm her. John and Lydia *had* become very wealthy after the discovery of the Blue John. Her fingers clutched at Brendan's arm as she struggled for breath.

It can't be true.

"The mine isn't on Pendleton's land, but *mine*." Brendan tenderly wrapped his arms around her, holding her tight to his chest. "I found the proof, Mother. It was Simon's father, John, who shot him." Brendan's voice caught, deceptively soft. "And Lydia helped. Simon has known the truth of it for years."

As Brendan finished speaking, he pressed a kiss to Marissa's temple before pushing her face against his chest in time to stifle the anguished scream erupting from her lips.

2

"My vision of a widower is an older gentleman with gout. He doesn't exactly fit the bill, does he? I'd no idea," a pause, "that *he* was *moldering* away in the country."

"I doubt very much he lacks for companionship, despite being so far from London. I wonder if he's looking for a wife. He has been gone from society for some time. Hopefully he hasn't brought those dreadful daughters along with him."

"I'm sure he has."

"I suppose a new wife could send them all off to boarding school." A twitter. "He's quite skilled in the bedroom, according to the gossips. Perhaps I shall take him as a lover."

The smile on Marissa's lips faltered at hearing the conversation behind her. The newspapers had been full of the handsome widower's return to society after so many years. Although, if he *was* looking for a new wife, Marissa wondered that he had to come all the way to London to find one. Haddon could surely have found someone closer to home. Although, she supposed London held a variety of amusements for an attractive, charming gentleman.

"Haddon has many admirers." The woman behind Marissa lowered her voice to a discreet murmur. "He'll have no trouble finding a wife among them."

A small speck of pain, unexpected and unwelcome, tightened across her chest. Marissa was sure she'd left anything akin to tender emotion behind in the Peak District. Purposefully.

"Marissa? What is it?"

Adelia, Lady Waterstone, Marissa's closest friend and confidant, peered at her, pretty face alit with concern. "I daresay you've become quite pale. Shall I pinch your cheeks?"

Adelia's tower of auburn hair tilted in Marissa's direction. Styled in an elegant display of curls and ribbons, her hair appeared to be more the topping of a cake than a coiffure. Diamonds swayed dramatically from Adelia's ears as she made a great show of examining Marissa for some defect.

"I don't need my cheeks pinched, Adelia. It is only all the smell of pomade in the air which makes me a bit ill. Reminds me unpleasantly of Cupps-Foster." Marissa hadn't cared much for her last husband, who had worn an excessive amount of pomade and whose breath had always carried the scent of peppermints and gin. Thankfully the marriage, like her first two, had been short-lived.

"*I* think you were listening." Adelia leaned over until one of her earrings nearly batted Marissa in the eye. "To the conversation behind you."

Marissa put a finger to her lips, quieting her friend and nodding. They both stayed perfectly still for a moment longer, but the two women's conversation had turned to the disparagement of Lord Talbot's waistcoat before the rustling of skirts met her ears and the women moved away.

"Germania Woodstock and Rowena Helmsworth. Two gossiping ninnies on the search for new lovers to ease their boredom with their husbands. They've gone to circle the refreshment tables and cast their nets elsewhere." Adelia looked at someone over Marissa's shoulder. "What had you so captivated, darling? Surely it wasn't Talbot's choice of clothing."

"I thought I overheard something of interest, but I was mistaken." The last thing she wished to discuss with Adelia was Haddon. Her friend would latch on to the fact that Haddon was not only attractive, but younger and speculate as to how Marissa had managed to meet such a gentleman. She'd ask endless questions, none of which Marissa wished to answer.

I've only just managed to put thoughts of Haddon aside.

Not completely, but—

"You're frowning." Adelia snapped her fan against Marissa's wrist. "Women our age can't *afford* the wrinkles so stop this instant." She nodded toward Marissa's dark hair swept up into an elegant chignon. "At least you took my advice. Your maid did an excellent job."

"She did. The apothecary mixed exactly the correct shade, as you said he would." Adelia had suggested to Marissa several weeks ago, when she was bemoaning the gray in her hair, to seek out a small shop tucked away in an alley just on the other side of Bond Street. Mr. Coventry's apothecary specialized in lotions, dyes and other tricks to assist in the illusion of youth or prohibit an unwanted pregnancy.

At least I'm in no need of those services. There were times

Marissa bemoaned the fact she could no longer have a child. It reminded her *unpleasantly* of her age.

"I don't know what I'd do without Mr. Coventry. The man is a treasure." Adelia espoused the virtues of the apothecary.

Marissa eyed Adelia's mass of auburn hair. She'd never seen a spot of gray. Her friend must spend a small fortune at Mr. Coventry's shop.

"Dear Lord, *who* is that?" Adelia stopped waving her fan, her eyes stuck on the far corner of the ballroom. "My *God*, look at those cheekbones." She made a low purr. "He has the look of a Viking or some other *delicious*. . .marauder."

"How would you even know what a Viking looks like? And they were rather barbarous, Adelia. Burning down convents can hardly be considered seductive."

Adelia shrugged. "Allow me my fun, Marissa. Not all of us are determined to become dull matrons. Especially when there are gentlemen like him floating about. My, he looks very *capable*, doesn't he?"

Marissa turned slowly, knowing the moment Adelia had extolled the virtues of his cheekbones it would be Haddon she'd see.

She was right. He *did* have the look of a bloody Viking, standing against the far wall with his arms crossed, his powerfully masculine form a contrast to the dandified gentlemen surrounding him. Spectacularly dressed in dark evening wear, expensively cut and tailored to fit him like a second skin, Haddon was drawing every feminine eye in the Cambourne ballroom.

And why would he not? Marissa took in the stretch of his coat across his broad shoulders, admiring the flex of muscles beneath the fabric. Haddon needed no padding, as some gentlemen were wont to use, in order to cut such a fine form. Marissa had traced the lines of all that beautiful sinew with her own fingertips and could testify to the fact.

A delicate shiver tickled her skin.

Marissa had been on the receiving end of Haddon's attentions, and despite her determination to put him from her mind, relived every second with pathetic regularity. It was really rather sad. She hadn't taken a lover since returning from her visit to the Peak District. Not since Haddon.

He looks smashing.

They hadn't spoken since that fateful day at Brushbriar, when Brendan had stormed into her room and informed her his father had been murdered by their hosts. Marissa had fled the estate after dressing, barely pausing to inform Brushbriar's startled butler she'd send for her things. The news of Reggie, the absolute *rage* filling Marissa at the duplicity of John and Lydia, had managed to blot out everything else.

Even Haddon.

She'd felt guilt over not speaking to him again, not even to tell him goodbye. But at the time, Marissa hadn't been capable of coherent thought. He'd written her, asking to call. But she'd ignored his letters, telling herself it was best they not continue their relationship.

It was not a relationship. It was a dalliance.

Marissa had only stayed in the Peak District long enough to arrange a quiet burial for Reggie. The tears she'd cried as he was laid to rest were full of more anger than grief. Her husband had been killed by his best friend. Not a unique tragedy, she supposed, but one she intended to avenge. She'd left as soon as Brendan had wed Petra.

Her eyes strayed to the angelic-looking young lady

hovering at Haddon's elbow, adoration shining from her pretty features as she gazed up at him.

Lady Christina Sykes, daughter of the Marquess of Stanton. Lady Christina was speaking to Haddon, her hands fluttering delicately as she sought to retain his attention. His dark head tilted in the direction of her shining gold coiffure, giving the appearance he was hanging on her every word.

Marissa had her doubts. Nothing Christina Sykes had ever said was of the least import.

Haddon chose that moment to look up, silver eyes flashing at Marissa from across the ballroom as he caught sight of her. A small frown appeared on his beautiful lips.

"Oh my." Adelia raised a brow, looking askance at Marissa. "You *know* him."

"Not well," she lied smoothly, wondering what Haddon was thinking. Warmth crept up her body the longer he watched her, as if she were sinking into a warm bath.

Adelia snorted in disbelief. "*Really?*"

"Don't make such a sound, Adelia. It's reminiscent of a pig." She ignored the quiet hiss of outrage from her friend, unable to tear her gaze from Haddon's. The attraction between them, the one she so desperately wished to ignore, sparked sharply to life. The flame snaked through the crowd of well-dressed society to embrace Marissa, just as it had during the house party at Brushbriar. She'd spent months telling herself they'd been drawn to each other only out of boredom.

How very wrong she'd been.

"I made his acquaintance while visiting Brendan this past summer," she heard herself say to Adelia. "At a house party, of all things. A rather dull one." Her pulse fluttered madly as Haddon excused himself from Lady Christina

Sykes and strode purposefully in Marissa's direction, stalking toward her as a hunter does its prey.

Oh, dear.

Lady Christina pouted dramatically at Haddon's departure, which made her even more exquisitely beautiful. Like a hothouse rose.

"Naughty girl. Taking up with a gentleman like that," Adelia murmured. "And not *telling* me. Here I was, growing concerned that you seem to prefer solitude or worse, that you only desire to surround yourself with bland, decrepit things like Enderly. Haddon shows *much* more promise."

"Enderly is far from decrepit." Enderly was a lovely older gentleman whose acquaintance Marissa had made upon returning to London. His interests were in politics and politicians, and he was particularly enamored with Viscount Pendleton. Marissa was marginally attracted to Enderly, but far more interested in his political connections. An affair with Enderly would be pleasant. He wouldn't devour her like a starving man nor threaten her heart in the least. An understanding with him would be considered appropriate *and* respectable.

Versus an affair with Haddon, which would not.

Adelia shot her a knowing look. "Tell me."

Marissa kept her expression bland. "There's nothing to tell, Adelia."

Adelia swatted her with her fan. "Liar."

Haddon stopped halfway across the ballroom to speak to two gentlemen, neither of whom Marissa recognized. One slapped him on the back in greeting and pointed in the direction of the room set up for cards. He smiled and nodded, but the silver gaze never wavered from Marissa.

"Goodness. I've torn the ribbon on my slipper," Adelia said from beside her.

"Adelia, don't you dare desert me at such a time." Marissa lifted her chin in polite inquiry, making sure her features displayed none of her inner turmoil. She instructed her heart to be still and not flop about in her chest as if she were having a fit of apoplexy. Had he affected her this way when she'd first seen him at the house party across the length of Pendleton's dining room table?

Yes. I nearly melted into a puddle as he watched me sip my wine.

"I must repair my slipper immediately, darling. I wouldn't want to trip when I'm claimed for a dance, as we both know I will be. You can thank me later. And I'll expect a full recounting." She winked, wandering off into the crowd though Marissa doubted Adelia would go any further than the refreshment table. She was far too curious.

"Damn," she said under her breath as he drew closer, automatically smoothing down the folds of her new gown. A stunning creation of sapphire with brilliants sewn across the bodice and skirt with silver thread, the color matched her eyes. An egg-shaped diamond, a gift from her father some years ago, hung from her neck, drawing attention to her dangerously low neckline and the swell of her breasts. Diamond and sapphire earrings dangled from her ears. And with a silent thank you to Mr. Coventry, not a spot of gray shone in her dark hair. She looked her best to greet her former lover.

Dalliance.

Despite wanting to forget him, the memory of Haddon never left Marissa, no matter how busy she had kept herself since her return to town. The destruction of Simon and his mother *did* take up a great deal of her time. And of course, she had holiday festivities to plan. Haddon shouldn't have entered her thoughts at all.

"Lady Cupps-Foster." The light, spicy scent Haddon favored hovered about his broad shoulders as he bowed before her.

Marissa inhaled sharply, filling her nostrils. Haddon's scent had stayed with her, lingering along with her memories of him and the night she'd spent in his arms.

He took her hand, eyes flitting across her bosom as he straightened, a soft purr of male appreciation coming from his chest. The brush of his lips against her knuckles sent a tendril of warmth from her core to slide between her legs. But the touch of his tongue made her knees buckle.

Marissa abruptly snatched her hand from his.

A mischievous grin crossed his lips, meant to disarm her and indeed any lady he bestowed it upon. It made him quite irresistible.

An image of Haddon walking toward her, naked, the same grin firmly in place on his lips, flitted before her eyes.

The ballroom had grown very warm. She resisted the urge to fan herself.

Realistically, for any woman her age, there was always *bound* to be someone in the room she had been involved with. Two of Marissa's previous lovers were at the Cambourne ball tonight, in fact, though she couldn't for the life of her remember how *they* looked naked, nor, upon greeting them tonight, had she felt as if her heart might burst from her chest.

"Lord Haddon, how lovely to see you again."

"Isn't it though?" His grin widened further. "Dance with me?" he said as the musicians began to play. Without waiting for an answer, Haddon took her hand in his and led her out to the dance floor, his grip on her fingers tight as the sapphire skirts of her gown wrapped around them both.

Marissa had always found the sensation of silk hugging

her to a gentleman as they danced to be mildly erotic, though much more so with Haddon than, say, Enderly.

Haddon was a graceful dancer, confident and agile. Turning her expertly, he brought Marissa closer to the lean lines of his body with each twist of his hips. They moved easily together, as if they'd danced many times in each other's arms.

In truth, they had only danced once before.

The warmth of his palm splayed intimately across the small of her back, fingertips pressing into the skin at the base of her spine.

The pressure was seductive. Enticing. Haddon had kissed that very spot during their night together, as well as a great many other places.

She saw Adelia out of the corner of her eye watching them with a smug look.

"How have you been, Marissa?" The husky growl of her first name sent bits of flame across her arms. "Enjoying London?"

"I'm quite well, thank you. I didn't realize you'd come to town." The tips of her breasts chafed against the fabric of his coat, stroking her nipples each time he turned her; it was distracting, to say the least.

A tiny smirk crossed his beautiful mouth. He knew she was lying.

"I don't come as often as I did before my wife died. My daughters require my attention, as does my estate. London does not."

Haddon had been married very young in a match arranged by his father. His wife had been sickly and bedridden during the latter part of his marriage, the birth of his youngest daughter destroying what remained of her fragile health.

In between bouts of lovemaking, they'd whispered to each other in the dark and Haddon had told Marissa of his marriage.

Another thing she hadn't done with a previous lover. *Dalliance.*

He had left out his former rakish reputation, and well he might. Though discreet, Haddon certainly had cut a swath through the ladies of London. But unlike most husbands who wouldn't have cared to be saddled with an ill spouse, he'd been with his wife when she died, at her bedside. After, he had not returned to London to pick up the threads of his life; instead, he'd stayed away from town, choosing to remain with his daughters in the country. Another thing most gentlemen would not have done.

"I brought Jordana to London with me." He mentioned his eldest daughter, to whom Marissa had been introduced to at Brushbriar.

"And how does Jordana like town?" Marissa found it hard to have a casual conversation with Haddon, especially when his hips kept brushing hers.

"As well as can be expected. But I thought she might enjoy some time here before making her debut. Ease her into things, so to speak. Jordana has a tendency to be stubborn."

Marissa thought that a gross understatement. Haddon's eldest had made it no secret at Brushbriar that she'd wished to be anywhere but there. Nor did she show the slightest interest in London or society. Haddon was wasting his time trying to introduce her to life in town. Jordana was defiant and prone to sulking, behavior that would not endear her to a future husband. She reminded Marissa a great deal of her niece, Arabella.

Haddon twirled her, the motion forcing her more fully

against his chest. The distance between them was only one tiny, heated inch.

"You left before I could tell you goodbye," he said, breath warm against her temple.

"Did I *need* to tell you goodbye?" Her own guilt at not doing so made her reply sharper than she intended.

His grip on her tightened. "I suppose not."

"After the discovery of my late husband's remains, I was in shock, as you can imagine." That was putting it mildly. The anger which filled her had frozen the blood in her veins until Marissa could think of nothing but how she would punish Simon and Lydia.

"I'm sure you were."

"I wasn't up to receiving callers, nor did I wish to receive polite condolences," she said.

"Of course," he agreed coolly.

Marissa bristled. Something about his calm manner, his instant agreement with her, smacked of judgement. It was clear by his attitude Haddon thought she *should* have received him. Sent him a note. Told him goodbye. She didn't care for him acting the discarded lover.

Dalliance.

"Ours was a *brief* acquaintance, Lord Haddon," Marissa said politely, allowing a hint of chill to enter her words. "Little more than a dalliance, if you'll forgive me for saying so."

He looked down on her, eyes like quicksilver. A touch of pink shone on his magnificent cheekbones, a sign of his annoyance, perhaps, though it could have been a trick of the light. "A dalliance?"

"A *tryst*, if you prefer."

"A tryst?"

Would he repeat everything she said? "Our relationship

would have invited speculation and unwanted attention, both things I don't care for. An older widow carrying on with—"

"Dear God, Marissa." He looked away from her, the corner of his lip lifting into something resembling amusement. "You didn't seduce some innocent young lad; stop behaving as if you did."

"*I* didn't do any seducing," she shot back.

"Debatable. I was under the impression we seduced each other, not out of boredom, as I'm sure will be your next point, but because we were *meant* to." His broad shoulders gave a soft roll.

Marissa stayed silent, uncertain how to respond.

"You know, I never really *considered* your *elderly* status at the time, but you brought it up so often during our *brief* acquaintance, perhaps your concerns have merit."

"They do?"

"You're a highly intelligent woman. Older and wiser than I. Shouldn't I listen to your counsel?"

The heat of him bled through the thick silk and layers of petticoats, caressing her skin as they danced. Each time he spun her, Haddon managed to notch the length of one muscled leg into her skirts and between her legs. Deliberately.

"Stop doing that," she hissed beneath her breath. A slow, honeyed ache followed the movement, driving her mad. "Do you intend to cause a scene?"

"What? This?" He pulled her a fraction of an inch closer and moved his thigh into her skirts again, sliding his leg in a sinuous motion. "I'm merely dancing."

A flutter of arousal slid down the length of her body at Haddon's very calculated teasing though Marissa was doing her best to ignore the sensation. Desperate to provide a distraction, she said, "I see you've made the acquaintance of Lady Christina Sykes."

"An incomparable beauty with an impeccable lineage," Haddon acknowledged. "A gentleman could do worse than to wed her. She's a lovely girl."

"She's very young," Marissa said, hating the prick of jealousy at the thought of Haddon dancing with Lady Christina the way he danced with her.

"You don't sound as if you approve. Shouldn't I seek someone closer to my own age? I'm barely out of the schoolroom, after all." The mischievous grin, the one she found so endlessly endearing, floated across his mouth.

Marissa forced herself to smile up at him. "I'm sure my approval is of no consequence. I'm only concerned."

"How very *maternal* of you, Marissa."

She deliberately stepped on his toe.

Haddon grunted in pain.

"Lady Christina is barely older than Jordana," she said. "But it is none of my affair who you deem a suitable bride. If your aim is to find a wife, Christina Sykes would serve as well as any." She forced the words up her throat though they left a bitter taste.

Spinning her about, he gave her a wolfish grin before murmuring, "The lady doth protest too much."

Her heel ground into the top of his foot. "Pardon me. I seem to have two left feet this evening. Goodness."

Haddon's fingertips dug into the silk at her hip. "I'm only acknowledging the *vast* difference in our ages. One you've brought to my attention repeatedly during our previous *dalliance. Are* you old enough to be my mother?" He pretended to consider the question. "Good lord, how depraved I am."

Marissa was going to slap him, right here in the middle

of a dance with most of the *ton* watching. "While there is an age difference, my lord, I assure you—"

"And in regard to Christina," he interrupted her tirade, "you also suggested during our *dalliance* that I need to remarry. Truthfully, I hadn't considered wedding again until you brought it to my attention. Again, I'm thankful for your guidance."

She bit her lip, knowing she couldn't refute his claim. Haddon was correct on all counts. She *had* been the one to bring up his need to remarry and produce a male heir. At that moment, Marissa could have cheerfully kicked herself for reminding him of his duty.

In addition to his age and his need for an heir, there was *also* the added complication of Simon and his murderous mother Lydia. Haddon and Pendleton were friends.

Haddon was wrong for her in every way she could imagine.

"I've something I wish to discuss with you, my lady."

"Oh?" There was a slight, hopeful leap of her traitorous heart before remembering it would be best if she didn't allow him to seduce her again. Haddon was far too dangerous. They could remain acquaintances and nothing more.

"May I call upon you? I would prefer not to have a private discussion here."

"Yes, of course," she agreed, ignoring the slight racing of her pulse.

The dance ended, and Haddon led her off the dance floor, a wisp of a smile hovering on his lips. But instead of leaving her where she'd stood with Adelia, Haddon purposefully took her to the opposite side of the ballroom; an area populated with elderly matrons, wallflowers and spinsters.

A strangled sound bubbled from her lips.

"Something wrong, my lady? Didn't you enjoy our dance?"

"I did. Immensely." If she wasn't sure it would cause a scene, Marissa would wrench her fingers from his.

Once he seemed satisfied Marissa stood with the most undesirable women in the room, Haddon bowed again over her hand, hiding his enjoyment at her discomfort behind a polite, bland smile.

"Enjoy the rest of your evening, Lady Cupps-Foster." Haddon turned and, without another glance at Marissa, sauntered back across the ballroom.

DAMNED DIFFICULT DESIRABLE WOMAN.

Trent Ives, Baron Haddon, flexed his fingers against his thighs and strode away from the only woman at this bloody ball who held his interest. He'd come tonight specifically hoping to see her, and he hadn't been disappointed. Dancing with Marissa, holding her in his arms until the warm vanilla scent she favored filled his nostrils, was worth having to listen to the people around him prattle on about their own self-importance.

Trent looked down at Lady Christina Sykes, the daughter of a marquess who was trying to amuse him with a story about a stray dog she'd found wandering about her gardens. He kept a polite smile pasted on his face as she chattered away, all the while watching Marissa from across the room.

He loved her in blue; the color enhanced her eyes, making them sparkle like sapphires. She'd been wearing a gown of nearly the same hue when they'd danced together at the Pendleton house party.

I had no idea how one dance would change everything.

He'd known who Marissa was, of course, when he met her at Brushbriar. Everyone in the Peak District knew the tragic story of the late Earl of Morwick's disappearance. And of his widow's grief.

When he'd come to her rooms later that night with a bottle of wine and one glass, intent on seduction, Marissa hadn't turned him away.

Instead I was ruined. His heart gave a thump.

An older gentleman was fawning all over Marissa, ogling her bosom, which Trent admitted was justified, especially in that gown. Trent rarely lost his composure, remaining calm even in the maelstrom of four rather high-spirited daughters. But unexpected possessiveness flared up as Trent watched her smile and place her fingers on another man's arm.

Trent turned his attention from Marissa back to Lady Christina, who had been joined by Miss Archer, both women busy smiling up at him and batting their lashes. His body was still humming with the awareness of Marissa, her scent still clinging to his coat.

Patience.

Something else Trent was good at.

3

"Oh dear, you don't look the least pleased," Adelia piped up from behind Marissa, casting a glance at an elderly matron whispering to her companion with ill-concealed distaste. "And you're quite flushed." Adelia linked her arm with Marissa's, walking them both away from the wall of undesirable women. "Your Lord Haddon is scrumptious."

"He's not a cucumber sandwich, Adelia," Marissa snapped. "And he's most definitely not *my* Lord Haddon. He's too bloody arrogant." Haddon had certainly made his point by depositing her amongst these women.

"Most men who look like that are, my dear. My darling young soldier is just such a man. Crooks his finger, and I can't help but rush to his side to be entertained." Adelia gave a small laugh.

"I shouldn't worry. A young lady as pedigreed and gently bred as Lady Christina Sykes will likely sob and collapse into a mound of ribbons on her wedding night. I'm sure her mother has taught her to *endure*. If Haddon were to marry her, he'd be bored within a fortnight, if not sooner. And he's much too delicious to be bored. I should offer him my companionship while he's in London."

Marissa snapped her head around. "You'll do no such thing, Adelia."

Adelia pursed her lips in pretend shock. "I was *only* joking, Marissa. My goodness, no need to be so...territorial."

"I'm sorry. It's only my head has begun to ache." She placed a hand to her temple. Her head did hurt, both from the press of bodies in the Cambourne ballroom as well as from seeing and sparring with Haddon. "My apologies for my ill humor." Marissa took Adelia's hand. "I fear I must take my leave, Adelia." She'd no desire to be at the ball a moment longer.

"Marissa, you *cannot* leave yet. The evening is young. You've only danced once."

Once had been enough.

"Enderly has just arrived." Adelia pointed with a flick of her fan to a distinguished gentleman.

Catching sight of Marissa, the older man changed course with a wave and headed toward her. Tall and fit for his age, Enderly's form held only a touch of softness around the middle. He still had a full head of hair, though it was not the rich brown of Haddon's but the color of new fallen snow. Enderly *did* cut a dashing figure, she assured herself.

Marissa cast a sideways glance to Haddon across the ballroom.

It was like comparing an aging Persian cat to a sleek black panther.

I'm being unfair. Enderly is perfectly respectable.

Enderly, member of Parliament and wealthy mine owner from Cornwall, was perfect for Marissa. Widowed and in possession of a slew of sons and grandchildren as well as an immense country estate overlooking the ocean, he was *significantly* older than she. Enderly would *never* stay up all night debauching her.

"Lady Cupps-Foster."

Marissa looked up to find Enderly taking her hand with familiarity. The pale blue eyes twinkled at her. He smelled subtly of pine and mint. Not the least exotic.

"Mr. Enderly."

Enderly spared a glance at Adelia but didn't take her hand. "Lady Waterstone."

Adelia made a muffled reply. She didn't care for Enderly.

"You're looking quite lovely, my dear." His eyes strayed to her neckline in appreciation of her bosom but didn't linger overlong. She thought he was probably more interested in the diamond around her neck.

There was no shock of excitement at Enderly's presence. No whisper of arousal sliding up her silk-clad legs.

No chance he might break her heart.

Marissa bestowed a lovely smile on him. "Thank you, Mr. Enderly."

"What a magnificent necklace," he said.

She'd been correct. His admiration had been for the diamond around her neck and not her bosom. Marissa tried to summon up a modicum of disappointment and found she couldn't. "A gift from my father on my twentieth birthday."

"A mere addition to the jewel of your beauty, my lady."

Nodding in acknowledgement of what was a weak compliment and ignoring Adelia's mutter of disdain for Enderly, Marissa said, "I wasn't sure you'd attend tonight."

"I wouldn't miss the Cambourne ball, my lady, though I'm here more to play cards than to dance."

Of course he was.

"You've saved me the trouble of sending you a note tomorrow. I've been invited to a small gathering next week at Lord Duckworth's and was hoping you'd allow me to escort you. Lord Pendleton is speaking about the bill he is trying to gain support for in Parliament."

"I'd love to attend. Lord Pendleton is a passionate speaker and his reforms of great interest to me. I've been following his career for some time given that my late husband's estate borders the Pendleton estate, Brushbriar."

Surprise colored Enderly's features. "I didn't realize you were acquainted with Lord Pendleton." Ambition flared briefly in his eyes; he was likely already deciding how his association with Marissa could benefit his own relationship with Simon. "He'll be delighted to see an old friend, I'm sure."

Marissa doubted that. "I haven't seen him in years," she lied smoothly. "It will be delightful to see him again."

"Wonderful. I'm pleased to escort you."

"I look forward to it."

Enderly, obviously realizing he'd ignored Adelia and ever polite, proceeded to ask her about the weather, a topic neither of them found the least interesting. But it did allow Marissa the opportunity to watch Haddon discreetly.

A pretty, overly endowed brunette appeared to have him captivated, whether by her display of bosom or her sparkling wit, Marissa wasn't certain. She was blushing and giggling as she looked up at Haddon, completely oblivious that Lady Christina Sykes seemed about to do her bodily harm.

Miss Priscilla Archer. The girl's name popped into Marissa's head. *And she has a spectacular bosom. Doubtless much perkier than my own.*

Haddon lifted his head and caught her watching him. His tongue flitted out to run along his bottom lip.

Marissa's body swayed of its own accord in Haddon's direction, like a plant desperately seeking the sunlight, drawn to him regardless of her feelings on the subject.

He took in Enderly, a spark of dislike shining in his eyes. Raw possessiveness flashed across his features, starkly apparent against the bold slash of cheekbones, before his chin jerked back to Miss Archer.

Marissa put a hand to her throat. Perhaps Haddon *did* have Viking ancestors. For just a moment he had looked quite . . . *savage*. A tiny thrill shot through her.

I should never have called him a dalliance.

It changed nothing, however. The pull between her and Haddon only reinforced Marissa's decision not to involve herself with him again. Such passion would certainly destroy her, especially when Haddon's interest dimmed as it was bound to do.

"My lady?"

She refocused her attention on Enderly, hoping the heat she felt creeping up her chest hadn't resulted in a flush across her skin. "I'm so sorry. I fear I've a terrible headache, Mr. Enderly, and must take my leave."

"My dear, I'll escort you home." His brows drew together in polite concern.

"There's no need," Marissa assured him, stopping his gallantry with the slight press of her fingers on his sleeve. "Stay and enjoy yourself."

"If you're certain?"

Adelia rolled her eyes at Enderly's false protestations.

"I am." She winced as if the pain in her head was unbearable.

"I've a mind to gamble a bit tonight at any rate. But only

if you're sure?" At her slight nod, he continued. "I'll call upon you soon, my lady. And look forward to our evening at Lord Duckworth's." Bowing to both her and Adelia, Enderly wandered off in the direction of the room set aside for cards, snaring a glass of wine from a passing servant as he moved through the crowd.

"Decrepit," Adelia said, tapping Marissa with her fan. "I find nothing to recommend Enderly. He looks like a wizened gull with all that hair. Though I suppose for a man of his years, possessing any hair is a point in his favor. Do you really mean to," Adelia lowered her voice, "take him to bed? When you've obviously—"

"Adelia," Marissa cut her off. "While I appreciate your assessment of Enderly as a lover, I am not yet at such a point that he is under consideration."

Her friend blew a puff of frustration between her painted lips. "Fine. Wallow in his feeble form and take pleasure in his ancient arms."

"Stop." She tried not to laugh at Adelia's antics. Adelia was unashamed and forthright about her tendency to take younger lovers with no fear of risking her heart, nor did she give a fig for any gossip directed at her.

Turning, she dared another look in Haddon's direction, but there was no sign of those striking cheekbones and broad shoulders anywhere in the ballroom.

"I saw the look Haddon gave you, Marissa," Adelia said in an urgent whisper. "Do not be a fool. He nearly set you aflame with merely a glance."

"Good night, Adelia." Marissa pressed a kiss to her friend's cheek. "Try to keep yourself out of trouble tonight."

"Trouble will find *me*." Adelia winked. "In the form of a ravishing young soldier with golden hair. I plan to inspect him for battle scars. He's no Viking though,"

Adelia whispered before moving off in search of adventure.

Marissa took her leave of the ballroom, wondering at Adelia's ability to move from lover to lover with little damage to herself. It was unfortunate Marissa couldn't behave in the same way. Or rather she could, only not with Haddon, for some reason.

Sighing with relief at the cooler outside air, Marissa caught sight of her driver and strode to her waiting carriage, the stale smell of powder and talc which often pervaded events such as these no longer invading her nostrils.

Settling herself against the leather squabs, Marissa's skirts ruffled, and a whiff of Haddon's spicy scent filled the inside of her carriage along with the memory of their dance tonight. He was a graceful dancer, the sinuous movement of his hips subtly commanding Marissa to follow his lead.

Haddon made love in much the same way.

Her heart raced as if she was still a schoolgirl in the throes of her first crush. Hopeful. Giddy. A heady feeling of intoxication, one she hadn't experienced since Reggie.

Marissa looked out at the dark streets of London as her carriage rolled toward home, thinking of Haddon and Reggie. Wanting Haddon felt like a betrayal. Silly, she knew, especially since her late husband had been gone for more than two decades. Reggie had been taken from her when Marissa was so young, she often considered his death to be the end of her innocence.

I was never truly innocent.

She sighed and leaned her head back. As the beloved daughter of the Duke of Dunbar, a man known for his brutality in dealing with those who opposed him, Marissa had learned early on the nature of deviousness. Of revenge. How to exact punishment on those who harmed the duke or his family. Henry, her father, had doted on Marissa, blatantly favoring her over her older brother, Phillip, the heir. Her brother had never understood Henry or what he was capable of.

Kelso, Marissa's first husband, had incurred Henry's wrath by ruining Marissa during a ball when she was barely seventeen. A notorious libertine, Kelso had kept a multitude of mistresses and had spent nearly every night in his cups with a whore on each knee. Marissa's marriage to him and his flagrant affairs had been the talk of London, humiliating her to the point she'd made the mistake of complaining to her father, though he likely already knew.

Henry knew everything.

Kelso died in a brawl soon after, in an alley just a block down from his club. He'd left her a widow with a small son at the age of eighteen.

Cupps-Foster, her third husband, was a hothead. She should never have agreed to wed him. He'd made the mistake of treating her poorly in front of the duke during a dinner party. Barely a week later, Cupps-Foster had found himself challenged to a duel by a mysterious gentleman at White's over the slightest of insults. The pistol Cupps-Foster had used for the duel backfired, blinding him. His dueling opponent finished the job, then disappeared from London.

Henry had detested Cupps-Foster as had Marissa. She didn't mourn him.

Only Reggie, her second husband, had truly loved her, but still, she'd never been first in his heart. Fossils. Ore. Nature. Trees. All took precedence over Marissa. But she'd loved him so much she hadn't cared. Perhaps it had been her youth which had allowed her to lose herself so completely in Reggie. She'd never contemplate such a thing now.

If Reggie was still alive, would we be happy?

Marissa wasn't sure.

But nothing changed the fact that Reggie had been murdered by his best friend for a mine full of Blue John. Lydia had sat in her parlor at Brushbriar for years surrounded by her wealth, all of it bought with Reggie's blood. Marissa knew she couldn't prove who had murdered Reggie, and even if she could, John had died years ago. But she *could* take the mine. Simon's career. Lydia's beloved Blue John and the wealth it provided.

I am my father's daughter, after all.

4

Marissa smiled indulgently while Arabella prattled on about Lily, as new mothers infatuated with their children were wont to do. She listened absently, systematically reviewing the list of projects before her, mentally checking off each completed task. Marissa prided herself on excellent organization.

Correspondence had been updated. Invitations accepted. A new butler, Greenhouse, had been hired and installed to run her household, though he was a bit staid for her tastes. She'd remodeled several of the upstairs bedrooms, knocking down a wall to create a large guest suite for Brendan and Petra when they arrived for the holidays.

The pair certainly couldn't stay with Lord and Lady Marsh. Petra still wasn't speaking to her parents.

A dozen new ballgowns had been ordered from her favorite modiste along with a gorgeous green velvet riding habit with a matching hat. Marissa *adored* hats.

She'd helped nurse Spencer, her eldest son, from the wound he'd received in an altercation shortly after marrying

Lady Elizabeth Reynolds, the details of which she still wasn't completely clear on. Elizabeth was a delightful girl who didn't tolerate any of Spencer's nonsense. Marissa wholeheartedly approved of her new daughter-in-law.

All her ducklings, as she called her two boys, niece and nephew, were now married. *Happily*. A true rarity in the *ton*. Four love matches. And they would all be together for the holiday season.

"When Rowan comes home," Arabella gushed at the mere mention of her husband, "Lily smiles up at him and makes the most delightful gurgling sounds."

Marissa nodded. Lily was most likely experiencing stomach distress and not actually smiling *at* Rowan. She was little more than an infant. But Marissa chose not to mention such a thing to Arabella.

Now, where was I? Oh, yes. She'd filed the survey map and asked her solicitors to determine validity and challenge Pendleton's ownership of the Blue John mine.

She didn't give a fig for the money or the mine, really. But what she *did* care about was that her request to determine ownership would be tied up in court for *years*. Requiring thousands of pounds for Pendleton to defend. His solicitors were bleeding him dry already.

"Aunt Maisy?" Arabella touched her knee. "Where have you gone?"

"Only imagining how lovely it will be to have us all together for the holiday season," she said, dragging her attention back to Arabella. "I know we should escape London, but I find town to be much more convenient than if we were to retreat to the country."

Her niece cocked her head. "Really? You are simply thinking of cooked Christmas goose and a seating chart for dinner?"

"Don't be silly. Whatever else should I be thinking of?" A pair of silvery eyes above striking cheekbones floated to mind. Marissa pushed such thoughts aside.

Arabella set down her teacup with a small clatter. "Brendan has written me."

Marissa took in her niece's smug little grin. It was no surprise her younger son would write to Arabella. The two cousins had been close for most of their lives. But had Brendan written her concerning Reggie. . .or his discovery of Marissa with Haddon?

"I didn't think you found his searching for fossils to be so entertaining," she hedged. Brendan, much like his father, adored fossils and rocks. He'd studied geology and spent most of his time in caves or scaling cliffs and had led a primarily solitary existence until meeting Petra. "I suppose you're disappointed you won't be able to torture Petra any longer without him objecting."

"I'll still torment my sister-in-law, only much more discreetly." Arabella gave her a prim look. "Petra and I have reached an understanding of sorts."

"I'm happy to hear it."

"Brendan told me about Reggie."

Marissa swished the tea around in her mouth, thinking carefully about what she should say to her niece, uncertain as to what Brendan had told her. The family had been informed of the discovery of the late Earl of Morwick's remains and his burial. But not of how he'd died, exactly. Or why.

"I see. And what did Brendan impart?"

"*Everything.*" Arabella's dark eyes flashed as she popped a biscuit into her mouth. "No wonder you and Lady Pendleton are no longer friends. She had your husband murdered for a bloody mine full of Blue John."

Marissa's hand trembled slightly at Arabella's assessment of the situation. It was still difficult, at times, for her to hear the truth spoken out loud. The sheer treachery of her former neighbors boggled the mind.

"I see he *has* told you everything. And since he has, then you must be aware Brendan promised he would not retaliate against Viscount Pendleton or his family," Marissa said.

"But *you* made no such promise, Aunt Maisy, did you?"

Marissa took another sip of tea. "No, I did not."

"Brendan left you a loophole. Intentionally, I think," Arabella said. "Unlike Viscount Pendleton or his mother, *I* am not so foolish as to assume you would not take matters into your own hands. Doesn't Lady Pendleton know who your family is?"

"Lydia has never been especially impressed by my heritage, I don't think, daughter of the Duke of Dunbar or not."

"Then she's very foolish. You've done a good job at hiding your true nature from her. Much better than I hide mine."

That was surely true. Arabella was a cunning little thing, though much less dangerous than before she'd married. And her niece was correct; Marissa *was* her father's daughter. She'd learned well from Henry how to slowly destroy an adversary in the most excruciating way possible. An education Marissa was putting to good use on Pendleton.

"I know Brendan made a grand gesture for Petra's sake—"

"He did," Marissa said.

"Brendan loves Petra very much," Arabella said. "I'm not sure exactly *why*—"

"You just said you reached an understanding with Petra.

I would think as part of that, you would have a better opinion of her."

"I have. But it doesn't detract from the fact I think her weak-willed at times and far *too* obedient. A true milquetoast. Still, I don't begrudge Brendan for wanting to protect her."

"Petra is far less demure and well-behaved than you remember her, Niece. You should watch your step in the future," Marissa warned. "Brendan worried far more for Petra's reputation than she did herself, but then, he knows Lydia. Lydia maintains a large network of friends here in London who would be only too happy to destroy Petra in retaliation for her throwing over Lydia's precious son. It brings her joy to ruin others. There are many ladies and indeed some gentlemen who can testify to the fact."

"I find it ironic given her own daughter's reputation."

"Indeed, but Lydia doesn't believe she has to play by the rules others follow. She managed to keep the worst of Catherine's peccadilloes out of the gossip columns. A distant relation at the newspaper was her key to doing so. Lydia exerted undue influence over him."

Not any longer. The Honorable Mr. Kensington has recently left for other opportunities.

Marissa allowed herself a small gleam of satisfaction.

"Piddling stuff." Arabella pursed her lips. "Viscount Pendleton, respected member of Parliament and rising political star, is *heavily* in debt. That is what is *important*, isn't it?"

"Indeed. I filed the survey Brendan found in Buxton and again in London shortly after I returned. Even Simon is not powerful enough to stop the court from freezing the proceeds of the mine until ownership is determined, which I may have suggested until the issue is resolved."

"Oh, Auntie, you *are* terrible."

Marissa shrugged. "It hardly matters what they agreed to when the information came to light. Simon, no doubt under his mother's tutelage, has already stopped paying Brendan the lease and giving over half the profits, as he agreed to do. What else could *I* do but ensure no one has access until the courts decide? Allow my son to continue to be robbed of his birthright?"

"Pendleton has markers all over London. I assume you've already started to purchase them?"

It didn't surprise Marissa her niece was well aware of Pendleton's money woes. Nor that she had ascertained the first part of Marissa's strategy. Rowan, Arabella's husband, was involved in a variety of financial ventures and would have mentioned it, considering Simon had nearly married Rowan's sister, Petra.

"A few." Discretion at this part of her plan was required. Marissa didn't want Lydia *or* Simon to catch wind of her intentions until it was far too late.

"Then allow me to handle the rest. Discreetly, of course. As you know, Rowan purchases the debts of others anonymously."

Marissa was well aware. Rowan used debt as leverage often for property or a business he wished to purchase. Her nephew, Nick, often said his brother-in-law considered all of England nothing more than a large chessboard in which Rowan was determined to be three moves ahead of everyone else.

Henry would have approved of Rowan.

"One of Rowan's solicitors can purchase Pendleton's markers. No one would ever suspect you, respected widow of the *ton,* are behind such a thing, and we'll keep it that way."

Marissa laughed at that. "I *am* a respected widow. He'll eventually suspect me, though I doubt he would consider me a threat. Simon doesn't have a high opinion of a woman's intellect."

"It will prove his undoing. My point is that *no one* outside of our family knows what really happened to Reggie. Brendan never even had the lease agreement drawn up properly by a solicitor."

"It would have raised questions. And he expected Simon to honor the bargain, which was naïve."

"Money isn't important to Brendan. You know that, Aunt. He has his rocks and fossils along with Petra. He's perfectly content. And he gave his word. My cousin expects everyone to be as honorable as he is."

Simon had not a principled bone in his body. Nor had his father, John. It was a pity John wasn't still alive. Had he been, Marissa would have cheerfully shot him herself and left him in a hole to die.

The *great* Viscount Pendleton. Who knew *all* about his parent's sins and did *nothing*. Treating Brendan with disdain while *stealing* from him. Marissa would enjoy destroying Simon's brilliant political career and making him the most impoverished politician in Parliament. The shock of being poor might even kill Lydia. Or she'd become an even bigger sot than she already was.

I am remarkably bloodthirsty.

"Pendleton will need to marry an heiress if he wishes to dig himself out of debt," Arabella mused. "One who is a paragon of virtue with not so much as a whiff of scandal attached to her skirts, and whose connections can help him politically. There's a limited supply of such girls circulating about." Arabella bit into another biscuit. "Of course, we cannot allow such a marriage to happen."

"*Absolutely* not. Lydia needs to be reduced to someone's poor relation living in a mud cottage somewhere." Arabella *would* be an asset to Marissa's plans. "If you are determined to help me, you must not allow Rowan to know. Or any of them." She waved her hand. "Nick, Spencer or Brendan." She named her sons and nephew. "I do not want or need their help." Marissa reached for her cup again. "My father taught me well enough."

Arabella's dark eyes flashed at Marissa in triumph. "I won't. I promise."

A sharp rap at the door interrupted any further discussion. Her butler, Greenhouse, stiff and priggish, marched in bearing an embossed card upon a silver platter. "My lady." He lowered the tray so she could read her caller's card.

The cup of tea paused on its way to Marissa's lips.

Haddon.

He had said he wanted to speak to her and had asked to call, but that had been over a week ago. She'd assumed he'd changed his mind. Marissa cast a look at her niece. It was bloody inconvenient he'd decided on today to visit. Her niece was far too intuitive for Marissa's tastes.

Pulse fluttering madly at the knowledge Haddon lay right outside the drawing room door, she gave a subtle nod to Greenhouse.

Arabella gave her a curious glance. "Aunt Maisy?"

Her niece waved Greenhouse over to her before Marissa could stop her. She picked up the card, eyes widening.

Apparently, Brendan *had* disclosed other, far more personal things to Arabella, if her niece's reaction was any indication.

"Please show in Lord Haddon," Marissa managed to say.

Greenhouse bowed and left the room.

"He's the gentleman from the Peak District," Arabella said in a low tone. "The one who you had—"

Marissa shot her a firm look, cutting off the rest of Arabella's sentence. A word would be needed with Brendan. He didn't need to go about telling *everyone* of her personal business or, in this case, gossiping about such things with Arabella. She was entitled to some privacy in regard to her personal life, as sparse as it was, though her niece didn't appear to be especially horrified at the thought of Marissa having had a lover.

Dalliance, she corrected herself.

Inclining her head in Arabella's direction, Marissa said, "Not another word, or I shan't allow you to help me."

Her niece sat back, lips tightly shut.

"Lord Haddon," Greenhouse announced, swinging open the door.

The air shifted in the drawing room as it does during a storm, just before lightning strikes.

Haddon stepped inside, his male presence immediately at odds with the delicate feminine décor of Marissa's drawing room. A wicked half-smile tilted his lips as he paused at the doorway, completely assured of his welcome. Dark hair lay tousled about his ears and a touch of pink lit his high cheekbones from the cooler air outside.

How dare he appear before her looking so . . . *delicious*.

"Oh, Auntie," Arabella said under her breath as she took in Haddon. "*Good Lord*."

"Lady Cupps-Foster." Haddon's gaze was focused on her mouth as he greeted her. "I hope I haven't interrupted anything important." A thick wave of hair fell against his forehead as he came forward to take her hand.

"Not at all." The light brush of his lips against her

knuckles was enough to turn the entire lower half of her body to jelly. "I hadn't expected you to appear today."

"My apologies. And here I thought you'd take me to task for my delay in calling upon you."

Arabella watched the exchange with interest, pretending to nibble at her biscuit.

"My niece, Lady Malden," Marissa said crisply.

Haddon greeted Arabella politely before settling himself in a chair just to Marissa's left, much too close for her comfort if the rippling of her skin was any indication. He leaned back, stretching out his long legs until the toe of his boot nearly touched her skirts.

Impudent rake. Awareness of him swirled, making her insides clench. *I should have informed him I was not receiving.*

"What a pleasure to meet a . . . *friend* of my aunt's." Arabella smiled, clearly enjoying Marissa's discomfort.

"Lord Haddon and I met during my visit with Brendan," Marissa said.

"At a house party, of all things." Haddon didn't look at Arabella as he answered, his attention entirely on Marissa. "Your charming aunt helped relieve some of the tedium."

Arabella took a large swallow of tea, hiding the smile tugging at her lips.

Marissa gritted her teeth at the innuendo behind his words. "Haddon and your cousin are friends."

"Unfortunately, I haven't seen Morwick in some time. A disagreement of a very *ancient* nature has put us at odds." The silver eyes twinkled with amusement at Marissa, daring her to contradict him.

She coughed delicately, wanted to hurl her teacup at him. "I've so enjoyed your visit, my dear," Marissa said, turning to Arabella. "I know you *must* be on your way. Give my love to Rowan and darling Lily."

Arabella stood immediately, wisely taking the hint. "My, I fear I have lost track of the time. I'll take my leave, Aunt Maisy. My husband will wonder where I've gotten off to."

Haddon stood. "Pray don't leave on my account, Lady Malden."

"Not at all." Arabella leaned forward to press a kiss to Marissa's cheek. "He's quite something," she whispered in Marissa's ear before straightening. "I'll bring Lily next time," she assured Marissa. "A pleasure to meet you, Lord Haddon."

"And you, Lady Malden."

Arabella took her sweet time leaving the room, perhaps hoping to overhear something salacious.

Marissa would need to have a very pointed discussion with her niece.

Haddon regarded her in silence until the door of the drawing room shut behind Arabella with a soft click. Removing his gloves, he laid them on the arm of the chair and crossed his legs at the ankle. His trousers pulled sharply against his heavily muscled thighs.

Drat.

It was a struggle for her *not* to look, which Marissa was certain was Haddon's intent. She had wondered during their previous *dalliance* what he did with himself which resulted in such a lean, powerful form. Her eyes were drawn to the large hands with their calloused blunt-tipped fingers, and she remembered the way he'd caressed her skin. *Not* with the hands of a gentleman, which were often as soft and pliant as her own and certainly—

"Marissa?" He watched her intently, one forefinger absently drawing a circle on the arm of the chair. "I see my appearance has surprised you. Are you well? You seem . . . distracted."

No, she *wasn't* well. If she was any closer to Haddon, she might burst into flames. "Perfectly fine, thank you." It was one thing to decide not to involve herself with Haddon. Quite another for her body to comprehend what that meant.

"Difficult," he murmured under his breath, almost too quiet for her to hear. His fingers started drumming.

Marissa was certain he meant her. She hadn't been called *difficult* by a man in quite some time. "If you are referring to me, I am well aware of my character deficits."

"I didn't say it was a deficit." He looked away for a moment before turning back to her. "I find it makes you more interesting. But then, I've told you such before."

While holding my hand as we lay beside each other after he ravished me at Brushbriar. I thought he would leave and return to his own rooms, but instead he held my hand and whispered to me in the dark.

"I would like to explain . . . after I found out about Reggie—"

"There's no need, Marissa." Haddon watched her with an odd expression.

Somewhat flustered, she lifted her chin. "I don't think it would be wise to continue our previous association. If you have come here to persuade me to continue our—"

"Affair?" he said in a helpful tone.

"Dalliance," she corrected. "And my answer is no." She nodded her head slightly and clasped her hands. He would not talk her out of her decision, despite his . . . annoying *magnificence*.

"I wasn't aware I'd asked you to dally with me again." A wrinkle appeared between the dark brows as his fingers continued to drum on the chair. "As alluring as I find you to be." His gaze briefly dropped to her breasts.

Marissa opened her mouth and then closed it, unsure how to respond.

"Your objections to continuing our *dalliance*, for your own reasons," he waved his hand, "are *exhausting*. I will bow to your *superior* wisdom in these matters."

"You will?" It appeared the pretty speech she'd prepared to refuse him wouldn't be needed.

"Of course, Marissa. Forgive me for being blunt, but I've no desire to pursue a *dalliance* with a woman who has been clear she doesn't want one. I didn't come here today to talk you into bed with me again." He shrugged. "*Ancient* history, as I said." His silver eyes gleamed.

Well, that stung a bit. More than she'd thought it would.

Haddon smiled at her, the small grooves around his eyes crinkling, making him even more handsome, if that were possible. "Perhaps I merely require your decorating acumen." He looked around the drawing room. "You've amazing taste. This room is beautiful and a lovely color. I like the floral arrangements." A large hand waved casually at a vase full of artfully arranged fresh flowers. "Your butler or a maid must be very talented."

"I arrange my own vases. A hobby of mine. But I doubt you are here to ask me about flowers or draperies."

"No, indeed. I find I am in need of your expertise in another area."

"My expertise?" She reached for her cup of tea. It had gone cold, but she needed to do something with her hands.

"While I was *relieving* your *boredom* at Pendleton's house party," his lips twisted into a mischievous smile, "you mentioned you might help Jordana one day if I brought her to London. I'm here to see if your offer is still good. I find myself in rather dire straits in regard to my daughter."

Marissa's hand froze, her teacup hovering just inches

from her lips. She *had* offered to help with Jordana, though to be fair, he'd been kissing his way across her breasts at the time. "I must have forgotten."

Haddon cast a lingering gaze at her bosom before his eyes returned to her face. There was no doubt he remembered the moment as well. "Forgetfulness is often a sign of *advanced* age."

Marissa sipped at the tepid tea, determined to ignore his baiting.

"An *experienced* woman, such as yourself, could help prepare Jordana to make her debut. She's awkward in society as unaccustomed as she is to it. Mrs. Divet has done her best, but I fear Jordana is in need of a firmer hand. And it would only be until my sister arrives."

Mrs. Divet and her husband were close friends of Haddon's and Mrs. Divet had taken over the role of aunt to his four girls. The woman was lovely, but Mrs. Divet was not out in society herself. She and her husband traveled much of the time.

"I see."

Helping Jordana would mean Marissa would be in Haddon's orbit for the better part of several months, being tempted by him.

It wasn't a good idea. Not in the least. And she already had several projects to keep her busy.

Haddon's fingers drummed again. "I would be *deeply* grateful."

Marissa's eyes followed the movement of his fingers. He'd moved them along her skin in the same way as they lay naked together, speaking quietly of their lives. Haddon had told her of his late wife. His daughters. He'd praised her for not only raising her two sons alone, but also her niece and nephew. None of her other lovers had ever expressed the slightest interest in Marissa's family or the struggles she'd endured. It was unusual for a gentleman to notice such a thing.

Yet, Haddon, casual dalliance that he was, *had*.

Her heart contracted, then stretched in his direction. *Damn it.* She wasn't going to be able to refuse him. Not with Jordana. Possibly not in anything. It was very worrisome.

"What *is* wrong with you, Marissa? I grow concerned that you are ill. You behaved oddly at the Cambourne ball as well."

"Headaches," she announced. "I've been cursed with them."

"Ah, that explains the flush to your cheeks." She doubted Haddon was fooled. She suspected he was well aware of his effect on her despite her attempts to keep her feelings hidden. "It means so much to me, Marissa. Your help with Jordana."

A light exotic aroma reminiscent of a bag of spices her nephew had once gifted her drifted into her nostrils as Haddon leaned toward Marissa, taking her hand in his larger one. "Thank you."

"You're welcome," she said, her pulse jumping at his touch.

Why must he smell so luscious? Why couldn't he smell of pomade and talc? It would make things so much easier.

One finger trailed along the inside of her palm.

"Haddon—"

If he asked her again to dally with him, or better still, pushed her back on the sofa and lifted her skirts, Marissa would be hard pressed to refuse him.

"I'll take my leave." He dropped her hand gently then stood, grabbing his gloves.

As he made his way around the sofa where Marissa sat,

Haddon paused, leaning down until his breath caressed her neck. "It was lovely to see you today, Marissa."

If she turned her head, their lips would meet.

This wasn't fair. Not at all. Her eyes fluttered closed. Perhaps the scandal of involving herself with Haddon wouldn't be that terrible. Adelia could certainly guide her. Maybe he'd never find out she was destroying his friend, Pendleton.

Maybe he is worth the risk to my heart.

Before she could stop him, Haddon reached the door.

"I bid you good day, Lady Cupps-Foster."

5

Enderly guided Marissa into the drawing room of Lord Duckworth's London mansion, his gloved hand hovering lightly against her back. Her heels clicked on the marble floor beneath her feet as she surveyed the immense space Duckworth had converted into both a speaking area and a place to discuss politics. The walls were burgundy, the windows outlined with gold cornices from which curtains a shade darker than the walls were hung. Duckworth's illustrious ancestors hung from the walls, their staid expressions looking down on the proceedings with mild censure.

Gentlemen stood clustered, their heated voices echoing as views were challenged, each interrupting the other as one opinion took precedence over another. A small group of well-dressed ladies whispered in one corner, like a flock of wrens who dared not make a sound lest the household cat should spot them.

They paused every few feet, their progress stopped by someone who wished for an introduction or desired to ask Enderly for his support. He greeted each request graciously, all the while puffing out his chest, filled with his own importance.

"Thank you for allowing me to escort you this evening, my lady. I realize much of tonight's conversation may not be of interest," he cautioned with an annoying paternal look. "The intricacies and politics involved in Parliament can be a bit complicated to follow. Ask me anything, and I will try to answer."

"I'm sure I'll be able to follow along," Marissa replied. When had Enderly become so patronizing? Perhaps he'd always been so, and she'd failed to notice.

Enderly's mouth tightened just a bit. "Even so, my dear, I am happy to share my knowledge should you have questions."

Pompous. Enderly was *pompous.* "I find my interests lean in the direction of the reforms affecting workers in textile mills, factories and mines."

"An unusual interest for a lady of your stature."

"My niece, Lady Malden, supports a variety of charities whose aims are to improve the lives of the widows and children of those working in the mines and textile mills. Often, if a worker is injured, the family has no recourse and is left penniless with no means of support."

"There's workhouses for such folk," Enderly said with the superiority of a gentleman who'd never set foot in such an establishment.

Sanctimonious. A better word for Enderly. "Have you been to a workhouse, Mr. Enderly? I assure you, it is not as charitable a foundation as you would think. Workhouses are only a way to punish an individual for being poor."

Marissa feared Enderly's indulgence toward her was rapidly turning to irritation. He generally behaved as if he adored Marissa's intelligence, until he found her opinions to be more than a woman should possess or worse, that they conflicted with his own.

"I think you've been misinformed, *my dear*. At any rate, you should enjoy the speech of my friend and your former neighbor, Viscount Pendleton. He is arguing that children under the age of eight shouldn't be subjected to working in mills or factories. Or mines. He wishes the age to be raised to at least ten."

How lovely of Simon. As if any ten-year-old child, no matter how poor, should spend his life below ground digging for copper or tin. Or in Simon's case, Blue John. She'd already informed her solicitors that one of the tenets to her ownership of the mine would be no children. If a child was thrust into the role of providing a living for his family, a position would have to be found *above* ground.

"How progressive of Lord Pendleton."

Enderly's nostrils flared slightly at the sarcasm tinging her words. He didn't care to have her disparaging a gentleman he supported and idolized. "He's wise in not offending his peers with his views," Enderly gave her a pointed look, "though you don't seem to find them progressive enough. By walking a fine line, he has managed to gain support in both houses." He took Marissa's arm, more reluctantly now, she thought. "Some are saying he could even be Prime Minister one day."

Not if I can help it.

How was it that Simon could fool everyone into thinking he was so *bloody* decent? She knew differently though. Even Haddon, whom she considered more perceptive than most, was friends with Simon. He'd even said he admired him. How could *he* not see through Simon's veneer of respectability?

And why had she not even had so much as a note from Haddon?

After leaving Marissa in a confused, slightly aroused puddle while securing her agreement to help with Jordana, Haddon seemed to have disappeared. One would think he'd want her to start *guiding* his daughter immediately given Jordana's awkwardness.

Perhaps he'd changed his mind about asking her assistance. Maybe he regretted doing so in the first place.

Enderly was looking at her in expectation, awaiting a reply. He must have asked her something and she'd failed to respond.

"I beg your pardon, Mr. Enderly. Woolgathering, I'm afraid. What did you say?"

Enderly proceeded to pontificate on some obscure banking issue Marissa didn't find the least bit interesting. Her niece would have, had she been there. Marissa nodded, pretending rapt interest. When Enderly began to gush over Simon, Marissa had to forcibly swallow down the bitterness filling her mouth. How he adored the great Lord Pendleton in all of his pretentious glory.

Enderly's hand fell down Marissa's spine, fingers caressing the lower portion of her back.

She casually stepped to the side, allowing his hand to fall away. Enderly had been hinting at his desire to be invited to her bed, but unbeknownst to the older man, he'd already outlived his usefulness. She'd found out nothing of interest about Simon from him. And the thought of actually having an affair with Enderly no longer held any appeal. She'd thought to put him off before tonight but reconsidered. Once Marissa's escort saw the mutual hostility between herself and Simon, Enderly would naturally cease in his pursuit.

"I'm quite parched." Marissa wet her lips and leaned over just enough for Enderly to catch a glimpse of the hollow between her breasts. She was not above such a thing when it was necessary.

The action had the desired effect.

"Of course, my dear." Enderly's pale gaze roamed over her neckline in appraisal. "How remiss I am. Would you care for something to drink? Sherry? Ratafia?"

Why did gentlemen always assume a lady wouldn't want something stronger? It was on the tip of her tongue to ask Enderly to bring her a whisky, but she thought better of it. His illusions of her would be shattered soon enough.

"You choose for me." She smiled. He looked so hopeful.

Poor Enderly. You are bound to be disappointed.

"I'll return in a moment." His fingers trailed along her waist before he moved off, his cloud of white hair disappearing into the well-heeled crowd. He'd probably bring her ratafia, which she detested.

Tonight, Simon would seek to gain traction for his bill among the titles gathered here, hopefully garnering the support he needed. His reforms, which Marissa didn't think went far enough, were still considered wildly progressive for many of his peers. Simon was building a reputation as something of a firebrand, arguing fervently for his opinions.

It was probably the only bit of passion Simon possessed.

Marissa had to admit most of his ideas had merit, though she didn't think he was helping the lower classes because he empathized with their plight. Ambition was what mattered most to Simon. Power. Prestige.

The buzzing in the room grew louder as heads turned in the direction of the door. Simon arrived, entering the room as if he were a conquering hero. His progress in her direction was halted by the throng of admirers who sought to shake his hand or offer their support. Marissa observed him dispassionately.

He hasn't done anything but hide murder and thievery.

Amid the hearty congratulations and pleasant conversation, Simon lifted his head ever so slightly in her direction. His lips parted, obviously shocked to see her in attendance. The lady at his side was speaking, her gloved hand hovering over his arm, though Simon ignored her. The brackets around his mouth tightened before he recovered from finding Marissa in Lord Duckworth's drawing room. A perfect mask of snobby politeness fell over his patrician features in a matter of seconds, the superior smile he bestowed on lesser mortals firmly back in place.

A portly man with a ginger mustache stepped forward, intent on gaining Simon's attention and momentarily blocking Marissa's view.

I hope I've ruined Simon's evening.

Enderly, white hair floating around his head like the puff of a dandelion, returned to her side, the offensive ratafia clutched in his hand.

"Here you are, my dear." He handed Marissa her glass. "The man of the hour has just arrived." He nodded in Simon's direction. "Shall we go and reacquaint you with Lord Pendleton?"

Marissa sipped her ratafia without wincing at the taste. "Yes, of course."

Enderly took her arm and led her to where Simon held court, subtly pushing aside the crowd. He introduced her to several people, one of whom was the ginger-haired man she'd seen earlier.

"Ho there, Enderly." The gentleman was barely Marissa's height, which put his eyes nearly on level with the tops of her breasts which swelled above her neckline. "You must introduce me to your lovely companion."

"Phineas, good to see you. May I introduce Lady Cupps-Foster. My lady, Mr. Phineas, an old school chum of mine."

Marissa inclined her head politely. "Mr. Phineas, a pleasure."

"I assure you," he took her hand in one beefy paw, "the pleasure is all mine." His gaze was anything but polite, though his smile was genuine. Despite looking like a plump elf, Marissa thought Mr. Phineas considered himself a bit of a rake. At least in his own mind.

Enderly wasn't paying the least attention to Phineas. He nodded to his friend, pulling Marissa along in his wake while trying to catch the eye of his idol, Viscount Pendleton.

Simon was watching them approach, his nostrils flaring slightly, as if Marissa were the Thames reeking in the middle of summer.

It was very difficult *not* to smile at his discomfort.

"Lord Pendleton." Enderly bowed. "Thank you for your kind invitation this evening. I look forward to your speech later."

"Enderly." Simon inclined his head. "The pleasure is all mine, I assure you. Your guidance in crafting some of these proposed reforms, as a fellow mine owner—"

Marissa made a small sound of derision.

"— has helped me to understand all viewpoints, especially those in the opposition. Your support has been instrumental."

Enderly preened under Pendleton's regard. "You are too kind, my lord."

"Not at all." Simon's unwelcoming gaze settled on Marissa. "Lady Cupps-Foster. How surprising to see *you* here this evening," he said, failing to take her hand in greeting. "I didn't realize you followed politics or were acquainted with Enderly."

"Lord Pendleton." Marissa nodded politely. "I couldn't resist coming tonight, especially after Mr. Enderly's kind invitation. It gives me an opportunity to apologize for leaving your house party so abruptly this past summer. I regret I could not thank you and your mother properly for your hospitality. But I'm sure it was understandable given the circumstances."

A tic appeared below Simon's left eye. "Of course."

"My son wanted me to send his regards. He *especially* enjoyed his stay at Brushbriar as you know. Why, if not for your house party, Morwick never would have met his lovely wife." A delicate laugh bubbled up. "He and Lady Morwick wanted me to express their congratulations on your success."

Simon's cheeks reddened, mouth thinning until his lips had nearly disappeared. The resemblance to his mother, Lydia, was notable though not especially favorable.

Enderly cleared his throat, gaze darting between Simon and Marissa. Her escort for this evening couldn't fail to notice the tension hovering in the air, though Enderly could be a bit unobservant. He'd failed to notice Marissa's lukewarm interest in him, for instance.

"A word, if I might, Mr. Enderly?" Simon dismissed her with a flick of his chin.

Marissa didn't mind his rudeness. She'd expected no less.

"If you'll excuse me." Enderly nodded to her and moved away, not waiting for her to answer as he followed Simon, his horror at discovering she and Simon weren't cordial shadowing his craggy features.

Simon and Enderly had wandered to an area at the far

end of the room. Every so often, Enderly would cast a glance in her direction. He didn't look pleased.

Good. It appeared she'd been right in her assumption that Enderly would leave her be with little effort on her part. Thankfully, she'd had the foresight to order her driver to meet her at Duckworth's. Her carriage was likely already outside.

Marissa intentionally moved in the opposite direction of Enderly and Simon, stopping only to study a portrait of a severe looking woman who very much resembled Duckworth, down to the matching moles they both bore on their chin. She pretended to sip her ratafia and finally gave up, setting the glass down on a nearby table.

Disgusting. Ratafia should be banned from being served in polite society.

Once Simon began what was bound to be a boring speech, Marissa planned to take her leave discreetly.

"Fancy meeting you here."

A delicious ripple rolled up from the base of her spine at the words coming from the darkened alcove to her left. Marissa immediately smoothed the velvet skirts of her gown as she turned, a nervous habit she'd had since she was a girl.

How long had he been watching her?

Haddon's lean form stepped out of the shadows, a glass of wine hanging from his fingers. His silver gaze flickered over her as he sipped the ruby-colored contents of his glass. When his eyes finally met hers, a lazy grin crossed his lips in greeting.

The pulse in her throat fluttered at the sight of him. "Lord Haddon."

"Hello, Lady Cupps-Foster. Imagine my shock at finding you lurking about a dull political gathering. Though perhaps not so strange given your familial connections."

The observation, coming from Haddon, didn't surprise Marissa in the least. He paid *attention*, to a great many things. Enderly had never asked Marissa about her father, the late Duke of Dunbar, nor the power he'd wielded, assuming, i*ncorrectly*, that as a woman, Marissa was oblivious to the workings of her family. As her niece had inferred, Marissa was just very good at hiding her true nature.

"Did you know my father, the duke?"

"I met him only once. I found him terrifying, especially when a gentleman referred to His Grace as the 'Old Spider.' The duke's eyes were so blue one could see them across the room." His voice lowered. "Yours are the same color."

Another flutter started in the space above her heart.

"Thankfully, I was well beneath his notice."

"Don't be too sure." Marissa laughed softly. "My father noticed everything about everyone. He believed that knowledge was *power*. Even more so than great wealth. My nephew is cut from the same cloth."

"The pairing of both is a dangerous combination." Haddon stepped closer.

Marissa's skin immediately prickled in awareness of him, lifting the fine hair of her arms.

"I will make sure to never underestimate you, as your friend, Enderly, no doubt does." Haddon tipped his glass in Enderly's direction.

He was so near her, if Marissa leaned just an inch forward, her breasts would catch against his chest. Just the mere thought tightened her nipples into peaks. Heat flooded up her chest and the column of her neck.

"I grow concerned for your welfare, Marissa." His voice was barely a whisper.

"Why? I'm perfectly fine as you can see and—"

"You look flushed much of the time. Overheated, perhaps."

Drat.

"I would think you were blushing except a woman of your *advanced* years . . ." the broad shoulders rolled into a careless shrug. "Well, such a thing is usually reserved for prim young misses."

Wretch. "Perhaps it is the ratafia." She nodded to her discarded glass. "It is not a favorite of mine."

"Then one wonders why you allowed your *friend* to bring it to you. I'm sure you'd find mine more enjoyable. Something French, I think." Haddon brought his glass to her lips before she could stop him.

The image of Haddon doing the same thing during their night together flashed before her. He'd brought a bottle of wine to her room, but only one glass. After each sip she'd taken, he had kissed her, eventually dribbling the wine across her naked breasts and—

"Good Lord, Marissa." His gaze was fixed on her mouth. "I grow ever concerned for your health. I'll search the room for a physician, shall I?" But he didn't move, instead he brought the glass to his own lips, tongue running across the rim as he did so. "Delicious," he said, but Haddon was looking at her.

Desire for him coiled tightly around her.

She took a step back, self-preservation screaming for her to place some distance between them. It was very difficult to think, her usual self-composure deserting her with Haddon so near.

"How is Jordana?" she said, shocked at the husky quality of her own voice. If this interlude continued, Marissa would find herself begging Enderly to rescue her before she made an idiot out of herself. "Have you decided you no longer need my assistance?"

"On the contrary, I seek your guidance now more than ever. Our delay in calling on you is the misfortune of a bad cold that has kept Jordana in bed the past few days. She is finally recovering. I'd thought to bring her to your home for tea this week, if that is convenient."

"Wonderful," Marissa lied. Part of her had hoped Haddon would decide he didn't want her to help with Jordana. If her reaction to him tonight was any indication, Marissa couldn't trust herself to be in his presence.

A loud clapping interrupted their conversation, breaking the soft bubble of intimacy surrounding them. Lord Duckworth was extolling the virtues of Simon and calling him to the podium.

Haddon looked toward the other side of the room. "Pendleton is about to speak."

"Then I won't keep you. I assume you've come to listen. You are friends, after all." Marissa meant to dash away the moment Haddon's back was turned.

"Oh, I wouldn't call us friends, exactly," Haddon said. "More wine?" The glass hovered near her lips.

"No, thank you. I was under the impression the two of you were quite close, and you held him in admiration."

"Were you? I admire his ambition, I suppose. I am a supporter of his reforms and what he hopes to accomplish as I have a vested interest in his proposals."

He'd neglected to directly answer her question. She searched his face for any clue as to what his comments meant, but Haddon was difficult to read, only allowing a hint of his feelings to show when he was angry.

As he'd been when I called him a dalliance.

"You own mines." Marissa had never asked Haddon,

assuming him to be involved somehow in tin, copper or lead. Most of the families in Derbyshire held some sort of interests below ground.

"Quarries. Are you sure you don't want another sip? You look thirsty."

"Quarries? You mean . . . *rocks*?" She allowed him to press the glass to her lips, moderately concerned someone might notice them tucked away at the edge of Duckworth's drawing room. Like Enderly. But everyone's attention was taken by Simon who was rousing those gathered with his fiery speech.

A low chuckle came from him. "You don't have to sound so appalled, Marissa. I don't do the digging myself, at least not anymore. I suppose stone isn't glamorous in the least. Not like Pendleton's Blue John."

"No." Marissa tensed at the mention of Blue John. "I suppose not."

"Or the tin mines your *friend*," he emphasized the word in an icy tone, "Enderly owns in Cornwall. I quarry limestone, granite, gritstone and the like. Someone has to provide building material for," he gave a negligent wave, "all these fine houses. For streets, garden walls and the like."

Stone had to come from somewhere, but she'd never given it much thought.

"I have two quarries which provide employment for most of the men in the small villages surrounding Buxton. I never have to despair I'm poisoning the water with lead, so I can sleep at night. I'll never be ridiculously wealthy on the level of Pendleton or your family, for instance, but I have more than enough for myself and the girls. And a wife." He winked at her.

"It sounds like a lucrative enterprise." The last thing she wanted to do was discuss Haddon's plans to take a wife, especially since the mere thought soured her stomach. Nor did she wish to debate the merits of Lady Christina Sykes who was probably the frontrunner in his quest for the new Lady Haddon. If only Marissa had not refused him—

He never asked to rekindle our affair.

The knowledge that he hadn't stung again.

"I'll allow you to continue with your evening, Lord Haddon." Marissa wanted to leave, to blot out the image of Haddon and Christina Sykes because it bothered her far more than she wished it to. "My carriage is waiting outside."

One dark brow lifted at that. "I can see you home."

"That isn't necessary, Lord Haddon. Please excuse me."

"As you wish." Bringing her knuckles to his lips, he murmured, "Good night, Marissa."

Marissa turned and walked blindly through the back half of the drawing room toward the door. No one noticed her exit; everyone in the room was focused on Simon expounding on his own wonderfulness. Sparing not a thought for Enderly, who might wonder at some point about her disappearance, Marissa made her way to the door.

She could still feel the press of Haddon's fingers against her own.

Drat.

6

Marissa pulled out two of the large ferns in the vase, put them aside, and rearranged the spray of peonies and roses. Sticking one fern back in, she stepped back to admire her handiwork.

"Much better."

Her household staff, though they certainly tried, couldn't make a decent floral arrangement if Marissa laid out a diagram for them. What was the point of spending a large sum of money at the flower market only to have them tossed in a vase without any care for how they looked?

Haddon was calling today.

She despised the trickle of anticipation at the thought. Of course, this time, he was bringing Jordana.

Marissa looked up at the clock. They were due to arrive shortly.

Fluffing a stray peony, she nodded to herself, satisfied at her handiwork. It shouldn't matter if her flowers were arranged so artfully, other than that Haddon had remarked on such a thing when he'd last been in her drawing room.

After arriving home from Lord Duckworth's, Marissa

had spent the remainder of her evening nursing a glass of whisky and convincing herself she must tell Haddon she'd changed her mind about Jordana. She'd prepared a list of excuses. Even written a note to Haddon.

It would have been the wise thing to do, refusing to take on his rebellious daughter, but instead she'd tossed the hastily written note into the fire.

Now here she stood, furiously moving about the peonies in some ridiculous belief her talent at floral arranging was something which would please him.

Greenhouse knocked and quietly opened the drawing room door at her summons.

Marissa turned to the doorway, heart beating about in her chest, expecting to see Haddon, but was only greeted by a sullen-faced feminine *replica*. She'd forgotten how much Jordana looked like him. The same quicksilver eyes. Matching cheekbones. The dark hair.

It was *unsettling*, to say the least.

"Jordana, how lovely to see you." Marissa came forward, peering into the empty hallway beyond, searching for any sign of Haddon.

"Good afternoon, Lady Cupps-Foster. A pleasure to see you again. Thank you for assisting me during my time in London." The words had the sound of a practiced speech. Noting the direction of Marissa's gaze, she said, "Father couldn't come. He sends his regrets. A previous engagement which he must attend to." Jordana gave a stiff, painful looking curtsey in Marissa's direction before flouncing over to the velvet-trimmed sofa to sit without being asked.

Marissa tried not to allow her annoyance show that Haddon had merely dropped off his troublesome daughter on her doorstep without so much as a note to her. After all, it wasn't Jordana's fault. She cast a look at her guest who was regarding Marissa's drawing room with interest.

"I see. Nevertheless," she smiled brightly at Haddon's daughter, determined Jordana not feel unwelcome, "*we* will enjoy our tea." Marissa gestured toward a servant who entered bearing a tray laden with tea and an assortment of small sandwiches and biscuits, setting it down on the low table in front of the sofa.

"That will be all," Marissa said to the maid, settling herself next to Jordana as the door clicked shut. "I suppose your father had a business appointment."

"He had to take Lady Christina Sykes for a ride in the park with Lady Stanton." Jordana made a face. She reached for a biscuit before waiting to be served, not bothering to place a plate on her lap or even take a napkin.

"Jordana," Marissa said firmly. "Please cease to act as if a lemon has found its way into your mouth at the mention of Lady Christina Sykes. She's a lovely girl and will be important for you to know."

A snort came from the other side of the sofa.

"And you will use a plate," Marissa stared pointedly at the biscuit clutched in Jordana's fingers, "and wait until I've poured tea. You should also wait to be asked if you'd like a biscuit and then I will place it onto your plate." She poured out two cups of tea. "I realize manners might be a bit lax in the country, but in London, sometimes manners are all one has to recommend them."

Jordana's chin took on a mulish slant, one which Marissa ignored.

"Would you care for a biscuit, Jordana?" Marissa handed her a plate, unsurprised to see Jordana chewing the already filched biscuit, her cheeks puffing out like a small squirrel.

The girl was immensely stubborn, as witnessed by her

earlier behavior at Pendleton's house party, but she couldn't be *any* worse than Arabella.

Marissa had vast experience in dealing with difficult young ladies.

Shifting her feet, the plate pitching about in her lap, Jordana seemed uncertain how to position her legs correctly, slouching and then straightening her spine in an abrupt manner.

Terribly awkward, poor little duckling. Marissa's heart immediately went out to her. Jordana *was* difficult, but only because she was lacking proper guidance. Marissa was acquainted with the tales of Haddon's daughters. He'd overindulged all of them, likely because he was outnumbered.

"Cream or sugar?"

Jordana watched Marissa's fluid, sure movements.

"Sugar," she mumbled. "Two, please."

Marissa purposefully dropped one into the steaming cup. "A young lady watching her figure should have only one."

"But . . ." Jordana stuttered. "I'm not watching my figure. Nor is anyone else." Her chin tipped dangerously again, her eyes, so like Haddon's, darkening to the color of old silver.

"And they won't," Marissa assured her, picking up her own cup, "should you persist in developing a sweet tooth."

Jordana glared at her but stayed silent.

"Tell me how your visit to London is progressing, Jordana. Has your father taken you shopping? Or perhaps to the museum?"

"I *hate* it here." Jordana's eyes gleamed as she plucked a sandwich from the tray, then catching Marissa's eye, placed it carefully on her plate.

"Hate is a strong word, dear, one usually reserved for an overcooked piece of fish or a gown a too brilliant yellow."

"I like yellow."

"Not with your coloring, dear. You'd resemble a hostile daffodil."

Jordana's lips twitched. Her shoulders softened, relaxing just an inch. "The only good thing is the park," she said. "I want to go home, Lady Cupps-Foster. I don't belong here. Can we just tell my father that you tried to," she looked toward the ceiling as if attempting to find the right words, "*mold* me, and I am unmoldable?"

"That isn't a word, dear. Nor is it true." Marissa sipped at her tea. "Your father has asked me to help you until your aunt—"

"Why?" Jordana said bluntly. "Why did he ask *you*?"

"I don't know," Marissa replied, making a mental note to curb Jordana's frank way of speaking. It was off-putting. "I suppose because I am well-versed in the ways of society, and"—she paused deliberately— "I have vast experience with challenging situations."

Jordana stopped chewing her sandwich. "Challenging?"

"Dear, please don't speak with your mouth full. Yes, challenging. *You* can't *possibly* be more difficult than *my* niece, Lady Malden, who I chaperoned for many years. She is legendary in the *ton*. Your obstinance doesn't frighten *me*." Marissa leaned forward. "If your plan is to be so completely lacking in manners, which I know for a fact you have," she gave Jordana a pointed look, "or if you seek to outsmart me, thinking I am just another pampered matron of the *ton*, you should reconsider. You'll find me a formidable opponent."

Jordana's eyes widened.

Good. Marissa had her attention. "Now, let me tell you

how my niece behaved at Lady Ralston's ball after she came out. It is a perfect example of how *not* to conduct yourself."

A SHORT TIME LATER, HAVING DEMOLISHED AN ENTIRE PLATE of biscuits, three sandwiches and two cups of tea while listening to the horrible behavior of Arabella, Jordana was reclining against the arm of the sofa. Not properly of course, but at least she was no longer set on defiance. Her lips had even contorted into what *could* be considered a smile.

Marissa leaned forward. "You are very pretty when you cease frowning, Jordana."

The high cheekbones, so like her father's, pinked. "I'm not. The most that can be said is that I'm handsome. Even Mrs. Divet has inferred as much."

Marissa cocked her head. "I disagree." Jordana's features were too bold for a young girl's face, but once she matured, Jordana would be stunning. Not beautiful, exactly, but striking in a way few women were. "And you are in *dire* need of a new wardrobe."

"I am?" Jordana looked down at the plain blue muslin day dress she wore.

"You are. That dress," Marissa nodded, "is perfectly appropriate for traipsing about the moors but *not* for paying calls in London. Never fear, I am already creating a palette for you." Marissa tapped her temple.

"A . . . palette?" Jordana swallowed, looking appropriately terrified.

It would do the girl some good to have a healthy bit of fear instilled in her instead of terrorizing everyone else. "Yes. A color scheme for your wardrobe."

A sharp knock sounded before Greenhouse entered, a tiny grimace tugging at the corner of his mouth.

Marissa was beginning to think that his patent 'butler' look. "Yes, Greenhouse?"

"Mr. Tomkin has arrived, my lady. He *claims* you are expecting him."

Oh Lord. She'd forgotten all about Tomkin. "Of course."

Greenhouse didn't budge.

Honestly, why must she pull information out of her own butler? It was becoming an annoyance. "Is there something else, Greenhouse?"

"Lord Haddon has arrived to fetch Miss Ives. His carriage has just pulled up."

Poor timing. She was endlessly the victim of such a thing. The two portions of her life colliding in the drawing room were a bit more than Marissa had planned for today. "Please put Mr. Tomkin in my study, Greenhouse, and show in Lord Haddon."

Greenhouse bowed. "Yes, my lady."

"You have a *study*?" Jordana regarded her oddly. "I thought ladies only had parlors or sitting rooms."

"Of course. Why should I not have a study? Do you think only gentlemen are capable of conducting business? There are a great many things which require my attention, Jordana. I need a place to work."

"You do not just pay calls and—"

"Flit about? Take on young, stubborn girls?" Marissa stood and took Jordana's hand. "No, my dear. There is no denying this is a man's world, and we must live in it, but I find it much better to be underestimated. That is your first lesson."

Jordana nodded slowly. "I will take heed, my lady."

"Splendid. But don't tell your father."

"Don't tell me what?" Haddon strolled in, hat in hand, handsome in fawn-colored riding breeches and a coat the color of burnt toast. He looked so beautiful, so incredibly male, a bolt of longing for him shot straight down between Marissa's legs.

A recurring problem.

His eyes surveyed the remains of the tea tray before he went to Marissa. "Lady Cupps-Foster. I trust you and Jordana had a nice visit?"

It was on the tip of her tongue to chastise Haddon for his absence, but she declined to do so. Marissa didn't want to appear jealous because he'd rather spend the afternoon with Lady Christina Sykes than herself. But she certainly felt the sharp sting of that horrible emotion. It wasn't pleasant, curdling the tea in her stomach.

"Jordana and I had a lovely afternoon, didn't we?" She smiled in Jordana's direction. "And accomplished much. Although we will continue our discussion while walking in the park—a more preferred venue."

Jordana nodded in agreement.

"I apologize—" Haddon started.

"There isn't any need." Marissa gave a wave of her hand effectively silencing him. "Jordana explained you had a prior engagement. As it turns out, I've another caller now, so I must beg my own apologies."

Haddon's gaze lingered over her, shuttered and polite. "Of course. Come, Jordana."

Had he seen Tomkin? Marissa thought he very likely had. He would wonder what a man like Tomkin was doing calling on her.

Let him wonder. Perhaps he would think Tomkin her lover.

Jordana stood to take her leave. "Thank you for the tea, Lady Cupps-Foster."

The girl *did* know how to behave, she just didn't wish to. "I enjoyed our conversation very much today, Jordana." This afternoon Marissa had learned quite a bit about Jordana, especially her story of trailing behind the lone physician close to Haddon's estate as the older man called on patients. There was also a local midwife with whom she was friendly.

Most alarming.

"I look forward to our walk in the park together. I'll send you a note."

Jordana nodded. "I look forward to it, my lady."

Haddon took his daughter's arm to lead her out, his gaze remaining fixed on Marissa. He seemed about to speak, but then the line of his jaw tightened, and he departed, with only a nod of the head.

Marissa waited for the sound of Haddon's carriage to pull away. Firmly pushing him out of her mind for the moment, she stood and made her way to greet Mr. Tomkin.

7

Mr. Tomkin stood stiffly in Marissa's study, hat in hand as he cooled his heels. He was a rather rough looking man, coarse and hardened, befitting a person of his profession. Tomkin was nondescript in the way street urchins and thieves were, his features undistinguishable from dozens of other faces in London.

Her father had often told Marissa the best disguise was to hide in plain sight.

Tomkin's cloak bore a thin line of mud at the edge, as did his boots. Bits of dirt fell from him as he approached her, bowing politely, a shock of graying hair spilling over his collar. The scar at his mouth wiggled as he greeted her.

Greenhouse, ever distressed, watched Tomkin with mounting disapproval, his eyes flickering to the specks of mud scattering across the expensive rug at her guest's feet.

"That will be all, Greenhouse. Thank you." Marissa nodded toward the door. God save her if Greenhouse thought his duty was to protect her from Tomkin. Her butler looked like an overstuffed Cornish hen with his chest puffed out in such a way. She doubted his thin arms carried enough strength to hold a pistol, if it came to that.

Not that it would. Marissa was completely safe with Tomkin. He worked for her nephew. And her father before that.

Once Greenhouse shut the door, Marissa waved for Tomkin to sit. "Should I ring for tea or would you prefer something stronger? Whisky perhaps?"

A grunt sounded from Tomkin as he itched his nose. "Please, my lady. If it isn't too much trouble."

"Whisky is never a bother, Mr. Tomkin." Marissa strode to the sideboard and poured out two glasses of whisky, one for each of them; his eyes widened when he saw she meant to join him. "I do appreciate a glass of good whisky, Mr. Tomkin. My father's doing, I'm afraid."

Tomkin's eyes widened further at the mention of the late Duke of Dunbar; he probably had not anticipated that this meeting would involve drinking whisky with the daughter of his former employer. "The duke did enjoy his whisky, my lady."

She'd engaged Tomkin's services after her arrival in London, quietly of course. It would do Marissa no good for her nephew to catch wind of her activities and attempt to be involved. Tomkin's attention to detail, his discretion and especially his loyalty to the Dukes of Dunbar had made him a very wealthy man, though one wouldn't know by looking at him. Tomkin *excelled* at gathering information, though Marissa was certain he possessed other skills, as the bulge of a pistol in his coat pocket could attest to.

The big man took a sip of the whisky, the glass looking diminutive in his massive hands. His eyes closed in pleasure. "You've excellent taste in whisky, if I may say so, my lady."

"You may. And if you've brought me good information,"

she said, "I'll send you a bottle or two." Marissa took a seat behind the massive yet delicately carved feminine desk dominating her study. Another gift from her father.

Her hands ran over the inlay of pearl around the edges. Ladies didn't have a study, but Marissa did. She found it a more convenient place to handle her correspondence and other business affairs, preferring certain matters, like Mr. Tomkin, not invade the sanctity of her private parlor.

"I have. At your request, my lady, I went first to Viscount Pendleton's home in the Peak District."

"Brushbriar." Marissa sipped, enjoying the fiery burn of the whisky sliding down her throat.

Tomkin nodded. "Lady Whitfield remains in residence." He cleared his throat as he spoke of Simon's sister. "She's had several visitors." The tips of his ears pinked which was disarming on a gentleman such as Tomkin who had no doubt seen the seedier side of life.

"Gentlemen callers, I'm sure." Catherine had always been a bit of a slut.

"*Many* gentleman callers. A Mr. Kendicott, in particular."

Marissa wasn't familiar with Mr. Kendicott. "And he is . . .?"

"Wealthy. He owns most of the land to the west of Brushbriar. New money. His family isn't distinguished in any way. Father was a pig farmer. Kendicott married a wealthy heiress who, to his great fortune, died barely two years after their marriage. The talk in Buxton is that he is courting Lady Whitfield."

Marissa placed a finger against her lips in thought, cradling the whisky in her free hand. There would be only *one* reason Catherine would ever consider lowering herself to attach herself to a man like Kendicott. *Money*. Simon's debts had to be enormous if Lydia meant to sacrifice her daughter to the son of a pig farmer. The stack of markers Marissa had acquired thus far were only further proof.

A pity Catherine wouldn't have to suffer the indignity of becoming Mrs. Kendicott.

"I'm afraid, Mr. Tomkin, that Kendicott will need to be apprised of Lady Whitfield's *other* gentleman callers. A shame. But we can't allow Kendicott to be married under false pretenses."

"No, my lady." The right side of his mouth tipped up.

"I assume, and forgive me for being indelicate, she is being attentive to one gentleman more so than the others?"

"Yes, a handsome gent named Doren. Works as paymaster for a local quarry."

What an odd coincidence to have one of Catherine's lovers in Haddon's employ. "Have you matters in hand, then?"

"Two of the maids at Brushbriar, a footman and a groom are all in my pocket, my lady. According to the footman, whom she has also *dallied* with"—he coughed—"Lady Whitfield favors a particular spot in the gardens for her . . . *activities*. I can arrange for her and Doren to be stumbled upon by Kendicott, with your permission."

This was excellent news. "You have it, Mr. Tomkin."

"If I may?"

"Pray, continue." Tomkin had more than earned his whisky. She made a mental note to have several bottles sent to him.

"Lady Whitfield, when not entertaining callers, took many of the more expensive furnishings of Brushbriar to Castleton where the entire cartload was sold at private auction. Blue John, my lady, most taken from Lady Pendleton's private sitting room. The auction was by invitation only and the source of the objects not disclosed, though I'm certain those bidding knew the items came from Brushbriar."

Marissa sipped her whisky. *This* was a cause for celebration. Not only was Lydia driven to accept a man like Kendicott as a son-in-law, but she was also willing to part with her precious Blue John, which Marissa suspected was far more dear to Lydia than her own daughter. Brushbriar was garnished with lavish displays of the mineral, carved vases, ornate eggs, windowsills, candy dishes and the like.

All things Lydia and her husband had murdered Reggie for.

"A terrible shame, to have to sell such precious items." A smile played at her lips. She could not be more pleased her efforts were bearing such immediate fruit.

"Indeed, my lady. And there is one *other* bit of news. Lady Pendleton is in London."

Marissa sat up in her chair. "Is she?" This was highly unusual. Lydia rarely left Brushbriar.

"Yes. I watched her coach depart Brushbriar and then passed her again on the road. She arrived at Pendleton's house late last night."

The *only* reason Lydia would ever have come to London was to ensure Simon married an heiress of *her* choosing, one wealthy enough to wipe clean the yawning hole of debt Lydia had driven the family into. And she would not have left Brushbriar unless she was assured Catherine had bagged Kendicott.

Poor, *poor* murdering Lydia, to have her old bones jostled in the carriage along the bumpy road to London. She'd probably stayed drunk the entire trip and doubtless hadn't felt a thing. Marissa covered her mouth to stifle the giggle that bubbled up. She only wished she could see Lydia's face when she heard the news that Catherine wouldn't be marrying Kendicott after all.

"You've someone watching Pendleton's home?"

Tomkin made a small sound of offense. "Of course, my lady. And two inside."

"Forgive me for questioning your thoroughness, Tomkin. I know you've planned well. I wish to know what events Lady Pendleton will be attending and if her son escorts her. Another glass?" Tomkin, bless him, had thought of everything. The man was a treasure.

"Regretfully no, my lady. I've business to see to." He reached inside his coat pocket and brought forth a small packet. "Everything's here. I've a man whom I trust handling things at Brushbriar for me. When he's sure Kendicott is no longer interested in Lady Whitfield, he'll send word to me."

"Very good, Mr. Tomkin. I'll have the funds deposited in your account. I hope you'll keep things just between us?"

Tomkin sat his now empty glass down on her desk and stood. "You may be assured. I will contact you when I have more information on Viscount Pendleton."

"Not a word to the duke," Marissa cautioned, her voice steely. Tomkin held her in healthy respect, but he was *afraid* of her nephew. Most people were. Sooner or later, Nick *would* find out what she was up to, but she hoped to be nearly finished by the time he did.

Tomkin bowed. "No, my lady. You may rely on my discretion."

After Tomkin took his leave, Marissa poured herself another glass of whisky and wandered back down the hall to the drawing room. The vase of roses and peonies wasn't quite perfect yet.

Marissa paced across the rug of the drawing room, taking in the spray of flowers from various angles.

Humming to herself, she strode back and forth, sipping at her whisky and wondering if Simon had received word yet from their solicitors that in addition to contesting the ownership of the mine and freezing all the current assets, she was also insisting that if the survey map was deemed an original, which it would be, that all the *previous* profits of the mine be reverted back to the estate of the Earl of Morwick.

Brendan had sent her a letter just the other day asking what the *bloody hell* she was up to because a court appointed overseer had taken over the mine.

Marissa had declined to answer. She'd tell him soon enough when he arrived with Petra for the holidays.

How fortuitous Lydia was now in London She would be able to hear the news about the freezing of her assets from Simon *firsthand*. Marissa hoped the news would send Lydia to bed for a week. Murderous bitch.

A rush of grief and anger filled her. *Reggie.*

The pain, while not as acute as it had once been, was still there, lingering on the edge of her heart. Reggie had *not* deserved to be murdered and left to die in a cave, shot by a man he considered his best friend. *Alone.* All so that Lydia could have an entire staircase made from Blue John. She hoped when every piece of the miserable stuff was sold, Lydia lost a piece of her soul.

I'm so sorry, Reggie.

Marissa slapped the table so hard the vase shook. One of the peonies fell out. Shoving the bloom back into the vase, she marched over to the couch, clasping the whisky between her hands. In her pique over Haddon's non-visit today and Jordana, along with the arrival of Mr. Tomkin, Marissa had nearly forgotten. Or perhaps she intentionally didn't wish to think about it.

She'd *dreamt* of Reggie last night, something she hadn't

done in years, not even after the discovery of his remains. They'd been in bed together, laughing at a joke he'd made, his back to her. Curled up behind him, her fingers had trailed over his shoulders before pressing her lips to the base of his neck.

Marissa tossed back the remainder of the whisky, her hand unsteady.

When Reggie had rolled over in her dream, fingers threading through Marissa's hair to pull her down for a kiss, it wasn't her long-dead husband's face she saw.

It was Haddon's.

8

T rent looked out the window at the trees, most bare of leaves, as his carriage neared the park. Marissa was bound to be surprised when she saw that he had accompanied his daughter today. She wouldn't be expecting him.

Good. Marissa could do with a few surprises now and again.

Stubborn.

She was testing the limits of Trent's patience, and considering he had four daughters, that was considerable indeed.

Challenging.

Trent had known the moment he took her in his arms and danced with her at Brushbriar, lifting her chin as if daring him to charm her, that they would be lovers. He'd sensed her vulnerability, well-hidden behind a sparkling wit, concealed nearly as well as the ruthlessness flickering in her sapphire eyes.

Clever.

The conversation between them had never lagged. Much

to his surprise, Marissa was not only well-informed on a variety of subjects, but her opinions were her own. His late wife had barely ever expressed an independent thought, nor had any of his previous lovers ever espoused their views. Marissa was an *intelligent* woman. One who, given her family's reputation, would be unwise to cross.

She was the most fascinating creature Trent had ever encountered. And his determination to have her, as evidenced by the hardening of his cock before he'd even kissed her that night, had only increased tenfold.

Shy.

When at last he'd pressed Marissa down on the bed in her room at Brushbriar, Trent's heart had ached at the sight of her. She'd been so lovely with all her dark hair spilling about the coverlet like a halo. Marissa had blushed as he'd untied the robe she'd worn, begging him, with no small amount of embarrassment, to please douse the candle.

Her inhibition had surprised him, as had the unexpected rush of protectiveness for her filling his chest.

Trent had taken the greatest care, wanting Marissa to weep his name as he bedded her, as he knew he would hers. This was no mere tryst, as the shaking of his fingers when he touched her had informed him. He'd traced the small lines radiating from her navel, proof she'd borne her two sons, then bent and trailed his tongue along each one, despite her protests.

Battle-scarred.

Nibbling at her warm, vanilla-scented skin, feeling her surprise as she climaxed at the mere brush of his thumb, Trent had breathed in Marissa. When he had finally settled between her thighs and thrust deep inside her, she'd cried out, her inner muscles clasping him so tightly, Trent had felt his heart stop.

"I'm sorry," she had whispered. "I'm—well, I haven't—it has been some time. Several years at least." A small laugh had escaped her. "I don't make this a habit."

"I don't either," he'd confessed, pressing a kiss to her open mouth, stopping her protests. Trent hadn't been with a woman in nearly two years before Marissa. Sex had ceased to be important to him, as meaningless as the act had become.

It was frustrating as hell she refused to acknowledge what was between them.

Which was why Haddon had been forced to use Jordana to keep Marissa close. She *had* offered to help his daughter, though Haddon had barely heard her at the time. He had been too entertained with running his tongue up the underside of one of Marissa's breasts.

The woman had a magnificent bosom.

Just the thought resulted in his cock thickening. He hoped he could get through their walk in the park without pulling her behind a tree to ravish her as he was sorely tempted to do. Overwhelming Marissa with sex would be far too easy.

I want all of her.

"I don't want to be late, Papa. Lady Cupps-Foster doesn't tolerate tardiness, especially since she kindly made time for me after rearranging her schedule. I promised to meet her at the spot where the path begins along the river."

"Don't worry. We'll be right on time."

"I'm not sure why you've come." Jordana eyed him with suspicion. "Don't make her angry as you did the other day."

"I thought I would take a moment to assure Lady Cupps-Foster that she must send any bills for your outings and purchases to me. She is my friend as well. And I fail to see how I made her angry the other day."

"She wasn't happy you left me to take tea with her alone even after I told her you'd a previous appointment which could not be avoided." His daughter gave him an innocent look.

Trent was, it seemed, surrounded by clever females.

"I'm glad you two have got on so well." He'd known they would. Marissa had wanted to refuse him, but she was far too kind not to assist a young girl in need.

Generous of heart.

Jordana *did* need guidance. But she could have waited until Trent's sister arrived in London with the rest of his girls. He'd brought Jordana with him purposefully, thinking his eldest daughter would enjoy the experience of life in town. And be of help if Marissa decided to be difficult.

Which she had.

Christ, he could read her like a book.

Trent *knew* she was older than he was; should he forget, he had no doubt she would remind him of the fact. He'd taken to making references about her age just to watch her reaction. Leaving her with the wallflowers and elderly matrons at the Cambourne ball had been inspired. The look on her face had been priceless.

No more than she deserved. Trent had turned *forty* at his last birthday. He wasn't some schoolboy. Couldn't the bloody woman see she could have been sixty and it wouldn't have mattered? His *heart* didn't care how old she was.

"Here, Papa."

Trent reached up, rapping on the roof to alert the driver.

He had given Marissa the space she'd needed after her late husband's remains had been discovered. It *had* pained Trent that she didn't send for him or reply to any of his notes. But when news reached him that Marissa had fled back to London, without so much as telling him goodbye,

Trent had taken a bottle of whisky to his study and thought long and hard about a woman whom he desperately wanted but who didn't seem to want him.

She's afraid.

He'd seen the way the sapphire of her eyes warmed when he'd approached her at the Cambourne ball. The way her luscious form bent in his direction whenever he was near, whether she realized it or not. Her jealousy over Lady Christina Sykes which she was incredibly poor at hiding. And the blushing. If he didn't know better, Trent would assume Marissa was constantly feverish.

She was *not* unaffected by him. The intensity of the attraction between them blazed stronger than ever. If it didn't, Trent would have already retreated. He'd had the misfortune of running into her youngest son, Morwick, in Buxton, shortly after Marissa had returned to London. Before Morwick had nearly taken his head off with his fist, he'd warned Trent to leave his mother alone.

"She's damaged, Haddon. Can't you see that? Find another woman to bed."

Marissa was *terrified* to fall in love again. Specifically, with him.

I need to be careful.

The carriage rolled to a spot just above the river path. Not another vehicle was in sight though there was a group of early morning riders ahead of them. Several pairs of young ladies walked the path, maids trailing behind them. A young boy escaped his nanny, stirring the leaves on the ground as he sped by, sailboat clutched in his hand. Trent saw no sign of Marissa.

"Are you sure this is the spot?"

"Yes, Papa. I'm sure. And should you inquire in the future, I much prefer the park to the *torturous* task of tea with Lady Christina Sykes and her mother." Jordana shot him a mutinous glare from across the carriage. "I hope taking her riding the other day will keep her from feeling the need to call again."

Trent stepped out of the carriage and held out his hand. "It was *one* time, Jordana. I thought it lovely she and Lady Stanton called on us. Perhaps you'd like to join us next time we ride in the park?"

Jordana made a face of abject horror at the mere mention of spending time with Lady Christina. "Please tell me you aren't seriously considering her, Papa. As a wife. I thought you said you'd never remarry."

His daughter detested everything about London but especially pouring tea and making small talk with a young lady of Lady Christina Sykes's ilk. Jordana's interests lay more in the direction of following about Dr. Choate, the local physician. Or helping the village midwife. When she was nine, he'd found Jordana assisting the head groom with the birth of a foal.

"Lady Christina is a lovely girl," Trent said, intentionally not denying her claim he was considering her as a wife.

"The Haddon Hellions will devour her in a matter of moments, Papa. She wouldn't survive a fortnight." Jordana hopped out of the carriage.

Trent smiled at Jordana's show of arrogance, though she was probably right. He adored his girls and never regretted leaving the lifestyle he'd cultivated for so many years to raise them himself. But it was possible he'd overindulged them, mostly out of survival.

Trent knew when he was outnumbered.

"May we go to Thrumbadge's tomorrow?" Jordana asked, taking his arm.

The only other place in all of London his daughter

remotely cared about, besides the park, was Thrumbadge's book sellers. Not for the rows of romantic novels, where most young ladies tended to linger, but for Thrumbadge's vast selection of medical books. Anatomy was currently a particular favorite of hers. The bookseller possessed a small collection of tomes for sale regarding how to treat *female* maladies. And childbirth. Something Jordana insisted most physicians cared nothing about.

"I believe we can manage a trip, though I'm not sure where these interests are leading you, Jordana."

But Trent *did* know when the curiosity and desire to help had taken root. Jordana had witnessed firsthand the agony her mother had gone through to bring Delphine into the world. Not long after, she'd assisted the midwife when the wife of one of Trent's tenants had bled to death giving birth, weeping for days because she hadn't been able to help the woman.

Another mutinous look shot from the pair of silver eyes so like Trent's own. "To my future."

Jordana was highly intelligent, brilliant, if he were being honest. But despite the aptitude she displayed, Trent knew of *no* medical school in all of England that would admit her. The most she might be able to accomplish would be learning the skills of a midwife. But even so, such an occupation for a girl of her station would be frowned upon.

"How do you know your future isn't in London?"

"It isn't," she said with certainty, sounding years older than she was.

They strolled in the direction of the river, passing a pair of young ladies who peered at Trent from beneath their lashes, giggling the entire time.

"I have nothing in common with these nitwits," Jordana hissed beneath her breath. "And I find it appalling I must watch my father be mooned over. You simply aren't that handsome." Two bright spots of red stood out on her cheeks. "It is *humiliating*, Papa."

"I apologize for any embarrassment." Trent tried not to laugh at Jordana as the wind ruffled through his coat. The morning was pleasant but cool, the sun struggling mightily to peek through the gray clouds littering the sky. The air smelled of grass and a hint of rain, along with mud. The river was just over the rise. As they turned and strolled between two large oak trees, neatly sidestepping a gentleman and his dog, Trent finally saw Marissa.

She was sitting in a handsome, horribly expensive carriage, drawn by perfectly matched ebony horses, their coats shining in the muted sunlight. The oval of her face peered through the window of the vehicle, sapphire eyes widening as she caught sight of Trent.

Her driver, a large mountain of a man, watched them approach before nodding and jumping down from his seat.

A ripple stretched across Trent's heart. It was the same every time he saw her.

Assisted by the driver, Marissa stepped out of the carriage, the indigo skirts floating above her ankles revealing fine calfskin half-boots. Her dark hair was pulled into a tight chignon at the base of her neck, only a few strands left to dangle against her temples. A small hat, festooned with an ornate twist of ribbon and flowers and tilted at a saucy angle, sat atop her head. She inclined her chin in his direction, as regal as any queen.

If I had any sense at all, I'd abscond with her and bed her until she surrenders.

"Lord Haddon." A girlish voice twittered from behind him. "Is that you?"

Jordana's displeasure was evident by the way her fingers twisted into his arm.

Marissa paused beside her carriage, a frown darkening her lovely features as her gaze focused on something beyond Trent's shoulder.

"Lady Christina." He turned and bowed smoothly as Jordana slipped her arm free. She spared a silent but polite greeting to Lady Christina before walking to greet Marissa who had moved several paces in Trent's direction.

Lady Christina watched Jordana's retreat, the smile gracing her rosebud mouth faltering when she noticed Marissa. Looking up at Trent, she composed herself. "Lord Haddon, how delightful. I had no idea you liked to walk so early."

"I like the quiet of the morning," he said. *And you've disturbed it.* He cast a sideways glance in Marissa's direction, willing her to come closer.

"I do as well. What a coincidence."

Trent didn't believe in coincidences, at least in regard to Lady Christina Sykes. "A lucky one," he said, blandly polite.

"May I present my cousin? Miss Regina Applewaite." Christina pulled the plump girl she'd been walking with forward.

"Miss Applewaite." Trent bowed again before nodding in the direction of Jordana and Marissa. "My daughter, Miss Ives. And Lady Cupps-Foster."

"His daughter's chaperone," Lady Christina informed Miss Applewaite before smiling up at Trent.

He kept his own smile pasted on his face, refusing to react to Christina's assumption. He supposed it was a natural conclusion for her to make. "If you'll excuse me, Lady Christina, Miss Applewaite, we were just about to take a turn around the path."

A frown pulled down the corners of Lady Christina's perfect, pink lips. She batted her eyes and waited for him to suggest she and Miss Applewaite join them. When he didn't, Lady Christina gave a small, quiet, barely noticeable sound of frustration. Looking again in Marissa's direction, she said in a voice that was sure to carry, "I'm pleased you've found an older widow to act as chaperone for Miss Ives, my lord. I had considered suggesting just that thing."

"Indeed?" Christina was barely older than Jordana herself. Trent found her know-it-all manner off-putting to say the least.

"I was relieved when my mother informed me that you'd engaged Lady Cupps-Foster to fill the role."

"I'm not sure how Lady Stanton came to such a conclusion." Trent had never referred to Marissa as Jordana's chaperone. Ever.

Christina's fingers fluttered boldly just above Trent's wrist. The tiny curls spilling from her coiffure and down her cheeks trembled in a fetching manner. "I grew curious, my lord, after seeing you dance with Lady Cupps-Foster at the Cambourne ball. And I drew an incorrect conclusion." She bit her lip. "But my mother assured me your interest in Lady Cupps-Foster could only be for the benefit of Miss Ives, as you are a widower."

"And how did Lady Stanton reason so?" Christina was unlikely to catch the hint of mockery in his tone.

"Well," Lady Christina stuttered, glancing at Marissa.

Marissa stared back, brow raised, one foot tapping with impatience.

Trent was certain she could hear *every* word.

"Lady Cupps-Foster is many years your senior which would preclude—that is to say—your friendship with her is more *professional* in nature. My mother has cautioned me on jumping to ridiculous conclusions, especially when it clearly isn't warranted."

A sound of feminine outrage came from behind Trent.

"It *is completely* acceptable for you to ask an older widow to help you," she hastily added, "in the absence of a Lady Haddon." The fingertip of her glove dipped to Trent's wrist. "Now that my mother has explained, I feel much better."

Trent took a deep breath, momentarily shocked at Christina's audacity. "If you'll excuse me, I fear my daughter grows impatient. I bid you both good morning."

"But they're already wandering off," Lady Christina said in a low tone. "They've left you in my care."

Miss Applewaite made a nervous twitter.

He turned to see Marissa and Jordana retreating down the path, leaving him to his fate which he supposed he deserved for giving Lady Christina even a modest amount of encouragement.

Marissa's skirts were twitching with agitation, her hips swaying with annoyance. She stopped abruptly and looked at him over her shoulder.

The sapphire eyes sparked with possessiveness as she took in Lady Christina and Trent. Jealousy flared sharply across her lovely features before Marissa turned her back on him. She straightened her shoulders, her attention returning to Jordana.

That gives me a fair amount of hope.

Trent bowed again. "Enjoy your walk. Lady Christina. Miss Applewaite."

Lady Christina made a poof of disappointment as Miss Applewaite took her arm, moving her back the way they'd come, a footman and maid trailing at a discreet distance.

Trent hurried away, lengthening his strides to catch up

with his daughter and Marissa. The two had their arms linked, and the sound of Marissa's laughter met his ears.

A wonderful sense of joy filled Trent at the picture the two made, with their dark heads bent together like conspirators, their skirts swaying in tandem as they strolled along the path.

He quickened his steps.

There was nothing Trent wanted more than to see the sight before him for the remainder of his days.

9

Marissa listened with half an ear to Jordana who was babbling away about something to do with body parts. Honestly, the girl seemed enamored of grisly details. But she didn't stop Jordana's earnest chattering. Marissa had been far too busy watching Lady Christina flutter about Haddon like an overprivileged butterfly. She'd heard enough of the conversation between them to know the little nitwit had dismissed Marissa as nothing more than an elderly matron, undeserving of attention from a man like Haddon.

A raw, biting possessiveness had filled Marissa so *sharply* that her fingertips had burned as if scorched by a hot pot of tea. Folding her hands into her skirts, she forced her features to relax. It wouldn't do for Haddon to guess at her feelings. She'd loved Reggie, but he'd never made her feel as if she needed to defend her claim on him.

But you don't have a claim on Haddon.

Marissa had to resist the urge to march across the grass and slap Christina Sykes on her pretty, pink little face and challenge her for Haddon. Pistols at dawn. Or swords. She'd even defended herself with a large frying pan once.

Little twit.

"Have I said something to make you angry?" Jordana said. "You're scowling."

Haddon was nearly at their side, his legs making short work of the distance to join them.

"What? No, dear," Marissa assured her, forcing a smile to her lips. "Whatever would make you think such a thing?"

"Papa says I'm far too blunt at times. I shouldn't have told you about the books I'd gotten at Thrumbadge's. I suppose the subject is somewhat grisly."

"Not at all, Jordana." Truthfully, she hadn't been listening. Something about the way blood pumped through a person's heart. *Very disturbing.* She'd tuned it out. "There is very little which offends me, else I would not have survived so long in society. But you must not discuss your interests with everyone you meet, especially in London."

Jordana was convinced she had every right to tramp around Derbyshire and assist in childbirth, the mere thought of which made Marissa swoon. If anyone was in need of feminine encouragement and direction, it was Jordana.

Even more reason for him to remarry.

The thought of a new Lady Haddon filled her with an almost unbearable melancholy.

Haddon finally reached them, his gaze lingering over Marissa, though she hadn't any idea what he was thinking. "My apologies for the delay. How wonderful to see you, Lady Cupps-Foster."

"You were otherwise occupied," she said in a crisp voice.

The pale of his eyes darkened like quicksilver, never leaving her face. "Unexpectedly detained."

Marissa told herself to breathe, a feat difficult enough with how tightly her stays were laced. And she was annoyed with him. He'd not even bothered to correct Lady Christina's assessment of Marissa as an elderly chaperone.

"Lady Stanton should have a discussion with her daughter on a more ladylike way of speaking. Lady Christina's voice is a bit shrill drowning out even the birds singing in the trees."

A tiny, knowing smile hovered at his lips. "Lady Christina sends you both her regards."

"How kind." Marissa savagely tamped down the jealousy snarling inside her. She told herself it didn't matter what Lady Christina or her mother thought. The end result was the same. Marissa had no claim on Haddon. And she *detested* being envious over Lady Christina's pert bosom and youthful glow. It wasn't becoming.

Marissa *was* the daughter of a duke.

The trio walked for several minutes with only the sound of their feet crunching on the gravel to break the silence.

Elderly widow. Chaperone.

A burst of laughter filled the air as they passed a group of gentlemen on horseback, one of whom hailed them in greeting.

Haddon waved back.

"I was telling Lady Cupps-Foster," Jordana began, "about the book I'd purchased at Thrumbadge's."

"Please tell me you're joking." Haddon shot Marissa a look of apology. The breeze ruffled the hair around his ears and caught against his collar.

Why must he be so bloody handsome? Couldn't he have a wart or some other unattractive disfigurement?

"She isn't." Marissa nudged Jordana to take out the sting of her father's rebuke. "I am hopeful to persuade Jordana to read something more appropriate. A fashion magazine, for instance."

Jordana stopped in her tracks as a gust of wind blew up sharply. "I would never."

A laugh escaped Marissa at the look on Jordana's face at the mere mention of reading *The Ladies Pocket Magazine*, or something similar before gasping as her clever little hat shifted, becoming dislodged from its mooring of pins.

"Drat." She reached up and adjusted the brim.

A rumble of thunder rippled across the park as patches of fallen leaves swirled and eddied in the gusting wind. Their time in the park would be cut short, it seemed, by the impending storm.

"I think we'd best turn around." Haddon peered up at the sky, his eyes the exact color of the gathering thunderclouds.

Marissa cursed under her breath. Next she would find herself composing an ode to his cheekbones or something equally ridiculous.

"My lady?" He quirked a brow at her, a grin tugging at his lips.

"I only said I was in agreement," she assured him.

Jordana looked up at the sky, sticking out her tongue as the first raindrops began to fall.

Another rush of wind, this one much stronger than the others, had Marissa holding down her dress lest all of London see her underthings. The hat rocked precariously, struggling to stay atop her head, before lifting from her hair and scuttling down the path.

"Bloody hell."

Neither Haddon nor Jordana showed the least bit of shock at her language which was mildly disappointing. "I apologize, Jordana, I should not have cursed."

"Oh, I've heard my father say much worse."

"*Much* worse," Haddon agreed, the mischievous smile Marissa so adored fixed firmly on his lips.

Marissa stomped to where her hat had fallen to the ground, sighing at the wet leaves sticking to the brim. Perhaps it could be repaired. She bent and tried to grab at her hat while simultaneously holding down her skirts which were determined to creep up her legs.

Another gust of wind blew across her ankles bringing several fat droplets of rain.

The hat slid away from her and across the wet grass, bumping over a large bush to land well out of her reach.

Damn and blast.

"Leave it," Haddon said from the path, taking hold of Jordana's arm. "The sky will open upon us at any moment."

Marissa was *incredibly* annoyed. At herself. At Haddon. At Lady Christina. *And at her bloody hat.* "I will not. It is one of a kind, made especially for me."

As she watched in horror, the wind took her precious, one-of-a-kind hat up into the air where it hovered for a moment before sailing toward an oak tree. The ribbons across the brim tangled on a low hanging branch, the hat swinging in the air, taunting Marissa.

Her new bloody hat.

This was what came of jealousy over the likes of Christina Sykes. She strode to the tree, ignoring the approaching storm and jumped up, the ribbon fluttering just out of her reach. A drop of rain fell right on the end of her nose. She was going to become a drenched, matronly—

"Jordana." Haddon spoke from behind her. "We've only just gotten you well. The doctor says you cannot afford to catch another chill which could settle in your chest. Get to our carriage and head home before the storm descends. The temperature has already dropped."

"But—"

"Now, Jordana. I'll see to Lady Cupps-Foster and her hat."

"Goodbye, Lady Cupps-Foster!" Jordana ran in the direction of Haddon's carriage whose driver, seeing the approach of rain, had already steered the vehicle further into the park to intercept them.

"Take her directly home," he yelled at the driver before turning to Marissa. "I may have to beg a ride." Haddon's voice vibrated down into her skin, dispelling the cold and warming her from the inside out.

"Why don't you just go?" Marissa didn't want his help. Nor was this about her hat. "*Elderly* widow that I am, I'm fairly certain I can retrieve this hat myself."

"I believe the term she used was *older* widow. I've no intention of leaving you here alone, jumping around like a mad hare." He looked back at his carriage which was pulling away now with Jordana tucked safely inside.

"There's no need, Haddon. Truly." She made another leap at the ribbon fluttering just out of her reach.

"You realize, Marissa, that no matter how hard you jump, you won't be able to catch it."

Marissa shot him a murderous look and continued to leap toward the branch, fingers spread to catch at the fluttering piece of ribbon.

An older widow. An appropriate chaperone. Is that all I am?

Isn't that all she *wished* to be to him?

"Christ, Marissa. It's only a hat."

I called him a dalliance, which is so far from the truth. I suppose we're even now.

Rain began to pelt them, the droplets big and fat. The

wind blew, no longer in sharp bursts but in steady, chilling gusts. They would both catch cold if they didn't leave soon.

"I don't need your help." Looking down at the rain spotting her dress and dripping down her shoulders in rivulets, with the hat ruined, and her hair sliding from its pins, Marissa gave a small cry of frustration.

Now she appeared to be an older *bedraggled* widow.

Haddon swept past her. Taking off his coat, he nestled it around her shoulders and handed her his own hat.

Marissa shivered in pleasure as the coat fell over her. The fabric was still warm from his body and smelled deliciously spicy, just like Haddon.

"I'll fetch it, Marissa. Your carriage is just down there. I'll get your hat and then see you home."

"No . . . I mean you don't have to."

Haddon ignored her and began to scramble up the tree as if he'd been born to climb. His shirt was soaking wet, the fabric clinging to the sculpted lines of his back and arms. There was no hesitation as he made his way up the tree, each movement imbued with graceful agility, sure and confident. He reached the branch from which her little hat dangled in a matter of seconds. Haddon would rival Brendan in his ability to climb. Her eyes lovingly traced every muscular line of his body, noting the way the rain made the ends of his hair curl about the collar of his shirt.

What had Adelia said? That Haddon had the look of a Viking marauder? Seeing him like this, a man against the elements, Marissa could well imagine him scaling the side of a castle with an axe clutched in one hand.

Desire for Haddon burst over her, settling with a dull, insistent ache between her thighs. It was going to be very difficult to resist him after such a masculine display.

A rumble of thunder shook the park followed by a quick flash of lightning.

"Hurry!" Marissa glanced around, unsurprised to find they were the only ones still there, besides her driver who was leading the carriage in their direction. "I don't care to be struck by lightning." Nor have Haddon become injured. Because she'd wanted that stupid hat and he'd gone to get it. *For her*.

Haddon was still hanging from the tree, cheeky grin in place, rain sluicing down his striking cheekbones. He deftly snagged her hat and waved it at her, clearly showing off.

Marissa's pulse skipped in an unbearable rhythm, her entire being aching with longing for him, along with something so much more complicated.

Water dripped down the lean lines of his body as he jumped from the tree and jogged in her direction. Haddon was smiling, his teeth brilliant against the light tan of his skin, proud of himself for rescuing her hat.

"Haddon," she whispered, looking into his beautiful face. "You bloody idiot."

He stood before her, bowing in the rain, before holding out her very ruined hat. When she reached for the brim, he jerked the hat back, making her fall against him.

And then he kissed her.

10

Trent hadn't meant to kiss her.

I couldn't help myself.

Marissa was so beautiful, waiting for him with raindrops caught on her lashes and in the dark curls of her hair. He'd just made himself promise to tread lightly with her. Allow her to set the pace to their courtship.

Of course, she had no idea he *was* courting her. Marissa was far too busy being annoyed over Lady Christina Sykes. As if he would ever prefer any other woman to *her.*

She shivered at the light touch of his mouth on hers but didn't pull away. On the contrary, a growl of pleasure escaped Marissa, a wholly feminine sound of desire which only hardened the length of his cock now clearly outlined in his wet trousers. Her lips tasted of tea and lemon. A hint of ginger. Delicious and warm.

He'd never wanted *anyone* or *anything* quite so badly in his entire life.

Only their mouths touched, the hat crushed and ruined between them. When he pulled away, Marissa's eyes fluttered open. The pools of sapphire shimmered in the rain like the depths of the deepest lake in the Peak District. There were tiny creases at the corners of her eyes which only made her more precious to him. Trent had the urge to press his lips to each groove but thought better of it.

"I fear your hat is ruined, my lady."

She blinked, moisture dripping from her lashes, looking at Trent as if seeing him for the first time.

"We should get out of the rain, Marissa."

"Yes. Yes, of course. Good Lord, what am I thinking?"

He took her hand and ran with her across the slick grass to the carriage. Her skirts curled around his legs as he helped her inside before sliding in across from her.

The carriage lurched forward as the rain began to increase, hammering the poor driver as well as the horses. The vehicle rocked as it fought with the wind outside.

"My house is fairly close," she said, her eyes fixed on the hollow of his throat. "Just on the other side of the park."

It was true. Trent's own house lay a good distance away. "Yes, it is."

"You can't," Marissa hesitated, wiping a wet curl from her cheek, "return home soaked to the bone, Haddon." Her voice held an undercurrent of something wicked. "You'll catch a chill."

"No. I don't suppose I can." His trousers, already tight, became increasingly uncomfortable. Marissa's dress, as wet as it was, left little to the imagination. *Christ*, he could see the points of her nipples. Unfortunately, her home was *so* close he'd not have enough time to ravish her in the coach. Which was what he wanted to do. Trent's fingers drummed lightly on one knee. Truthfully, he was the furthest thing from being chilled.

"The least I can do for the rescue of my hat is to offer

you tea. You can warm yourself before the fire while your clothing dries."

"I think I'd prefer whisky." *And you naked beneath me.*

A blush rose up her cheeks despite the cold air. Trent found the way she flushed adorable. "I, too, prefer a good whisky. Much more than ratafia."

His cock twitched against his leg.

They sat in silence on the short ride to Marissa's town house, neither willing to interrupt the fragile acceptance of what was going to happen. Trent was afraid if he spoke, Marissa would change her mind, something the deep ache between his legs wanted to avoid at all costs.

Once the carriage slowed, Trent ran up the steps, Marissa's hand clutched firmly in his, not caring which one of her neighbors spied them out their parlor windows. Once inside, Marissa's ruffled butler greeted them, nose pointed high in the air at the water dripping all over the floor.

"Greenhouse, send word to Lord Haddon's daughter we've arrived safely. He will be home after his clothes are no longer dripping wet, and he's been warmed."

The wet trousers pulled tighter though he didn't think she'd meant the words as an innuendo. Trent turned, pretending to observe the large vase of greenery and purple flowers to his left. Marissa still had his coat around her shoulders.

"Have tea and something to eat brought to my parlor."

"Your private parlor?" Greenhouse looked appalled. He watched Trent with suspicion. "Are you certain, my lady?"

"I did not stutter, Greenhouse, did I?"

The butler's lower lip pulled tight. "No, madam."

"Make sure the fire is *roaring*, Greenhouse. I'm freezing."

Greenhouse clapped his hands and a maid appeared. He

whispered instructions to her before the girl sped off in what Haddon guessed was the direction of Marissa's parlor.

"Lord Haddon is soaked to the bone, as am I. My son left behind a dressing gown in the large armoire in the guestroom. Lord Haddon can avail himself of it while his clothes dry. Please retrieve it immediately. And send my maid to me."

The butler stared at her, eyes bugging out. "In the parlor?"

"I'll meet her upstairs, Greenhouse." She clapped her hands. "Hurry."

Trent watched in bemusement as the butler fairly sprinted up the stairs, eager to do her bidding. His hand trailed down the line of Marissa's back, gratified at the way she arched into his touch. "Marissa—"

"Don't speak, Haddon. Not yet."

Once Greenhouse returned with the robe, a silken thing with dragons embroidered on it, Marissa thrust it into Trent's hands before gesturing him to follow her to another innately feminine room he felt too large to be stomping around in. He caught sight of a pair of discarded reading glasses and a book, tossed atop a blanket that looked as if a child had knit it. The thing was full of holes and loose yarn. The furniture, in contrast to her drawing room, was older. Worn. Comfortable.

This was Marissa's private domain.

She took his discarded coat from her shoulders, shaking it out before the fire to dry, and turned to face him. Gone was the woman who'd ordered about her household staff with military precision. She was regarding him cautiously, the blush from earlier still staining her cheeks, as if undecided about what she should do.

"I'll leave you to dry yourself and make use of the robe. I'll return momentarily." A slight tremble lit her words.

"You don't wish to stay?" Trent stepped before the fire, stoked and roaring as she'd instructed. Before she could answer, a knock sounded at the door and a servant wheeled in a cart stacked with sandwiches and pastries along with a steaming pot of tea.

Once the door to the parlor was shut again, Marissa cautiously approached him, the dark strands of her hair slithering out of her coiffure to fall upon the peaks of her breasts.

"Tea?"

"I thought we were having whisky," he said quietly.

Marissa nodded and went to the sideboard. "I've only one glass." The words were husky. "We'll have to share."

The sound of the whisky splashing in a glass met his ears before she turned around and came back toward him. She held out the glass, tilting the whisky against his mouth for him to drink, then took a mouthful herself.

Trent watched her swallow, wanting to taste the whisky on her lips.

He shrugged out of his waistcoat before sliding the cravat from his throat. "You have good taste in whisky."

Marissa's mouth parted slightly, the pink of her tongue flashing between her lips. "So I've been told. My nephew sent it to me."

Taking a seat on the ottoman before the fire, Trent relieved himself of his boots before his fingers slid to the buttons of his shirt. His eyes never left hers as he tossed the sodden garment over his head. Once everything was laid before the fire, Trent stood and faced her. He was nearly naked, and Marissa hadn't yet objected.

He undid his trousers, peeling the damp fabric down over his hips.

"I—" Marissa blushed furiously again, something Trent found endlessly enchanting. She stared at his chest, her fingers fluttering as if she wished to touch him and was afraid to do so.

"Marissa."

Taking a deep breath, she looked up to meet his eyes. The motion strained the fabric of her bodice, pushing the tops of her breasts against the modest neckline of her dress. Water dripped from the edge of her skirt to the floor, dampening the rug.

"My dress," she said, her breath hitching. "Is wet and—"

Trent shucked off his trousers to stand naked before her. "Take it off."

11

She was only human. And Haddon had just disrobed while she watched.

Completely.

And he was *bloody* magnificent. Every inch of him. A thrill ran through her, fingers twitching, remembering the feel of all that lovely muscle and warm skin pressed against hers.

There was no doubt of Haddon's intentions as he stood before her in the privacy of her small parlor, a place she had never brought any previous lover. Poor Enderly hadn't made it past the drawing room.

Her eyes flicked below Haddon's waist where his *intention* jutted in her direction.

Arousal snapped and curled between her legs, suffusing her entire body. There was no use any longer at pretending she didn't desire him. Haddon would see through the lie in a matter of seconds. Dear Lord, her *nipples* were poking through the wet material of her chemise and gown, something he couldn't fail to notice. Haddon wasn't blind.

Haddon was like a hurricane, whipping about Marissa

with such intensity he left her dizzy and breathless. It pained her to know her feelings for Reggie paled dramatically compared to Haddon, as if she were betraying her late husband somehow.

He's just a dalliance.

She tried to cling to her paltry dismissal of him, told herself that this was only a casual encounter brought on by the weather and his heroic exploits in the rescue of her hat. He'd been marvelous climbing up that tree. There wasn't a woman alive who wouldn't want him in her bed after such a display.

Haddon crooked a finger in her direction. "Come here," he purred.

Drat.

Marissa obeyed without thinking, taking a step toward Haddon, unable to take her eyes from his naked body, his skin painted gold from the flames licking up the supple lines of his hips and torso. She approached cautiously, determined to stay in full command of her wits. Laughable, under the circumstances.

"Lift them." He nodded to her skirts. "Petticoats and all." The words rasped against her skin.

"What—?"

He waved his hand up. "Do it, Marissa. Lift them. Now."

Heat erupted again inside her. With shaking hands, she lifted the hem of her wet skirts, exposing a great deal of her silken-clad legs . . . among other things. The warmth of the fire glanced off her thighs as Haddon reached out to trail a finger from the side of her knee up her thigh and into the soft hair of her mound. His finger ran along her crevice, exploring the already moist flesh, gaze fixed firmly on her face, daring her to look away while he touched her.

The caress of his finger was light, barely more than the pressure of a butterfly alighting on a flower.

Moisture seeped between her thighs and she bit her lip. "I—"

"Shh. Don't move," he whispered before pressing an openmouthed kiss to the slope of her neck.

Marissa clutched the fabric of her skirts tighter. She couldn't have moved even if she were on fire. Which, technically, she supposed, she was.

His teeth grazed her neck while his finger slid back and forth against her in a languid manner, searching and teasing until a soft moan escaped her.

"I can't wait to taste you again, Marissa." He took the whisky clutched in her hand.

Honestly, Marissa couldn't believe she hadn't dropped the damn glass what with holding her skirts and—

Her hips rocked forward as one of his fingers slipped inside her. Holding the glass of whisky in his other hand, he gave her a sip, making sure some spilled across her mouth. Haddon used his tongue to catch the drops of whisky before his mouth fell on hers.

I will drown in him.

The last bit of sense she still possessed fled as his lips trailed over hers. The kiss was gentle, unhurried, but spoke of months of hunger and longing. His fingers never stopped moving against her, stroking and teasing until she made a small sound in her throat.

Haddon's mouth left hers. "Is there something you wish to say, Marissa?"

"No." Her thoughts were a floating, jumbled mess. "Only that I'm—" Her words halted as his forefinger found a particularly sensitive spot and a soft moan left her. "Wet."

"Yes. You most certainly are." His fingers cautiously

circled the small pearl hidden in her folds. The hand holding the glass of whisky gently tipped up her chin, forcing her to look at him as he toyed with her flesh. The thick length of him seared the skin of her thigh.

Marissa swayed on her feet, skirts twisting in her fingers. "I was under the impression—you weren't interested in—" Her breath caught as he sunk another finger inside her. "Me."

"I *never* said that, Marissa." His thumb flicked against her until she whimpered with need. "You *assumed* I didn't want you." The pressure increased. "I only said your objections were exhausting." Haddon nipped at her bottom lip. "Which they are."

"But—"

"I've two questions." His tongue returned to her mouth, running along her lower lip.

"Yes?" she said in a shaky voice. Pleasure spiraled up inside her, tightening into a small knot. Unbearably close. She strained toward it, her legs trembling as she struggled to stay upright.

"Are your servants discreet?"

"What?" Oh, dear God, he was pressing a spot with his thumb and moving his fingers in and out, until she thought she might— "Yes. Of course."

"Good." He loomed over her, sinking a third finger inside to join the others, tips grazing against a spot which sent bolts of sensation shooting out across her body.

Haddon was *very* good at this. Seduction. Touching. Caressing. Dear God, no wonder half the women in the *ton* were chasing him.

"What is the second question?" Her voice raised an octave on the last word as his fingers curled again. "Please," she whispered.

"Not yet, my love." His lips brushed hers. "But soon. Is this dress a favorite?" He leaned over and set down the empty whisky glass.

"No," she said, too focused on what his fingers and thumb were doing to her. "I only chose the dress today because the color complimented the hat."

"Good." His hands slowly fell away, stroking her lightly before he did so.

Marissa panted softly. Haddon would drive her mad with want. "No. Please." She was very close to begging him.

A large, warm hand moved to cup the underside of one breast. He pressed a kiss to the exposed skin above her neckline before two knuckles sunk into the deep valley between them.

A tearing sound cut through the air as he jerked his hand, ripping the dress down the front.

"Oh, dear. I mean—" Marissa was aroused. Flustered. She'd never had a man want her so much he'd rip the clothes from her body.

The ache between her thighs intensified.

Pushing the wet dress from her shoulders, Haddon continued to tear at the poor garment until Marissa stood in nothing but her damp chemise and stays. He palmed one of her breasts, brushing his thumb against the tip of one hardened nipple. Then the heat of his mouth followed, sucking the small peak through the thin cotton of the chemise.

"Oh." Her hands sunk into the damp strands of his hair. Tiny bursts of sensation radiated out from her breast, her inner muscles clenching, begging for the release only Haddon could give her.

His free hand took hold of her hip, teeth grazing over the taut bud of her nipple.

A knock sounded at the door. "My lady?" The muffled voice of her maid came from the other side of the door.

"Tell her to leave your dressing gown," Haddon growled against her breast.

"Leave it outside, Felice. I'm enjoying," her voice raised again as Haddon's hand cupped her mound, "the fire."

"Yes, my lady." Footsteps moved away from the door.

"Don't move, Marissa," he admonished her again.

"I won't," she whispered, curling her fingers at her sides now that she was no longer holding her skirts. She refused to think of anything past this moment with Haddon.

Her eyes closed as he left her and went to the door to retrieve the dressing gown, throwing the lock as he did so. Not that her servants would have dared come in here.

Haddon tossed the dressing gown on the worn sofa. He hovered behind her, purring in satisfaction like the large panther she often imagined him to be. The length of him, hard and thick, teased her buttocks through the damp material of her chemise.

A charge of excitement shot up her spine as she felt the tug at the laces of her stays.

Haddon cursed, a vile oath, before bending to nip lightly at her shoulder. The heat of him left her back as he padded to the fire where Marissa had hung his coat.

The firelight caressed him as he moved, glancing off the muscle lining his buttocks and thighs. Haddon was sculpted, like one of the dozens of statues that seemed to populate everyone's homes and gardens. Marissa hadn't ever thought of a man being beautiful, until Haddon.

"The curve of your hip is lovely," she blurted, half ashamed she'd said such a thing out loud, especially because she sounded like a nitwit.

A sound of satisfaction came from him as he turned

back toward her, holding up a small pocketknife. His free hand splayed over his hip. "I'm beautiful here?" The hand moved, his fingers wrapping around the hard length between his legs. "Or here?"

Marissa inhaled softly, feeling the answering throb between her legs. "Both."

Laughing softly, Haddon came toward Marissa again and pressed a kiss just beneath where her hair was gathered in her now battered chignon.

A pop sounded as the fastenings of her stays were cut.

Torn dress. Stays cut from me. Whatever will I tell Felice?

As the remainder of her stays fell away from her waist, Marissa took a deep breath. *Heavenly.* Almost as lovely as the slow burn of kisses Haddon was placing at the top of her spine. His fingers tore her chemise, pushing it down over her shoulders, until it, too, fell into a damp pile around her ankles.

Fingers toyed with her garters.

"I think we'll leave these on," he murmured against her neck as two hands came from behind her to palm the underside of her breasts, squeezing as if testing the weight.

"You have the most delicious bosom ever created." A thumb flicked against one taut nipple. "So perfect." His blunt fingers rolled the globes of flesh back and forth. "I'm a great admirer."

Marissa trembled as a sigh of pleasure escaped her lips at his ministrations. She was standing nearly naked—oh, very well; she supposed still wearing stockings couldn't actually count as being partially clothed—in her parlor with Haddon.

I'm naked.

Suddenly conscious of the fact, Marissa tilted sideways toward the sofa, kicking away the remnants of her clothing.

She grabbed at the blanket she'd left there last night, a terrible use of good yarn with more than a few holes. But Arabella, in a fit of domesticity when she was all of thirteen, had knit the blanket for Marissa.

Her niece had many skills, but knitting wasn't one of them.

The blanket was a study of slipped stitches and uneven edges. One corner had nearly unraveled. Still, Marissa grabbed at it, determined not to stand naked before her lover—

"You are beautiful to me." Haddon's eyes slid down her shoulders to where she'd clasped the blanket against her breasts. "Please don't hide from me."

Tilting her chin up with his thumb, Haddon's mouth fell on hers. Urgent. Hot. With no shred of the gentleness or patience he often displayed. It was as if he'd been starving for months and finally been presented a banquet.

Fingers sunk into her hair, releasing the remainder of the thick, wet mass until it streamed in disarray over her shoulders. Droplets struck her cheeks as he cupped them and pulled Marissa forcefully against him.

The blanket dropped to the floor.

"I thought I could wait. Drag this out for several hours. But I want you too much." His words were a dark hiss against her lips.

Marissa's back arched, groaning as her breasts pressed against the heat of his chest, her taut, sensitive nipples, catching at the whorls of dark hair on his torso. Shamefully, she rocked her hips against him, already near mindless from the assault he'd made on her body.

Mouth not leaving hers, he brought her down with him as he sat on the sofa. Haddon's eyes had gone the color of old pewter, glinting softly in the muted light of her parlor.

He took hold of her hips and positioned her across his lap. Pulling her forward, Haddon's thumb sunk beneath her folds, rotating and teasing.

"Trent." A broken whisper left her.

His mouth latched onto one nipple laving the taut peak as he entered her with one hard thrust.

"Jesus." A grunt of pleasure came from him. "Marissa."

Marissa became a wild thing, her body writhing against him, hips rocking to meet every thrust. Haddon filled her. Absorbed her. Forced her to accept the truth.

He pushed down with his thumb, his mouth swallowing the scream of pleasure she made as she climaxed. Her body jerked, inner muscles fluttering and pulling him deeper.

A groan left him.

The pleasure was so intense, Marissa's mind went still for a moment, something that rarely happened.

Haddon flipped her over until she lay on the sofa beneath him, still buried inside her body. He held still for a moment, nuzzling the side of her neck before crooking one of her legs over his arm and took her with full, deep thrusts. When her pleasure began to build inside her again, Haddon sensed it and smiled.

Each thrust became slower, more deliberate, as their bodies rocked together, dragging out each exquisite sensation. Haddon looked down at her as he found his release moments after she again found her own, his eyes shining like quicksilver, her name on his lips. The feeling of completion, of finding the lost part of herself, was so overpowering, Marissa almost didn't breathe.

It was absolutely terrifying.

Haddon's breath was warm and ragged against her neck. He shifted slightly to take his weight from her, leaving her cold and wanting him.

This is what happens. I'll grow to need him, and then he'll disappear.

He pulled her close, his skin heated beneath her cheek, the beating of his heart strong and fierce.

Why him? Not even with Reggie—

Marissa firmly pushed the thought away. While Haddon's desire for her was intense at the moment, it would fade in time. One day soon he would tire of her, especially given their age difference. Most affairs ended in disinterest on the part of one partner or the other. If her three marriages and infrequent affairs had taught Marissa anything, it was that *nothing* was forever. She had her family. Her friends. Great wealth. If her life wasn't blissfully happy, it was at least somewhat content. Or would be once she destroyed Lydia and her priggish son.

Yes, but Haddon—

Had to stay nothing more than a dalliance. Unfortunately. She wasn't like Adelia who could flit from lover to lover without having her heart compromised.

Marissa touched her tongue to his skin, wanting to savor the taste of him. A tear ran down her cheek. When Haddon ended the affair, *and he was bound to*, it would be far worse than losing Reggie.

"Please don't be afraid, Marissa," Haddon said quietly, his arms tightening around her.

Horrified he'd guessed at the direction of her thoughts with so little effort, Marissa struggled to be released, feeling exposed.

A sigh of frustration came from him, but he let her go. His eyes followed as she slid along the sofa until she was behind him. Snatching the poorly constructed blanket, Marissa wrapped it around her body, hiding herself as best she could.

Haddon sat up, completely unabashed to sit naked in her parlor with her standing before him. He reached for her, lips tilting in a grin, but Marissa danced away.

The smile faded. "Who made you that blanket?"

What a thing to ask at a time like this. She grabbed the corner to wrap it more tightly around her, frowning when it unraveled in her hand. "My niece, Arabella, when she was thirteen. It was a gift to me on my birthday. One of her first efforts."

"That explains the craftsmanship. By the way, your left nipple is popping through one of the holes."

He needed to leave. What had *possessed* her to bring him here and then—

"This was a mistake, Haddon," she said firmly. "It *cannot* happen again."

"I was a dalliance, now I'm a mistake. I suppose," he bit out, his voice frosty, "that I'm to be dismissed yet again. Now that I've served your needs."

"Served my needs?" How incredibly . . . *ugly* that sounded. And derogatory. Couldn't he sense how difficult this was for her? But perhaps it was for the best he assume she thought so little of their relationship.

Her heart gave a dreadful lurch.

"You didn't seem to mind," she shot back in the voice she used when dissecting someone who had earned her wrath.

Haddon stood abruptly, picked up the empty glass he'd discarded earlier and brushed past her on the way to the sideboard. He spilled a healthy dose of amber liquid into the glass. "You don't mind, do you? Thirsty work and all." The very tops of his cheekbones had pinked, a tell-tale sign of his mounting anger.

Well, she was rather annoyed herself. How dare he make this her fault. "I didn't kiss *you* in the park."

The glass hovered at his lips. "You asked me here."

"To warm up after you rescued my hat," she snapped back.

Lord, that sounded ridiculous.

Haddon snorted in disbelief and downed the whisky. Setting the glass down with a clatter, he said in a bland tone she instantly detested, "What did you think would happen, Marissa? We were going to sip tea and eat these sandwiches? And for the record, I don't care for watercress."

"Yes. Not for . . ." She waved a hand in the direction of his perfect, naked body. "This."

"We made love, Marissa. *Christ*. Just say it."

"It was only sex, Haddon. And it must not happen again." Her voice faltered at the lie.

"I see." He walked to his still damp clothing, jerking on his shirt and trousers. Throwing on his waistcoat, Haddon shoved his cravat into a pocket.

Marissa shut her eyes for a moment. If her heart would just stop reaching in his direction, this conversation, as hurtful as it was, would be far easier.

"This would never work." She pointed at the two of them. "An indiscretion with a much younger man—"

"Indiscretion. Mistake. Dalliance. Make up your mind. I think you fear it would work far too well. I never took you for a coward, Marissa Tremaine." He pulled on his coat and shot her an icy look.

Coward? Her own anger, both at herself and him, bubbled up her throat. "You think I'm unaware of your intention in coming to London? I know it isn't only for Jordana."

Haddon paused in the act of pulling up his boots, not bothering to look at her.

"You're here," Marissa said, annoyed he didn't even have

the courtesy to look at her when she was speaking, "to find a wife, aren't you? You need an heir. You didn't come to London to have a *meaningless* affair with a notorious widow, many years your senior. Of that, I'm certain."

The large body grew still. His hands stretched over the top of his thighs, fingers curling ever so slightly. When he finally spoke, his voice was thick and hoarse, as if it were painful to speak.

"You have no idea what my intentions are in London, Marissa. You've *never* asked." When he finally deigned to look at her, his silver eyes shone with misery. The absolute anguish at her rejection of him, her assertion they meant *nothing* to each other was laid bare for Marissa to see.

Pressure filled her chest, a terrible suffocation in which she struggled for air.

Marissa reached out her hand. What had made her say such an awful thing? It *wasn't* meaningless to her, and it certainly wasn't to him. How could she have made such a dreadful miscalculation? "You misunderstand. What I meant is—"

"I don't. Misunderstand, that is. You've made yourself *abundantly* clear, my lady." Without meeting her eyes, Haddon strode to the door. "Thank you for the whisky, Lady Cupps-Foster. Unfortunately, I can't stay and avail myself of the repast you've had prepared. I deeply appreciate your time and efforts in befriending Jordana. She's grown very fond of you in a short time, and I don't wish to disrupt her progress."

Marissa hated the clipped tone of his speech, nor did she care for the detachment he regarded her with. It was as though a large wall had been erected between them, one made of ice and frost.

"I would consider it a great kindness if you would

continue in your plans to help Jordana with her new wardrobe. I assure you, once my sister arrives in town, she'll take Jordana well in hand and leave you to other pursuits. In the meantime, I'll trouble you no longer, my lady. You may send the bills for the dressmaker to me and any other expenses you incur while assisting my daughter."

Haddon.

He was taking himself from her life. Just as she wished. But there was no elation. No feeling of relief she would be spared the temptation. Only a terrible, aching loneliness. "Thank you. I appreciate your consideration, my lord." Now that he was leaving, Marissa had no idea how to fix things between them and take back the awful words she'd spoken.

I didn't know. I didn't realize.

Haddon strode to the door, purposefully avoiding her as Marissa pulled the tattered yarn of the blanket around her shoulders.

He didn't bother to say goodbye.

12

"Miss Clare Higgins," Arabella whispered to Marissa as they settled themselves into their seats at the Chenwith Society. A well-known physician, Dr. Linwood, was speaking of the health of those who toiled away below ground, especially children. After his remarks, there would be an auction.

Marissa was pleased to see an item donated by Lady Pendleton. A small egg of Blue John. Her nemesis would be here today just as Tomkin had informed her.

She smoothed her skirts and took in the room, filled to the brim with society's wealthy ladies, all of whom had taken a break from their exhausting ritual of calling on each other to throw their support behind one of Arabella's charitable causes.

A cause Simon, and his mother, Lydia, were supposed to give a fig about, given his efforts in Parliament. Though, Simon's bills stopped short of *actually* caring for the physical well-being of the children who worked in the mines. But the Chenwith Society was very high profile, with many prominent donors. Viscount Pendleton *had* to give a show of support.

"She's the daughter of—"

"The Honorable Sir Richard Higgins," Marissa finished for her niece. "Member of Parliament and owner of several banking institutions in Cornwall." Enderly had mentioned the name to her on more than one occasion when he'd escorted her about, though she'd not seen him since the evening at Lord Duckworth's. "Sir Richard is well thought of, in addition to being powerful."

"Quite so," Arabella mused. "Miss Higgins *also* possesses an enormous dowry along with her political connections. Her father has a habit of collecting politicians and keeping them in his back pocket. I'm sure the thought of having a son-in-law to count among that number is making him positively lightheaded."

Marissa plucked a loose thread from her bodice. She'd have to have a word with Felice. Her maid had manhandled the lovely new dress of striped brown silk.

Yes, but nothing compared to what Haddon did to the dress I wore to the park.

Pain nipped at the edge of her heart. No good would come of thinking of Haddon.

"He was made a knight several years ago," Arabella continued, "and seeks a much loftier title to elevate his family, like that of viscount."

"Sir Richard will be disappointed." Marissa was *adamantly* opposed to Simon marrying little Miss Higgins. Her dowry would save Simon and Lydia the horror of their mounting debts, of which Marissa owned nearly all.

"How will you stop it?" Arabella whispered. "I know you meant to discredit Pendleton in some way but unlike most politicians, he seems a most honorable man."

Arabella paused. "Aside from his duplicity involving the Blue John mine. He has never set foot in Elysium or any other gambling hell I could name. He does not keep a mistress. No perverse tastes we could exploit. It is difficult to catch him in a compromising position if he never puts himself in one. Higgins will not be put off by Simon's financial straits either, not when his daughter can be a viscountess."

"I'll find another way," Marissa answered. Mr. Tomkin was still digging, but Simon, for all that he had stolen from her son for years, had otherwise not taken a wrong step. Marissa had at least managed to interrupt the courtship of Simon's sister and Mr. Kendicott of Buxton. Shamefully, Catherine had been discovered with Mr. Doren, another gentleman caller, *in flagrante*, among the well-tended flower gardens of Brushbriar. Kendicott had been *horrified* and was busy ruining Catherine's reputation all over Derbyshire.

Shortly after Kendicott had ceased his pursuit of Simon's sister, another cartload of Blue John from Brushbriar had found its way to private auction in Castleton.

"Pity that more can't be made of Catherine's behavior," Arabella said. "But she was known for her indiscretions during her marriage." Her niece put a finger to her lips. "I can't remember whose ball—"

"Lord and Lady Rutland's," Marissa answered automatically.

"Yes, Lady Rutland's. Do you recall Catherine's gown? The bodice was cut so low, that when she curtsied to the Marquess of Vere, her breast popped out."

"Yes. It was quite the stir."

Utilizing her contacts, Marissa had made sure the scandal involving Catherine and Mr. Kendicott was alluded to in the London papers. But no one seemed shocked by

Catherine's behavior nor did it reflect badly on Simon. Everyone knew what a slut Catherine was.

"It was never about Catherine's reputation," Marissa said to her niece. "Though it would have been lovely if his sister's reputation caused Simon some embarrassment. I simply wished to avoid Kendicott bailing Simon and Lydia out of debt."

"You succeeded," Arabella said with a nod.

The claim for the Blue John mine was making its way slowly through the courts, something Marissa was doing purposefully in order to drag out the process and cost Simon as much money as possible. Until ownership was decided, the mine remained open and the profits put into a trust. She'd not wished to take away the livelihood of the men working the mine, only Simon's.

She was sure Lydia was anxiously waiting to see whether or not Marissa would make the claim public, which would make Simon the recipient of untold attention.

Let her worry. How long did Reggie wait, dying in a cave, for rescue?

Timing was everything. The markers would be called due first. Shortly thereafter, Marissa meant to make the lawsuit public. She would also feed the gossip hounds of London with conjecture about why the ownership of the mine was being disputed. With so much negative publicity, Sir Richard was bound to call off the courtship of his daughter, especially when Simon's brilliant career became nonexistent. His supporters would leave him. He would be destitute and hardly considered a catch any longer. Lydia would have *no hope* of ever being saved.

Just like Reggie.

The noose was tightening. It should have brought her much more joy that her plans were coming to fruition. But all she could think of was Haddon. She could not shake the memory of his face after she'd called their relationship meaningless. Marissa had hurt him, far worse than she could have imagined.

But he seemed to have recovered quickly, if the gossips were correct.

"How is your Lord Haddon?"

Marissa didn't answer her niece right away. She knew he was well; certainly Jordana, who showed up to have tea with Marissa several times a week, would inform her if he was not. Haddon's daughter took great pains to never mention anything about her father, foiling several attempts on Marissa's part to glean more information. But she'd heard the gossip. The handsome widower's attention to the daughter of the Marquess of Stanton, Lady Christina Sykes, was no secret. Nor was his interest in several other young ladies.

"He's not my Lord Haddon."

"Indeed not, if the rumors are true." Arabella gave her a sympathetic look.

"Ours was a brief association, Arabella." Sending Haddon from her, dismissing him from her life, hadn't stopped Marissa's heart from breaking. Instead, she seemed in a constant state of melancholy. "I was a novelty to him, nothing more."

"And what was he to you, Aunt?"

The answer to her niece's question was complicated and fraught with danger for Marissa. She refused to think too hard on it. "While it was amusing to have a younger man pay me attention, Haddon was no more than a dalliance, as he could only be for a woman my age."

"You make yourself sound quite ancient, which is ridiculous. You are far from being an elderly matron along the lines of the Dowager Marchioness of Cambourne. Besides," Arabella's voice softened, "I saw the way he looked at you."

Marissa's eyes burned with tears she refused to shed. "Haddon is in the market for a wife. He's got four daughters and is in need of a son."

"Are you sure of that, Aunt?" Arabella shrugged when Marissa didn't answer. "At any rate, I find Christina Sykes to be an annoying creature. She twitters."

"She does indeed."

Thinking of Haddon and Lady Christina Sykes did nothing to brighten Marissa's mood.

"Well, look who has arrived." Arabella nodded in the direction of the door. "I thought she might accompany Lady Higgins."

So had Marissa.

Magnificently coiffed in a gown of pale gray silk, Lady Pendleton sidled into the room like an overdressed crab. Pale skin stretched taut across the sharp bones of her face, drawing attention to the sunken hollows of her cheeks. Lips thinning, Lydia took in the assemblage gathered in the room.

Marissa smiled. Lydia had little charity in her heart for anyone. How annoyed she must be, forced to attend with Lady Higgins, a woman Lydia most certainly considered beneath her.

Next to Lydia and Lady Higgins stood an unremarkable looking young girl, several years older than Jordana. Simon's intended bride was perfectly suitable at first glance. She was incredibly average in every way possible. Slender, but not painfully thin. Dark brown hair like dozens of other girls. Wide blue eyes above gently rounded cheeks. Tiny rosebud of a mouth.

Lydia said something to Miss Higgins and the girl immediately looked down at her slippers as if studying the stitching across the top.

A frown tugged at Marissa's lips. *Horribly docile.* Probably lacks the ability to think on her own. Exactly the sort of young lady Lydia would deem perfect for her precious son.

If nothing else, I need to save that poor girl from having to endure Lydia as a mother-in-law.

Lydia gave a roll of her shoulders, one of her patent disingenuous laughs filling the air while her head tilted back as if horribly amused. Her head jerked sharply as she caught sight of Marissa sitting across the room, Arabella at her side.

"Oh, dear. She doesn't look happy to see you, Aunt. I can't imagine why," Arabella said with a small laugh. "I *do hope* she simply detests meeting me and realizes she cannot so much as give me a sour look. Lady Higgins holds this charity very near and dear to her heart. And I'm the largest donor in attendance, besides Lady Higgins."

"Are you? I didn't realize you'd found miners to be worthy of your charity, Arabella. You've never shown concern for their plight before."

"Well," Arabella nodded in the direction of Lady Higgins, "Cornwall is *full* of miners and also mine owners, most of whom do business with Sir Richard Higgins through one of his banks. Lady Higgins considers herself to be quite the philanthropist, as evidenced by her support of the Chenwith Society, to which I am now a generous contributor."

"Clever girl, aren't you, Bella?"

"My husband thinks so. Besides, Rowan has interests in Cornwall."

Of course he did. Arabella's husband had his hand in a great many *interests*, the multitude so great, Marissa found it boggled the mind. How in the world did anyone think Rowan merely a lovely gentleman who charmed the ladies of the *ton* and drank scotch with their husbands?

"I am not surprised at the news of Rowan's interests in Cornwall."

Arabella gave a soft chuckle.

Lady Higgins's gaze landed on Arabella, fairly beaming when Marissa's niece inclined her head in the woman's direction. It was clear Lady Higgins was thrilled to see Arabella attending a gathering of the Chenwith Society.

As well she should. The patronage of the Duke of Dunbar's sister would give Lady Higgins and her projects, including the Chenwith Society, a great deal of support and attract the patronage of other wealthy ladies.

Taking her daughter's arm, Lady Higgins whispered to Lydia before proceeding toward Arabella.

Face soured with displeasure, Lydia peered around the room as if looking for a way to exit gracefully before her eyes fell on Marissa again. She stiffened her narrow shoulders, resigned to the inevitable.

Marissa wanted to giggle at her discomfort. This was *most* enjoyable.

Arabella stood gracefully to greet Lady Higgins.

"Lady Malden." Lady Higgins bobbed politely upon reaching them. "Pardon the intrusion." She looked at Marissa in apology.

"Not at all, Lady Higgins." Arabella bestowed a gracious smile. "May I present my aunt, Lady Cupps-Foster."

Lady Higgins was a perfectly lovely woman whose dark brown hair and blue eyes were the same as her daughter's. She was well-dressed in a simply cut dress the color of amethyst, her jewelry tasteful and not ostentatious. Lady Higgins, though visibly impressed with Arabella, did not seem inclined to pander to her niece, and Marissa liked her all the more for it.

It was a shame she would have to ruin her daughter's courtship.

"A pleasure, Lady Higgins." Marissa greeted her with a touch of her hand. "My niece was just mentioning to me your work with the Chenwith Society. I find your interest in the welfare of others to be inspiring."

Lady Higgins colored with pleasure at the thought Arabella had been speaking of her.

Lydia's mouth pursed and wrinkled, clearly displeased.

"My daughter, Miss Clare Higgins," Lady Higgins continued, "and our dear friend, Lady Pendleton."

"A pleasure." Arabella greeted them both politely. "I adore your dress, Miss Higgins. Very becoming."

The girl blushed prettily. "Thank you, my lady."

"Lady Pendleton," Lady Higgins said, "is visiting us all the way from Derbyshire. You may be familiar with her son, Viscount Pendleton."

"I am indeed as I am with the lady herself," Marissa said. "How lovely to see you again, Lady Pendleton." At Lady Higgins's surprise, she said, "My late husband's estate borders that of Viscount Pendleton. We are old friends, aren't we?" She placed a hand on Lydia's forearm as if in affection, gratified when the old witch flinched as if Marissa had seared her with a poker.

"A pleasure to see you, Lady Cupps-Foster." Lydia sounded brittle, as if chips of ice were lodged in her throat. She stepped back just enough for Marissa's fingers to drop from her sleeve.

Marissa gave her a sweet smile.

"Lady Malden," Lady Higgins started, "I wanted to thank you personally for your generous donation to the Chenwith

Society. Your patronage has come as such a pleasant surprise. We are a small organization and there are those who feel our charity isn't needed, but we do very good work." Lady Higgins beamed, her passion evident. "So many of our miners lack proper food and medical care, as you will hear when Dr. Linwood speaks. Worse, if they perish while toiling away, their families are left to starve with little recourse. Or sent to the workhouse. And I don't believe any childhood should be spent digging for tin." The small curls dangling against her temple quivered in subtle indignation.

"I've always felt it a duty," Arabella placed a hand on her chest, "to help others when we can, regardless of their station in life. You are to be commended, Lady Higgins, for your generous heart."

Another blush of pleasure pinked Lady Higgins's cheeks. "I *knew* we were of like mind, Lady Malden. Sir Richard has been ridiculed by some of our acquaintances because he *does* care for those less fortunate. Viscount Pendleton has fortunately embraced such reforms."

"I understand him to be one of Parliament's brightest stars," Arabella said.

"I've never seen anyone so passionate and devoted to the welfare of others," Lady Higgins said, her admiration for Pendleton evident.

"How gratifying for you, Lady Pendleton," Marissa said, struggling to hide her amusement as Lady Higgins extolled Simon's virtues. She wouldn't be quite so effusive in a month or so.

"Incredibly so. Pendleton has made *something* of his life." Lydia's eyes, like bits of flint, glared at Marissa. "Unlike other young, overindulged gentlemen who due to their *poor* upbringing lack the discipline to finish their studies and make something of themselves. Breeding itself is no guarantee a gentleman won't fall in with disreputable company. One wonders how such men avoid the gallows given their cutthroat tendencies."

Lydia really needed to work on her insults. Perhaps she was out of practice. Her mild slurs against Brendan and Spencer barely roused Marissa's anger.

"True. I do wonder how Lord Pendleton became such a paragon, but then I recall you had an excellent nursemaid for him. And a governess." She smiled sweetly.

Oh dear. When Lydia's eyes bulged, she was very *unattractive.*

"Are you enjoying the round of parties this season, Miss Higgins?" Marissa turned to the girl Lydia meant to have as a daughter-in-law.

Miss Higgins, shy to a fault, murmured something adequate and stared back down at her slippers.

Marissa had the inclination to shake the docility right out of prim little Miss Higgins. She didn't subscribe to being well-mannered to the point you disappeared. A girl must possess some spirit.

She cast a sideways glance at Lydia, taking note of her bloodshot eyes and the deeply etched brackets around her lips. A whiff of the air around her brought forth the scent of spirits.

Brandy.

Arabella purposefully placed her hand on Lady Higgins's forearm, leading the woman and her daughter away, asking if they'd been to the opera.

Her niece disliked the opera.

As soon as Lady Higgins and her daughter moved several paces away out of hearing range, Lydia pounced, as Marissa knew she would, curling up to her like the venomous snake she was.

"If you *think* you've somehow outsmarted me, Marissa, *think again*." The brandy on Lydia's breath was sharp. "No court in London will entertain your ridiculous request that we repay the proceeds of the Blue John mine dating back over twenty years, especially since you can't prove the mine even *belongs* to the Earl of Morwick." Lydia gave a flutter of her beringed hands. "All you have is an old survey which is likely a forgery."

"If you feel that way, Lydia, one wonders why you would have bothered to murder my husband all those years ago."

Lydia's left eye twitched. "Hearsay," she hissed, the brandy fumes floating out in a cloud. "You've not a shred of proof save a private conversation overheard by some *tart* your worthless son married."

"That *tart* is now the Countess of Morwick," Marissa reminded her. "She outranks you."

"Sour grapes. She'd say anything to hurt Simon after he had to end their betrothal. What else was Simon to do? Especially after she debased herself with your son. No one will believe her. I can't wait to drag her reputation through the mud now that I'm in town."

"But Simon gave his word." Marissa blinked, wide-eyed. "I can't imagine. Your son is so incredibly honorable." A snarl flitted about her lips. "Like his father."

Lydia flinched. "You can do *nothing* to us. I won't stand for your *nonsense* another minute, Marissa. I'm not sure what you hoped to accomplish with your little stunt. My husband has been dead for years, and you've no proof. The entire case will be thrown out of court."

Marissa nodded as if agreeing. "Perhaps. Or *maybe*," she moved closer to Lydia, "I'll drag this dispute out for *years*. I've scores of solicitors who'd like nothing more than to waste my *substantial fortune* on such things. Whereas *you* can ill afford a lengthy court battle if the rapid pace at which you are selling off your valuables is any indication. Goodness, next you'll be prying the Blue John from the fireplaces of Brushbriar." She shook her head. "You should have told me, Lydia. I would have happily bought up the entire lot."

"You—" Lydia's eyes bulged dangerously again.

"Have the resources of my very powerful, *wealthy* family at my back. You always seem to forget I started life as the daughter of a duke," Marissa said with false disbelief.

"An infamous one. Your family is *reviled* in London."

"I prefer respected. *Feared*." Marissa's voice hardened. "And with good reason. You'd do well to remember that, Lydia."

Lydia faltered slightly, her slender figure wavering as if buffeted by the wind. Spittle formed at the corner of her mouth as the scent of brandy and breath mints filled the air above her. "Is that your game, Marissa? Will you hide behind your nephew and hope to frighten me?"

Marissa shrugged. "*Frighten you?* Perish the thought. I've better things to do. By the way, how *is* your daughter's pursuit of Mr. Kendicott progressing?"

Lydia paled until she resembled a bowl of day-old, curdled cream.

"Oh *dear*." Marissa made a tutting sound. "Are you feeling well, Lydia? You look as if you could use a glass of brandy. I'm sure you assumed you could sneak a nip into your tea today, perhaps when Lady Higgins turns her back. Or are you planning to disappear for a moment to . . . *collect yourself*?" She nodded to the stylish reticule hanging from Lydia's wrist. "Is there a tiny flask in there? You should be very discreet." Marissa lowered her voice. "I understand Sir Richard is a teetotaler."

"How dare you," Lydia snarled.

"I'm only *concerned* as your former neighbor. Miss Higgins possesses an *enormous* dowry which you are in *dire* need of. Dear Lord, I hope nothing happens to scare her away as it did Kendicott." A small laugh bubbled up. "I mean by something other than *you*, Lydia. I bid you good day, Lady Pendleton. I'm *sure* we'll see each other again."

Lydia's eyes narrowed to slits, glittering with unrestrained malice. Had she a gun handy and a cave nearby, there wasn't a doubt Marissa would be treated to the same fate Reggie had suffered.

But as Lydia was doubtless finding out, Marissa was possessed of the same malice and rage.

Lydia and her children *deserved* to live the remainder of their days in utter ruin. She felt not the least bit of guilt in destroying all of them.

Miss Higgins was overly absorbed in plucking a string from her skirts as Lady Higgins and Arabella conversed. The pitiable girl looked as if she wished to be anywhere but here. And who could blame her? Spending the day with Lydia had to be excruciating. Did Miss Higgins bear Simon any affection? Or was she only doing her duty?

Marissa thought the latter. Simon was a cold fish, much like his mother.

Arabella, finally running out of things to say about the opera, led Lady Higgins back to where Marissa and Lydia stood, Lady Higgins hanging on her niece's every word.

"Lady Higgins, I fear I've taken you away from your guest. What poor manners I have. I hope you'll forgive me." Arabella took Lady Higgins's hand. "But I've *so* enjoyed our conversation. You and your daughter *must* come for tea soon. We've so much more to discuss. And to find out our husbands are already well acquainted." Arabella shook her head. "Malden is so forgetful. He never mentioned such a thing to me."

Lady Higgins twittered, obviously overjoyed to be invited to call on Arabella. "It would be our great pleasure, Lady Malden. Wouldn't it, Clare?"

Miss Higgins nodded. "Delightful, Lady Malden." Her glance flitted up to regard Arabella as if she were some exotic creature.

The brackets around Lydia's mouth deepened further; she likely couldn't bear the thought of Arabella pouring tea with the girl she'd selected for her precious son. Marissa could practically smell the fear rolling off Lydia in waves. One of Lydia's gloved hands disappeared inside the reticule dangling from her wrist.

"Come, Aunt." Arabella took Marissa's arm. "There's someone I wish to introduce you to. Good day to you Lady Higgins. Miss Higgins."

Arabella pointedly ignored Lydia, but Lady Higgins was far too enamored of becoming a close friend of the sister of a duke to notice. Marissa's niece had learned well how to be charming and inviting to others, a stark contrast to the sour, staid woman she'd been before her marriage to Rowan. What a change love had wrought in Arabella.

I was right about Rowan. Marissa allowed herself a congratulatory moment.

She and Arabella returned to their seats, settling their skirts around them. The chairs were terribly uncomfortable and devoid of any padding. Her back would be aching in a matter of minutes. Another result of growing older.

Arabella leaned toward her and whispered, "What in the *world* did you say to Lady Pendleton? I nearly mistook her for a corpse until she blinked. And was that brandy on her breath?"

"She smells like a Christmas punch. And I only reminded Lydia she could ill afford to scare off Miss Higgins. I may have also mentioned the scores of solicitors at my disposal who were intent on dragging out the court proceedings. But I was at all times polite."

"Oh, you are *dreadful*, Aunt." Arabella squeezed Marissa's arm. "It's one of the things I love most about you."

13

"Lord Pendleton to see you, my lord. Shall I send him in?"

Trent sat back in the leather chair before his desk, pushing aside the small pile of invitations he'd been replying to. Lord Stanton had invited him to the theater, doubtless at the bequest of his daughter Lady Christina. Before the day in the park with Marissa, Trent would have refused.

He scratched off an acceptance. "Send Lord Pendleton in."

At least Pendleton would provide a distraction because he was in dire need of one. He'd seen little of the viscount since arriving in London save for the one political gathering Trent had attended. And he'd only gone to Duckworth's because he suspected Marissa would be in attendance with Enderly.

A tiny squeeze pinched his heart.

"I hope I'm not interrupting you." Pendleton wandered into Trent's study with his customary superior attitude and took a seat on the leather sofa. His gaze flitted about the comfortable yet hardly luxurious room, probably comparing Trent's study to his own which was covered in expensive furnishings and the obligatory Blue John.

"Not at all."

Pendleton always assumed visits from him, rare though they were, would take precedence over anything else Trent was doing. Pompous ass.

Was Pendleton's snobbish behavior a contributing factor to Marissa's blatant dislike of the man? He could understand why Pendleton didn't care for Marissa; after all, her son *had* ruined the young lady Pendleton had planned on marrying last summer. The woman in question was now the Countess of Morwick. But it was Marissa's animosity toward Pendleton that had genuinely surprised Trent because it contrasted so sharply against her earlier behavior at Brushbriar. Watching the two interact from across the room it was hard to mistake the deep undercurrent of loathing between them. The sight unsettled Trent because he didn't know where such hostility had come from. Or why.

Thinking of Marissa brought with it the expected wave of hunger for her. A gnawing ache which refused to go away. He'd not seen her since she'd dismissed him, yet again, from her presence, though Jordana continued to visit Marissa.

I'm still very angry at her.

Trent possessed a temper, one which he had learned to keep in check over the years. Another flaw of his he'd had to learn to control when raising four girls. The entire countryside wondered at his idiocy at not immediately remarrying or keeping nursemaids for his daughters. But fatherhood had made Trent a better person, one he would not have been had his wife lived.

The selfish rake he'd once been wouldn't have deserved Marissa.

Hell, I'm not sure I do now.

Pushing aside his thoughts, Trent made his way to the sideboard. A visit from Pendleton required spirits. "Scotch? I may even have some brandy somewhere."

"Yes. I'd love a glass. Scotch."

Trent raised a brow. His unexpected guest rarely had a drink before dinner, and it was only mid-afternoon. In fact, in all the years Trent had known him, Pendleton had *never* sought Trent out for a drink *or* friendly conversation.

So why was Pendleton here?

Trent splashed scotch into two glasses and handed one to his visitor before taking a seat in a chair across from Pendleton.

Pendleton sat with his legs spread, rolling the crystal glass between his palms, a sure sign of some distress. It was rare for him to show a lick of emotion. The only exceptions were the passionate speeches Pendleton gave or when he defended his stance against the opposition. Trent was convinced the only thing Pendleton truly cared about was achieving his dream of Prime Minister. Everything else was a very distant second to that desire. The broken betrothal to Petra Grantly was only an inconvenience to a man like Pendleton.

Trent wondered if Pendleton even remembered her name.

"I find I'm rather . . . *embarrassed* to be here, Haddon." Pendleton tossed back the contents of his glass before pinching the bridge of his nose between his fingers as if in terrible pain.

That was something different. "Because I don't think your current bill goes far enough?" Trent said, sipping at his drink.

Pendleton gave a snort. "No." He waved a hand

dismissing Trent's comment. "A difference of opinion and one you'll see I'm right about. You fail to see the larger picture, as you so often do. The greater good must be served."

Christ, Pendleton thought himself the savior of all of England.

"What can I help you with? Is Lady Pendleton well?" Trent cared little for Pendleton's mother, a disingenuous woman he had never liked. Once his wife had died, Trent had declined to spend much time in Lady Pendleton's company. She was a grasping, selfish woman with an over-inflated ego and an air of superiority her son had inherited. Pendleton's mother had never had much use for Trent which was why the invitation to her little house party had been a complete surprise.

Except, Pendleton's sister was . . . not *discreet* in her . . . friendships. Trent supposed Lady Pendleton saw an opportunity to foist off her scandal-ridden daughter on some unsuspecting country bumpkin. Like Trent.

As if I'd have Pendleton's sister around my girls.

"My mother is fine," Pendleton said. "She's here in London. Arrived a few weeks ago."

"Oh? I wasn't aware." Ignorance had been bliss. Now that he had been informed of Lady Pendleton's presence, manners dictated he call upon her. He would put it off as long as possible.

"Another, if you please, Haddon." Pendleton held up his empty glass. "This isn't a social call to discuss my mother."

Well, that was a relief.

"I'm only here," Pendleton's lip curled a bit, "because there isn't anyone else I can turn to without an enormous scandal erupting—something I wish to avoid."

Trent got up again but instead of taking Pendleton's glass, he went to the sideboard and just grabbed the decanter. Pouring out nearly half a glass, Trent set the decanter on the small table between them before handing Pendleton his scotch. "Things must be dire indeed if I am your only hope."

Pendleton glared at Trent over the rim of his glass.

Trent and his girls were only *tolerated* because Trent's late wife had been related to the current Lord Pendleton's father. A familial tie not widely known, largely because Lydia didn't wish it to be. She found the connection be of little use to her and thus not worth her acknowledgement.

Unless Lady Pendleton needed something from Trent. Like his presence to round out a house party.

A vision of Marissa, her lovely face turned in his direction as she slept, the tangled mass of her hair stretching across his chest, filled his mind. He could have watched her sleep for hours that night. Trent had traced the line of her jaw with his fingertip, marveling at the precious gift he'd found at Lady Pendleton's stupid little house party.

Can I not go more than a few minutes without her invading my thoughts?

No. No he could not.

"I require a favor." Pendleton regarded Trent with determination.

How mortifying that must be for him. Pendleton far preferred lording over all the lesser beings in his orbit and bestowing favors upon *them*. And he considered Trent to be a much lesser being.

Trent leaned back in the chair. "A favor?"

Pendleton's gaze had grown downright chilly, his nostrils flaring out until he resembled an annoyed bulldog. "As you know, I'm courting the daughter of Sir Richard Higgins."

"Congratulations." Higgins owned several banks and was well known in political circles. Ridiculously wealthy,

Higgins sought influence and power, which he would have after buying Pendleton for his daughter. "Which one?" Trent asked. Higgins had more than one daughter. Five, to be exact.

"The girl in the middle. Clare."

A resounding vote of affection if Trent had ever heard one. If Higgins decided to switch out one daughter for another, would Pendleton even notice?

Unlikely.

"I'm assured my suit will be accepted. Higgins and I are in complete agreement."

Apparently, Miss Clare Higgins had not been consulted. Pendleton *had* assumed the same thing about Petra Grantly, but Trent thought it wise not to bring up Pendleton's past assumption.

"I'm sure you'll be very happy."

Pendleton opened his mouth to speak and then shut it again, lips thinning as he took in Trent.

My God. He really does dislike me. Quite a bit.

"We are family, Haddon, are we not?" Pendleton said in a slightly malevolent tone.

Trent suddenly had a *very* bad feeling about this conversation. "In a manner of speaking."

Pendleton gave a negligent wave of his hand. "We've had our differences, I know. But at the end of the day, we *are* family. I find myself in a bit of an unwelcome *situation*. If my *situation* became widely known"—he lifted his palms—"it would reflect poorly on me. Maybe even damage my effectiveness in Parliament. My opponents would have something to use against me." He took another sip of his scotch. "All those bloody reforms you so adore wouldn't stand a chance without my support."

"I concur." On that point, Pendleton was correct. While

Trent often thought his reforms didn't go far enough, those bills wouldn't exist at all without Pendleton. "What is this about?"

"My estate is deeply in debt. My mother and sister have been overspending for years and it is only recently I've managed to tighten the purse strings, but it is too late. If my sister could have managed to marry Kendicott, I wouldn't be sitting here. But," his lip curled in disapproval, "she's managed to muck things up with him. The son of a *pig* farmer. I should toss her out."

"How unfortunate."

Pendleton's eyes slid over Trent, searching for signs of mockery. Satisfied there were none, he continued.

"I've been selling bits and pieces. Items my mother had made from Blue John. Ridiculous little objects she had to have. It's all worth a fortune, but still, it isn't enough. I've markers all over London, Haddon. *Large* sums." He pierced Trent with a hard look. "The duns are already beating at my door. Imagine my embarrassment."

How mortifying for Pendleton who would see himself above such things.

"The vein of Blue John has finally run its course?" Trent asked. Pendleton's Blue John was the second largest deposit in England.

"No. The mine is still profitable." A choked laugh came from Pendleton. He ran his fingers through his close-cropped hair and across his face.

Trent waited, but Pendleton said nothing further concerning the Blue John or the mine.

"I have ambitions, Haddon. Melbourne will not be Prime Minister forever. I cannot afford to become destitute and thrown into debtor's prison. Nor do I wish to be called a fortune hunter while trying to secure Higgins's daughter. The girl is skittish enough. And I need Higgins's support."

"No, of course not." *Get to the point, Pendleton.* Even in his anxiety and begging a favor, the man still managed to be long-winded, as if Trent had nothing better to do but listen to him.

"My markers are being bought up, Haddon. Anonymously. My fear is one person, possibly with political motivation, is behind the collecting of my debt. This individual could seek to use my debt as leverage. Possibly even try to wield power through me, and thus into Parliament. And I'll have little choice."

"We all have a choice, Pendleton."

"How naive you are." An ugly choked sound came from him. "You've *no* concept of the workings of government. How one hand rubs the back of another."

Trent was liking this conversation, and Pendleton, less and less.

"Your late wife knew how things worked, for all that she'd been raised in the country. Anne wasn't shy about running to *my* father when you were in trouble. An accident at the quarry. You also had nowhere else to turn, as I'm sure you recall."

Trent's fingers tightened on his glass. "I do."

Barely twenty-four, with a small child and another on the way, Trent had only just buried his father and become Baron Haddon. His inheritance had consisted of an estate that was barely solvent and a struggling quarry. Trent's sister needed a dowry and his younger brother's tuition at Harrow was a small fortune. He was already in dire financial straits *before* the accident.

Trent's father had *refused* to modernize the lone quarry he owned. *Fifty* men had died during the cave-in, buried alive beneath an enormous pile of rock, leaving their families destitute. It had been an obligation for Trent to provide for those men's wives and children. The quarry was also the largest employer in the area for miles. If the quarry didn't reopen, not only would Trent become impoverished, but so would most of the families in the area. So many lives had depended on him. Anne, against Trent's wishes, had gone to her great-uncle, Lord Pendleton, who was flush with cash from the Blue John mine his family owned. It was assistance Trent hadn't wanted to accept, but he'd had little choice.

"So, you see why I've come. My father never asked you for repayment for the funds he gave you, but I believe, honorable man you are," Pendleton narrowed his eyes, "that you insisted you would return the favor one day. In fact, you wouldn't take the money until he agreed."

Trent knew very well what had been said; Pendleton need not remind him. The burden of being indebted to Pendleton for so long had weighed heavily on him for years.

"You were so bloody grateful, throwing around such a promise. My father never had need for a favor, but I do."

The scotch soured in Trent's stomach despite the fact he now wanted to drink the entire bottle.

"Don't worry, Haddon. Unlike your agreement with my father, I will make this only a *temporary* loan. I plan to repay you. Once I secure Clare Higgins and her dowry. I've already had my solicitor draw up papers to that effect."

"That isn't necessary." Pendleton was a prig, but he *was* honorable. It was literally the only thing Trent found likable about the man.

"Already done." Pendleton's mouth contorted into a semblance of a smile. "I don't want to cause you any undue distress. We are family, after all."

How fucking noble of him. After the completion of this

transaction, Trent meant to sever all contact with Pendleton once and for all. "How much?"

Pendleton's carefully constructed façade cracked for a moment, the fear at his circumstances bleeding through.

"A great deal."

14

M arissa shifted in her chair, desperate to get comfortable. Her back was already aching. She must remind Spencer to have his box at the theater updated with furniture that one could actually relax in.

Lifting her chin to better see the stage, Marissa winced as the leading lady began an overblown speech to the actor playing the gentleman who was courting her, though she loved another.

Marissa adored the theater, though not this play. The strident voice of the actress below grated on her nerves, reminding her unpleasantly of Lady Christina Sykes. Which in turn made her think of Haddon. Something she was trying desperately not to do.

I never took you for a coward, Marissa.

Marissa's fingers folded into her lap. She hadn't taken herself for one either.

"I said, Mother," said a voice laced with sarcasm, "I'm planning on assassinating the entire cast because the play is terrible. I've seen better performances in the private rooms at Elysium. Will you wait with Elizabeth while I do so?"

Marissa blinked, still thinking of Haddon. "Don't be ridiculous, Spencer."

A dark laugh came from her eldest son. "What has you so preoccupied that you cannot even spare me a moment of your attention? I've been gone from London for literally years, and I can't hold your interest for the length of this poorly acted play?"

Spencer was being dramatic. "If you will recall, I *show-ered* you with attention when you first arrived. You were so appreciative of my efforts to nurse you back to health that you asked your wife to tell me to leave. You referred to me as *Smother* and not *Mother* for an entire week."

An appalled look crossed his handsome face. "I did no such thing. I can't believe my wife would disparage me to my own mother. But Elizabeth is a sneaky little thing. Don't be fooled by her innocent demeanor." He nodded in the direction of the elegant, ebony-haired young woman seated next to him, who was listening in rapt attention to every word the actors on stage spouted.

The expression on her son's face spoke of his utter adoration for her. Spencer was completely besotted with Elizabeth. As well he should be. Elizabeth smoothed out Spencer's caustic edges, bringing him out of the darkness that so often surrounded her son. Marissa thought her newest daughter-in-law quite marvelous.

"I would even go so far as to call her *dictatorial*." Spencer bent down pretending to inspect something at his wife's feet.

"Kelso," Elizabeth hissed under her breath, cheeks turning red as she spared a discreet look at Marissa.

"Remove your hand from beneath my skirts this *instant*. I am trying to enjoy the play."

Marissa turned her head with a smile, pretending not to hear Elizabeth's rebuke. Her son and Elizabeth were very much in love, despite Spencer's reputation and the age difference between them.

I never thought you a coward, Marissa.

Haddon and the words he'd uttered, the slash of his cheekbones tinted pink with anger, invaded her thoughts more often than she wished. She had a terrible, gnawing suspicion she'd made a mistake that day, one which could not be fixed. It didn't help that every time she opened the papers, the gossips linked him to Lady Christina Sykes.

Spencer snapped his fingers before her nose. "Mother, stop this instant, or I'll get the smelling salts."

Marissa gave him an indulgent look. How she'd missed him while he was on the other side of the world for so many years. All of her ducklings, her sons, niece, and nephew, were *happy*. Marissa saw that as a personal achievement. And they would all be together during the holiday season for the first time in years. Her heart *should* have been full. Marissa *should* be happy.

Yes, but I am not.

"Now that you are no longer instructing Arabella how to be a young lady, a useless task in my opinion—"

"Not so," Marissa said, her eyes still on the play.

"My cousin is as *horrible* as ever. Malden has only taught her how to hide it behind affability. Every time she smiles, I'm frightened out of my wits. Her pleasantness is unnatural."

"Spencer." Marissa shook her head. "Arabella is content."

"At any rate, she tells me you've taken another difficult

young lady under your wing. Truly, Mother, you are a glutton for punishment."

"I am only offering my guidance."

Spencer's lip twitched with amusement. "Will you start a school, Mother, for wayward, mercenary young women in the hopes of turning them into demure little ladies? My wife could benefit from your guidance, I'm sure. Spending years in a convent didn't make the least impression on Elizabeth. When can I expect you to take her on?"

Elizabeth twisted, pinching Spencer's upper arm, before returning her attention to the play.

"Ouch." He leaned over and pressed a kiss to his wife's cheek.

"Elizabeth is perfection as you well know. She is a master at dealing with adversity already. I fear there is little I could teach her."

Elizabeth leaned sideways across her husband's lap. "Thank you, Marissa, for noticing my struggles. Every moment is a trial. I pray daily for strength."

"Sassy little nun," Spencer muttered.

"Honestly, dear," Marissa said, placing a hand on Spencer's arm. "I'm more concerned Arabella has turned into such a gossip. One would think with Lily's birth and her involvement in Rowan's various enterprises, she'd be too busy to worry overmuch about me. My life is *lacking* in excitement. Some might even say I'm boring."

"You are the furthest thing from boring, Mother. In fact, it is my understanding," a tiny snort left him, "that you are the life of the . . . *house* party."

Bloody Hell. These were *not* topics Marissa wished to discuss with her adult children. "Was it Brendan or Arabella who told you? The two of them gossip like a pair of elderly ladies over tea."

Spencer, her dangerous, deadly son, a former assassin and a man few would cross, was giggling like a schoolboy beside her. As if the idea his mother had been caught in a compromising situation with a gentleman was the most humorous thing he'd ever heard.

"Brendan told me. He was *appalled* by your lack of discretion." Another snicker.

Damn it.

"I wonder that your brother didn't just put an announcement in the Times. He's told nearly everyone," Marissa said in a crisp tone. "I think Nick may be the only one who has not poked fun at me," she said, referring to her nephew, the duke.

Spencer took her hand and brought it to his lips. "I'm only teasing, Mother. You've every right to a life of your own. I'm actually glad you're enjoying yourself. And though Brendan was a little upset at the time, he likes your . . . *friend*." A giggle erupted from him.

Marissa snatched back her hand. What an appalling conversation to have with Spencer, though she was relieved somewhat to know Brendan thought highly of Haddon. "It was only a *dalliance*, at any rate. It wasn't as if I had an understanding with him."

Spencer cocked his head. "Is that why you're squiring about Lord Haddon's daughter? Because he was merely a dalliance?"

Marissa swallowed and turned her attention back toward the play where the leading man was overacting in a dreadful manner and skipping across the stage.

This really is a terrible performance.

"His daughter, Jordana, is without the instruction of an older female. The poor thing is terribly awkward, having been raised in the country and without any guidance. I've only stepped in until Lord Haddon's sister arrives in town to take charge of her."

At least, that was Marissa's assumption. There had been no communication between her and Haddon since their argument in her parlor.

I called him meaningless.

An image of Haddon that day refused to leave her. He'd been not only angry but utterly wounded. Marissa pressed her fingers over her heart. She hadn't meant to hurt him. Hadn't known until that moment that she could.

"Well," Spencer said, bringing Marissa's attention back to their conversation, "your work with Arabella certainly speaks for itself."

"Your cousin is very happy. Her marriage is a love match though they had a bumpy start."

"I blame Malden for her improved manner and not you." He shrugged. "Still, I was surprised to hear you'd taken on another project. One would think you busy enough with what you're doing to Pendleton and his mother."

Marissa pursed her lips. She didn't even bother to ask how he knew. It seemed she was to have no secrets at all. Now they would all be meddling. "And what is it you think I'm doing?" she whispered in his ear, not wanting Elizabeth to overhear her.

Spencer lowered his voice. "Be quicker if I just slit his throat. I'll make it look like an accident. *Very clean.* Unless you wish him to suffer."

Marissa closed her eyes, taking a deep breath, and shook her head. "No, dear. No murder." She'd forgotten how *blood-thirsty* Spencer could be. "You promised Elizabeth you won't do such a thing again."

Spencer scowled. "I did. But she might allow an exception given the circumstances." He shot a glance at his wife who seemed enthralled with the play, though Marissa was certain Elizabeth was listening. "I heard Lady Pendleton's a sot. Had a bit too much to drink the other night during a dinner party Pendleton held for some of his political allies."

A recounting of the incident had been in Tomkin's last report to Marissa. The thought of Lydia drunkenly waving about a glass, drops of wine flying across to sprinkle the guests at a political dinner while her son watched in horror, was priceless.

"Sent his mother up to her room before the last course was served. Can't afford to have his betrothal to Miss Higgins ruined by Lady Pendleton's drunkenness, though I understand the girl's father has agreed to the match and the contracts signed. But I expect the betrothal is about to be broken despite Pendleton's best efforts, isn't it, Mother?"

"Perhaps."

"It's unfortunate you don't have another son to ruin the girl for you."

"Your brother *ruined* Petra because he loved her. Her relationship with Pendleton had little to do with it." Simon had moved quickly to secure Miss Higgins before Marissa had had an opportunity to stop the courtship, and now the contracts had been signed. He'd have the money to pay off his markers, which Marissa now owned. She'd been careless, taunting Lydia at Arabella's charity event and should have anticipated how Simon and his mother would react.

I wasn't thinking clearly because of Haddon.

Her revenge had now become more complicated, but not insurmountable. A compromising position would have to be arranged for Miss Higgins with a gentleman who was not Viscount Pendleton. It would take some planning and must be executed flawlessly, but it *was* possible.

Miss Higgins would only have to be coerced, *gently*, into betraying Simon, but it shouldn't be too difficult. He hadn't bothered to even court Miss Higgins, just her father. Any gentleman who paid the poor girl a bit of attention could likely seduce her.

"It isn't a love match, Spencer," she said a bit defensively.

In fact, the instrument of Miss Higgins's future ruination was, at this moment, sitting in a box with Marissa's friend, Adelia. She meant to make his acquaintance, in spite of Tomkin advising her against doing so. But she'd insisted. An ex-soldier, the gentleman in question had served with Tomkin's son somewhere in Canada. Ironically, he happened to be the same gentleman tupping Adelia.

The world was full of coincidences.

"You'd ruin that poor girl just to get at Pendleton?" Spencer looked incredibly disapproving, which Marissa thought hypocritical of her son given his past.

The guilt she'd been trying to ignore reared up.

"I didn't think you so moralistic, Spencer. Besides, how else am I to ensure they don't marry?" Marissa *did* feel horrible she might harm Miss Higgins and destroy the girl's reputation. She'd be forced to return to Cornwall in disgrace. "At any rate, I'm still working out the details."

"I'm hardly what one would consider a moral, upstanding citizen, as you well know. But you've always seen yourself as a protector of young ladies." Spencer paused as his brows knit together. "I find it entirely out of character for you to harm one." He took her hand and leaned close again until his lips brushed her ear. "I'll get rid of him. And Lydia. I'd enjoy doing so. Elizabeth need never know. They had the audacity to murder your husband and steal from my brother."

"No," she said softly. "I need to do this for Reggie." She pressed his hand to her cheek. "And myself."

Spencer leaned back slightly, still scowling at her. "Very well. You've called in his markers?"

"I did this morning. I've given him until the end of the month to come up with the sum, which he will not be able to do."

"Why not force him to pay immediately?"

"I want them to suffer." Marissa's voice turned brittle. "Worry. *Fret*. I want Lydia stumbling about drunkenly, terrified of being poor. She'll have a measure of relief thinking her son has bagged Miss Higgins. Which will make the loss of her that much sweeter."

Spencer regarded her thoughtfully for a moment.

"What is it?" Marissa patted his hand.

"I just never noticed how much you remind me of Grandfather." He took her fingers, pressed a kiss to the tips and returned his attention to the play.

15

Thank goodness the lights were flickering for intermission. Marissa tapped her foot as she waited for the curtain to come down.

"I believe I'll stretch my legs and visit Lady Waterstone for a moment." Marissa stood. "I did promise if I attended tonight, I would stop by her box."

Spencer glanced at her, disapproval still hovering at the edges of his mouth. Her son could go *hang*. How dare he condemn her actions while simultaneously offering to garrote Lydia with her string of pearls for Marissa. *She* wasn't going to murder anyone.

Marissa meant only to meet Captain Ross Nighter, the man Tomkin had hired. Perhaps she'd have an opportunity to speak to him and outline her expectations for Miss Higgins. She didn't want the girl harmed in any way by Nighter.

No, you'll handle that part yourself.

The voice in her head sounded suspiciously like Reggie.

Marissa wasn't having any of it. She was conflicted

enough about what she meant to do. She pushed the voice aside along with her guilt.

When she arrived at Adelia's box, her friend was sipping wine, her buxom figure draped over a large, bulky shape in a chair facing the stage.

Captain Nighter.

Marissa came forward. She'd not confided the circumstances of Reggie's death to Adelia, only that his remains had been found. It was one thing to discuss lovers and children, quite another to inform your closest friend you were ruthlessly destroying one of London's most brilliant politicians because his father had murdered your husband decades ago.

Adelia wouldn't understand Marissa's need to avenge Reggie. Just as she wouldn't comprehend why Marissa had refused Haddon.

Damn it. Stop thinking of him.

"Marissa, darling." Adelia rushed forward, resplendent in an emerald gown which was the perfect foil for her auburn hair. "I was hoping you'd stop by. It's a dull play, don't you think?"

"Atrocious," Marissa agreed.

"But the leading man is delicious, is he not? Who cares how poor his acting is?"

"Adelia, you're incorrigible. Aren't you already otherwise engaged?" Marissa nodded in the direction of the chair facing the stage. She could just make out the profile of a man. Aquiline nose. Strong jaw.

"Yes, but one must always be prepared for the inevitable," she said. "Until then, I'm enjoying myself immensely." She tugged at her bodice. "Nighter is very impatient, but I knew you'd be coming by." Fluffing the lace at her neckline, she said, "He's here, you know. I saw him as we came in. Those magnificent cheekbones are impossible to miss."

"Who is here?" Marissa said, pretending indifference.

"Your Lord Haddon." Adelia shook her head, the ringlets at her temples bouncing vivaciously. "You've taken the daughter but not him. Foolish girl." Adelia wagged a finger. "Now he's taken up with that little twit. He's in Lord Stanton's box tonight."

Marissa's heart thudded painfully at the words. "Lady Christina Sykes?" It wasn't unexpected, given the way their names were linked in the gossip columns. What was surprising was how much Marissa hated hearing Adelia confirm their relationship. Up until now, Marissa had been able to pretend it was nothing more than gossip.

"And Miss Ashley. Or Miss Higgins." Adelia laughed. "Your Lord Haddon certainly is making his way through this season's debutantes. Though not we merry widows. I can't seem to catch his eye though I've been trying. Perhaps he doesn't care for redheads."

A low sound came from Marissa before she could stop it.

"Well?" Adelia lowered her voice to a whisper. "*You* aren't interested though why that is I can't imagine. Haddon has that look to him. Every inch a man." She wiggled her brows.

"Adelia—" Marissa warned.

Adelia leaned back, smug smile firmly in place. "Well, it does seem such a waste. But very well, I'll keep my distance. Don't be cross with me, darling."

Marissa's fingers flexed. She was horrified to find both hands had been curled into fists. The thought of Adelia, or anyone else, bedding Haddon was so abhorrent, she nearly slapped her closest friend. She'd always assumed Spencer had gotten his bloodthirsty tendencies from his grandfather, the 'Old Spider.'

Apparently not.

"You were saying something about Miss Higgins?"

Adelia spared a glance in the direction of the balcony, where a disgruntled sigh filled the air from Captain Nighter. "*Regina* Higgins, the younger sister of the lady whose engagement to Viscount Pendleton will be announced soon. She's developed a *tendre* for your handsome baron."

"Adelia." A masculine grunt came from the chair. "I'm *bored*."

The dark outline stood, taking the shape of a towering, well-built gentleman.

Adelia giggled and went over to take his arm, propelling him forward, but Nighter's eyes remained on Marissa, one brow quirked in question.

He was breathtakingly handsome, much more so than Marissa had expected, though Adelia had always displayed good taste in men, if not judgement. Candlelight glinted on the burnished gold of his close-cropped hair, dipping to trail across his exquisitely sculpted features. His mouth was full and wide—sensuous lips with just a hint of cruelty tipping up one end.

He was quite possibly the most beautiful man Marissa had ever seen.

It was Nighter's eyes that tipped Marissa off and belied his angelic looks. Pale blue, like the crust of winter's first snow, and just as devoid of any warmth. Or humanity. How old had Adelia said he was? Twenty-five? Much too young to have become so . . . *soulless*.

Nighter stood over Marissa, his immense, muscular form dominating the small space of the box. The full lips twisted into a charming smile, chilly gaze lingering over her bosom before lifting to take in her face.

Marissa stared down her nose at Captain Nighter. Or as

much as was possible with a man of his height. She put aside her initial misgivings. Tomkin trusted the young captain, telling Marissa that Nighter was an honorable man who did dishonorable things.

Like compromising a young girl for a purse of gold.

If Nighter so much as curled a finger in Miss Higgins's direction, the poor thing would melt into a puddle at his feet. Exactly what she was meant to do.

"Aren't you going to introduce me?" The gravelly voice echoed in the box.

"Captain Nighter, may I present my dearest friend, Lady Cupps-Foster." Adelia twirled about nervously.

Nighter didn't bother to hide his blatant assessment of her. "My pleasure, Lady Cupps-Foster." He took her hand politely, holding it a moment longer than necessary while Adelia fumed at his side.

"Captain Nighter. How lovely to make your acquaintance."

Releasing Marissa's hand, Nighter turned to Adelia. "I'll go fetch us some more wine, shall I?" He didn't wait for her to answer before he headed out of the box.

"Yes, Nighter," she said to his retreating back. "Thank you."

Marissa turned to her friend, who was still staring in the direction the captain had gone. What on earth was Adelia thinking taking up with a man like Nighter? "Goodness, Adelia. He's younger than both my sons." *And so very broken.*

"He's twenty-six." Adelia shrugged, fanning herself. "And he's an old soul. Trust me." She took Marissa's hand. "Don't pout, Marissa. You'll get little lines around your mouth. Besides, I'm enjoying myself."

"I know . . . just be *careful* with him. At any rate, I only stopped by to say hello and ask you to join me for luncheon tomorrow." She hadn't intended on inviting Adelia over, but the excuse seemed as good as any. "Haddon's daughter will be coming as well. I would love for you to meet her."

"Haddon's daughter? She's probably blessed with the same divine bone structure. I shall be there." She kissed Marissa's cheek. "But not too early, darling. Nighter is a *demanding* lover."

"You really are quite horrid, Adelia," Marissa said, smiling at her.

With a wave at Adelia, Marissa made her way out of the box, and toward the stairs. Spencer and Elizabeth would be wondering where she had gotten off to. The hallway was dim, the lights having been turned down in anticipation of the play resuming. Haddon was here, somewhere in this theater, with Lady Christina clawing at him with her perfect gloved hands.

The thought did not improve her mood.

"My lady."

A dark rasp came from the shadows at the very top of the stairs. The darkness moved, taking the shape of Captain Nighter.

Lying in wait for me. Marissa's pulse jumped at his sudden appearance.

Bunched muscles tightened beneath the fabric of his evening clothes as he bowed to her. Nighter was a big man, much like Nick and Brendan, sucking up all the available air in the hall with his presence. There was a hint of well-bred snobbery in his manner—the sort a person possessed when they'd been born into wealth. Nighter, according to Tomkin, was the disgraced nephew of a wealthy marquess, though she'd neglected to ask which one. His familial ties were of no importance to Marissa. Only the fact that he was at loose ends and needed money mattered, though it had reassured her somewhat to know he'd been born a gentleman.

"Captain Nighter." The hall was empty save for her and Nighter, something which gave her pause. The play had started. She could already hear the screeching of the lead actress. Marissa lowered her voice to ensure anyone who might chance upon them couldn't eavesdrop.

"I assume you will be attending Lady Ralston's ball," she murmured.

"If that is your pleasure, my lady." The icy gaze traveled over her breasts.

Marissa didn't care for his chilly perusal of her bosom. Nighter was undoubtedly well-versed in the seduction of women, though it was unlikely he had to work very hard at the task. Any young lady would be grateful for his attention if one didn't notice the absolute desolation in his eyes.

"I will arrange for the two of you to be caught in an indiscretion at Lady Ralston's. But you must seek her out prior to attending the event. Flirt with her. Garner her trust so that she will meet you without question in some darkened room at the ball. There will be *no* seduction of her person, only the *appearance* of one. The young lady in question is not to be physically harmed in *any* way," she stressed.

An odd look flitted through his ice-blue eyes, surprising Marissa before Nighter caught himself and placed his chilly mask firmly in place. But not quick enough.

Sorrow. Grief.

In that moment, Marissa caught a glimpse of the man Nighter must once have been. Before becoming this crueler, darker version of himself.

"I would never harm a woman physically. You have my assurance." The words hovered in the air like bits of snow and ice. "I won't betray Mr. Tomkin's trust in me nor would I ever be stupid enough to incur the *interest* of *your* family, my lady."

"Very good."

What happened to you, Captain Nighter?

There had been no mistaking the absolute heartache shadowing his striking features, if only for a moment. She'd seen it in her own face often enough after Reggie's death.

"The lady in question," he was careful not to mention Miss Higgins by name, "will have her reputation damaged only enough to break a betrothal and nothing more. I will seek her out in the park tomorrow. She always takes the path furthest from the river but closer to the woods."

Marissa nodded. Nighter had done his research on Miss Higgins. "I will find you at Lady Ralston's." She felt *marginally* better, assured Nighter wouldn't harm Miss Higgins physically, although her stomach continued to pitch about at the thought of destroying her reputation.

"Good evening, Captain Nighter."

"Until we meet again, Lady Cupps-Foster." He bowed politely but made no attempt to take her hand before heading down the stairs.

Marissa waited, counting to ten before placing a hand on the railing to assure Nighter had enough time to sneak away. Hand trembling against the iron, she made her way down the stairway, the implication of the series of events she'd just set in motion firmly fixed in her mind.

The guilt was the worst of it.

I'm doing what I must. For Reggie.

No, this is not for me, Reggie's voice whispered in her head.

"Shush. It is for you," she muttered under her breath. *Good Lord*, anyone coming upon her would think her addled, speaking to herself in such a way.

As she took a step down, the heel of her slipper caught against the hem of her skirt. Swinging her foot in irritation she sought to dislodge her shoe from her skirts, but instead the velvet wrapped around her legs. Marissa's knee buckled, trapped amid the layers of her skirts.

Perhaps I won't have a chance to avenge Reggie.

Arms spinning like a small windmill, Marissa held out her hands in a futile attempt to avoid falling to her death and conveniently resolving her guilt at harming Miss Higgins.

Of all the idiotic ways to break my neck. On a staircase. At the theater. And it isn't even a good play.

Marissa closed her eyes as the staircase spun, certain she was about to perish when she landed against a familiar, muscular chest that smelled of shaving soap and spice.

Haddon.

16

Trent had taken the long way back to the Marquess of Stanton's box after the intermission ended, using the excuse he wished to have a cheroot and take some air. What he'd really needed was a respite from the stifling atmosphere of Lord Stanton's box and the gentleman's quiet disapproval. Lord Stanton didn't think Trent a good enough catch for his only daughter, which was fine with Trent since he'd no intention of marrying Lady Christina Sykes.

He had enough on his mind tonight besides trying to garner the approval of his host, something Trent didn't give a shit about anyway. Pendleton's markers, consolidated into one giant, enormous sum, had been called due. As Pendleton said they would be.

I have beggared myself.

True to his word, Pendleton did have his solicitors draw up a document detailing the loan repayment. The documents had been delivered to Trent just this morning by special messenger. Of course, repayment was entirely contingent upon Pendleton marrying Miss Higgins.

Pendleton had assured Trent that *nothing* would impede his marriage to the girl.

Just as Pendleton had assumed before when Petra Grantly was ruined beneath his nose.

Miss Higgins seemed a level-headed young lady. He'd met her only moments ago as Pendleton, escorting the highly reserved girl, had visited Stanton's box. Though shy and soft-spoken, Miss Higgins appeared somewhat intelligent. Dutiful. She'd clung firmly to Pendleton's arm as he'd paraded her about.

Christ, let's hope so.

If something were to halt Pendleton's marriage to Miss Higgins, Trent would be returning to Derbyshire *permanently*. His home in London would have to be sold immediately. His daughters would be left with only small dowries if even that. And the quarries?

A heavy weight settled in his stomach.

Gone.

The work of three generations would be foreclosed on by the banks and Trent would be reduced to sheep farming. Or raising pigs. He was equally terrible at both, so he supposed it didn't matter. Trent and his daughters would become yet another ancient family with nothing to show for themselves but a bankrupt estate and good breeding. His girls would be raised in genteel poverty.

Trent had lain awake several nights contemplating the sheer stupidity of helping Pendleton, but at the end of it, he always came to the same conclusion. Honor, a stupid overused sentiment, would nonetheless dictate his actions. He owed Pendleton. At least there was the promise of repayment in writing. And thinking of Pendleton and the loan had pushed Trent's thoughts of Marissa aside for the better part of a week.

He rounded the corner to go up the stairs, certain Lady Christina was pouting at his absence, when he heard the hum of a low-pitched conversation above him. The stairwell was dark, the lamps having been dimmed once the curtain went up and the play resumed. The quiet corner at the top of the stairs was the perfect place for an assignation since most of those in attendance had returned to their boxes.

Trent paused, not wishing to interrupt the pair. He could take the stairs at the opposite side of the theater, but just as he turned to do so, a gentleman came down the steps. Tall, with the bearing those with military experience often displayed, he nodded politely, brushing past Trent before moving into the main hall.

Resolved to return to Stanton's box and endure the remainder of the evening, Trent had only placed his foot on the stair when a small cry met his ears. A flurry of burgundy velvet and a spray of feathers fell toward him; without thinking, he reached out his arms. He was either being accosted by a giant bird, or a lady had lost her footing on the stairs.

Feathers tickled his nose as a soft, generous form fell into his arms with a whoosh. Trent recognized the luscious body pressed so delightfully against him immediately. He was intimately acquainted with every inch of her.

"Oh, dear. Thank you," Marissa said, breath uneven and lips parted. She clutched at his coat, as she struggled to regain her footing.

Trent couldn't take his eyes from her mouth. The luscious plum of her lips cried out to be claimed.

One kiss.

His head tilted and his mouth moved toward hers before their last conversation, her words ringing in his ears, rushed back at him. Stiffening, he took Marissa by the shoulders, and set her firmly back on her feet.

Marissa stared up at Trent, blinking as if he were some sort of a hallucination. "Lord Haddon."

Trent raised a brow. "You look disappointed, Lady Cupps-Foster."

"No. I mean—I wasn't expecting—thank you." Her fingers were still curled into the lapels of his coat, seemingly reluctant to release him.

God, she was beautiful. Her sapphire eyes were luminous as she looked up at him, the decorative spray of feathers fixed in her dark locks listing dangerously to one side. His entire body hummed at being near her, his heart throbbing painfully inside his chest. What was it about this one woman that made Trent lose every bit of sense he possessed?

"Have a care, Marissa. You could have broken your neck." The words came out harsher than he'd intended but only because jealousy, so thick he feared he'd choke on it, flooded up his throat.

Marissa had been the woman at the top of the stairs.

Her body arched, just enough to push her breasts, which were *bloody* magnificent, against his chest.

Trent's arousal was immediate. *Painful.* His cock didn't seem to care he'd just caught her in an assignation with another man.

"Perhaps you should have your *dalliances* in an area with better lighting lest you injure yourself." Trent disengaged her fingers from his coat, ignoring her small sound of surprise at his actions. Anger and jealousy were mixing together, fueling the temper he so often kept under control. He didn't trust himself to speak or be so near her. Trent took a pointed step back.

Marissa's mouth popped open. "No. He's not—that is to say—"

"You owe me no explanation, my lady," he bit out. "Excuse me." He brushed past her to move up the stairs. "Enjoy the rest of your evening."

"MY HEM," MARISSA SAID STUPIDLY TO HIS RETREATING BACK, hoping he wouldn't leave just yet. "I fear it caught in my heel. I should lodge a complaint. The stairs aren't lit properly."

Haddon looked down on her, the dim glow of the lamps glancing off his sharp cheekbones. "A fine idea."

Her breath paused, eyes greedily soaking up every inch of him. She made a great show of brushing a bit of feather which had come loose from her styled hair, off the sleeve of her dress. Everything caught on velvet; she wasn't sure she'd have another gown made from the fabric.

Terribly inconvenient.

As inconvenient as Haddon seeing her with Nighter and assuming the worst.

What else would he think?

"I'm glad I could be of service. *Again.*"

Marissa looked away. There was so much acrimony in those few words and all of it directed at her. All of it deserved. Did he really believe she'd only used him?

I called him meaningless.

"It was fortuitous you were here to catch me." She looked up at Haddon, speaking to stop him from dashing up the stairs and away from her. Wanting his forgiveness but too afraid to ask for it.

"Next time, I won't be," he said flatly.

"No, I don't suppose you will." Marissa lifted her chin, hating everything about this conversation though loath to end it. "He isn't my lover if that is what you are assuming." She couldn't tell him the truth. "Captain Nighter is involved with my friend, Lady Waterstone. I was just visiting her and—"

"I don't *care*, Marissa."

Her heart fluttered madly. He clearly *did* care.

"I only find it ironic. He's far younger than I."

Marissa looked up at the face of the man she'd carried with her from the Peak District to London. A man she dreamed of nearly every night. Desolation filled her at the thought of Haddon being forever gone from her life. The last few weeks with Jordana, the only remaining reminder of him, had left Marissa feeling torn and ragged. Her eyes took in the sheer masculine beauty of Haddon, tracing the lines of his shoulders to his face and the magnificent slash of his cheekbones—dark smudges beneath quicksilver eyes.

Worry filled her the more Marissa studied Haddon. He looked leaner, as if he hadn't been eating properly in addition to not sleeping. Jordana had certainly not volunteered any information that would cause Haddon to be in such a state.

"Haddon, is everything all right? Are the girls all well?"

Did I do this?

His expression was cool. Unfathomable. Politely reserved. Effectively closing himself off from her. A chilly block of ice looked back down on her. "Good evening, Lady Cupps-Foster."

Not only did Haddon *not* wish to disclose whatever troubled him, he was violently opposed to discussing it with Marissa.

She came forward before he could take another step. "Haddon." Marissa placed a hand on his sleeve to stop him, ignoring the hostile look he gave her.

"Is there something more? Lady Christina will be expecting my return to her father's box."

Marissa flinched. "Yes, there is something. I'd nearly forgotten. I meant to send you a note." She gave him a smile.

It was not returned.

"But now that we've run into each other," she said in a rush, "I wished to let you know I'll be taking Jordana to Madame Fontaine's later this week. To fit her for a new wardrobe."

"I'm aware. Have a lovely time on Bond Street. My sister will arrive in a few weeks and will relieve you of your duty to Jordana."

He was so *bloody* angry. "She isn't a duty," she snapped, suddenly comprehending how unbearable being separated from Haddon had become. Marissa bit her lip, struggling to find a way to make him understand. He wasn't meaningless. All she managed was his name.

"Trent."

Haddon brought his jaw up sharply, eyes narrowed as if he couldn't bear the sight of Marissa a moment longer. "Good evening, Lady Cupps-Foster," he repeated, this time with even more hostility than before. He turned his back on her, jogging up the stairs, clearly unwilling to be in her presence a moment longer.

Marissa blinked back the tears filling her eyes. She reminded herself of all the reasons she and Haddon could not be together. His age. His need for a wife who could provide an heir. His friendship with Pendleton.

Her *bloody* heart which couldn't stand to be broken again.

Except it already was.

17

"Come, Jordana. Madame Fontaine is just down the street." Marissa waved a gloved hand at her charge. "We don't want to be late. *Madame*"—she affected a slight accent—"doesn't care for clients who aren't prompt. Lateness sets her off. She's temperamental. And French."

"Isn't that the same thing, my lady?" Jordana stomped beside her, steadfastly *refusing* to be hurried no matter how Marissa prodded her. They'd gotten a late start today, mainly due to Marissa rising at an exceptionally late hour. She hadn't slept much last night, tossing and turning in her bed until the wee hours of the morning. Between the ache in her heart over Haddon and her guilt over Miss Higgins, Marissa wasn't getting a lot of rest.

Only Haddon made her weep, though.

Felice had put cold compresses on her eyes this morning while Marissa had tried to convince her maid the excessive dust in the bedroom had caused the redness and swelling.

"Is your father enjoying London?" Marissa bit her lip.

What a question to ask Jordana, who she suspected knew much more than she let on.

Jordana shrugged. "I suppose he is. I'm sure if he wasn't, we'd return home."

A purposefully bland and useless answer. Marissa had the urge to shake Jordana. "I ran into Lord Haddon at the theater the other evening. He looked rather tired."

"My father keeps much later hours in London than he does in the country." Jordana paused before a small coffeehouse, looking through the window with longing. "May we stop for tea or perhaps hot chocolate?" She turned to Marissa. "Look at these tiny cakes, my lady. I adore pink icing."

Late hours? "No, dear. Possibly after we are done at Madame Fontaine's." *He's probably busy dancing attendance on Lady Christina Sykes.* "Not now. Do hurry along, Jordana." Taking her charge's arm, she pulled Jordana away from the window.

All of London must be out shopping today. The streets had been so congested her driver had been required to park the carriage a bit further away from Madame Fontaine's than Marissa would have liked, although the walk was surely doing her and Jordana some good.

"You must hurry along as well," she called over her shoulder to the young footman tagging along behind them. He was a gangly lad, all elbows and long legs. Marissa couldn't remember his name. She hazarded a glance at his ill-fitting livery. A conversation with Greenhouse was warranted.

Jordana rolled her eyes, not bothering to hide the fact she didn't care about a new wardrobe nor about offending one of the most exclusive dressmakers in London. "I've never even been to a modiste. Seems a waste of time."

Marissa was aghast, stopping in her tracks. "Who makes your clothing?"

"There is a seamstress in Buxton. We visit her several times a year and she takes our measurements. Mrs. Divet usually accompanies us. I pick out some fabrics and she makes me suitable clothing."

Marissa started moving again. "Very like a modiste. It isn't as if you've been sewing your own clothing, Jordana. You nearly gave me a fit at the thought."

Jordana frowned. "At going to a seamstress or stitching my own underthings?"

"We don't say such things in public, on a street," Marissa reminded her. Jordana blurted out her thoughts at the slightest provocation.

"No one heard me. And I truly don't see the point in visiting Madame Fontaine. I don't need any more clothes. I've plenty of dresses. I doubt I'll attend any balls while I'm in London. You've seen me dance. I don't do it well." Her dark brows knit together. "And I've no desire to make some grand debut."

"We've been over this *several* times, Jordana. If what you wore when Lady Waterstone came for luncheon is *any* indication of the contents of your armoire, then you are in dire need of something decent. A proper lady *never* has enough to wear. You can always benefit from another riding habit, for instance. Hurry along." She picked up her pace. "You simply must have something other than sprigged muslin to wear in London. We are not in the wilds of the Peak District, climbing gritstone."

"I wish I was." Her eyes held a faraway look. "I don't belong here."

Jordana was stubborn, but *not* devious, as Arabella had

been. It was the only positive thing Marissa could say about her latest project.

Still grumbling, Jordana allowed herself to be dragged behind Marissa as they approached Madame Fontaine's. The modiste was only the *first* stop. Jordana must have new gloves. Bonnets. And Marissa needed a new hat to replace the one which had been ruined.

He'd been marvelous, climbing that tree to save my little hat.

Marissa didn't even attempt to push away her thoughts of Haddon, nor the bits of him which filled her mind at the oddest moments. *Everything* reminded her of him. Marissa had hoped to catch a glimpse of him when she'd called to retrieve Jordana for today's excursion, but Haddon had remained absent.

He thinks I'm having an affair with Nighter.

"This way, Jordana." Marissa deftly steered her into a brick storefront. At least there was enjoyment to be found in shopping for clothes. What woman didn't want a new wardrobe? Besides Jordana? Marissa herself had already ordered three additional ballgowns which should be ready today.

As they entered Madame Fontaine's, Jordana grew silent, taking in the clusters of women looking at fabrics and ribbons with mounting horror. While she'd improved, Jordana was still terribly awkward among society, especially with young ladies her own age. Marissa had been hoping it was only shyness that kept her from making friends, but she was starting to realize Jordana truly had no interest in the things most girls valued. Dresses, paying calls, finding a suitable husband; none of those things mattered to Haddon's daughter.

One of Madame Fontaine's assistants saw Marissa enter

and approached, bobbing politely to her before taking in Jordana.

Jordana treated the poor girl to a scowl.

"Lady Cupps-Foster." Her English held a charming French accent. "It is my pleasure to greet you today."

"Bonjour, Claudette." Marissa smiled at the girl. Claudette was one of Madame Fontaine's proteges. "This is Miss Ives."

"Madame is expecting you both. This way, please."

As she and Jordana made their way through the shop, Marissa pointed out the groups of women, reciting their names and titles to Jordana.

"Over there is Lady Ralston and her daughter, Emily," Marissa whispered. "She's to be married shortly to the eldest son of the Earl of Devon and her mother is giving a grand ball to celebrate. I myself will be in attendance. *Everyone* will be there."

Jordana's lips puffed in agitation. "You're always spouting off everyone's names and titles as if you expect me to remember them all. As if it were of importance. Which I don't believe it is."

Jordana was being particularly difficult today.

"Perhaps we should purchase you a small notebook to take down the things I tell you." Marissa patted her arm. "I leave myself notes all the time to help me remember what is important."

"I still won't remember because I don't *care* to."

Marissa pursed her lips. She'd made progress with Jordana, but there was still much more work to be done. Jordana seemed determined *not* to engage with society and *not* to marry. She delighted in informing Marissa she meant to spend her life as a *midwife* or something equally disagreeable.

"Ah, Lady Cupps-Foster." Madame Fontaine came forward and kissed Marissa on both cheeks. "I see you've brought me another young lady, no? Lady Malden wasn't enough?"

Madame Fontaine towered over Marissa and every other woman milling about her establishment. Taller than most men, the modiste favored red painted heels which added several inches to her height. Along with her tower of hair which was often full of the pencils she used for sketching, Madame Fontaine resembled an overly large, fashionable porcupine. The gossips whispered the modiste had left France after murdering her married lover.

The story seemed suspicious, especially when the modiste's accent slipped. No matter the truth of her origins, Madame Fontaine was one of the most sought after modistes in London. Her original designs were nothing short of stunning, her taste impeccable.

Marissa adored her.

Madame Fontaine plucked a pencil out from the mountain of her hair. Glancing first at Jordana and then back to Marissa, her tongue flicked over the end of the pencil, a small leather-bound notepad appearing from her pocket.

"May I present Miss Ives." Marissa brought Jordana forward.

"Miss Ives." Madame Fontaine peered down from her great height at Jordana.

"Madame." Jordana's eyes had widened to the size of saucers taking in the modiste.

"She will need a new wardrobe, from scratch, as I explained earlier." Marissa produced a list from her reticule and handed the paper to Madame Fontaine. "Perhaps you have two or three dresses which can be fit for her today while the rest can be delivered later? Something appropriate for paying calls?"

"I have just the thing." Madame looked down her long nose, studying Jordana while taking notes. "Blue-grays, perhaps. Or violet. Periwinkle. Her eyes are a most unusual color. We must take advantage."

Jordana shot the modiste a defiant look.

Madam Fontaine laughed softly. "Oh, my dear Lady Cupps-Foster, I find your new charge very similar to Lady Malden in temperament." She tapped the pencil against her temple. "I remember the dark colors so favored by your niece. I wept every time she came in for a fitting," the modiste said dramatically. "Staid, matronly fashions which gave no hint of her lovely figure. Such *atrocious* colors for such a gorgeous creature. Now she *adores* crimson." Madame Fontaine lowered her voice. "As does Lord Malden." Her long graceful fingers waved in invitation as she began to move in the direction of the fitting rooms. "Come, come."

Jordana hesitantly stepped behind the curtain as directed by Madame Fontaine, shooting Marissa a look of reproach.

Marissa gave her a not-too gentle nudge.

Madame Fontaine clapped her hands and two assistants immediately appeared, rushing forward to remove Jordana's dress and take her measurements.

Jordana stood frozen, eyes looking up at the ceiling briefly before her gaze settled on Marissa with no small amount of hostility.

Marissa ignored her and settled herself on a damask-covered settee. Accepting a glass of wine, she began leafing through a pattern book as she waited for fabric swatches to be brought to her.

"Is this necessary?" Jordana blushed furiously on the small block while the two girls stripped her down to her chemise. She shifted on the balls of her feet, jerking as if in the throes of a fit, clasping what remained of her clothing around her.

Marissa was half-afraid Jordana would leap from the podium and run half-naked from the shop to avoid being fitted. *Goodness*. The last thing she expected from the girl was such extreme *shyness* what with her having three sisters, not to mention her unnatural interest in . . . *body parts*.

She looked *so* miserable.

"Jordana," Marissa said, putting the wine aside. "If you tolerate being pinched and pinned without complaint, I will take you to Mr. Coventry's. The apothecary."

"Truly?" she said in a blissful tone, lips tilting up at the corners.

"Jordana, I'm shocked. You appear to be *smiling*."

"Perish the thought, my lady." Her mouth immediately resumed the usual tight-lipped scowl. "And I should like nothing more." She slapped at the assistant who attempted to measure her waist. "Sorry," she murmured to the girl. "You startled me."

Marissa pressed her fingers to her forehead. Jordana would try the patience of a saint. "You must stay still, dear, and allow your measurements to be taken *without* injuring Madame's assistant," Marissa admonished. "In case I was not clear before."

"Fine." Jordana stoically fixed her gaze on something across the room, ignoring the small flurry around her. "You promise?"

"I do indeed. I must stop there and pick up something for myself, at any rate." Marissa had mentioned Mr. Coventry's establishment during one of the girl's recent visits. Jordana had been in the midst of describing a drink the local midwife had mixed for Jordana's mother after her sister Delphine's birth when Marissa had brought up the apothecary. Jordana had been pestering Marissa to visit Mr. Coventry ever since.

Marissa regarded Jordana standing on the block, her shoulders stiff and unyielding, facing the world with a stubbornness few females her age possessed. She admired Jordana's single-minded purpose in wanting to become a physician because she knew where it came from—the agonizing death of her mother. But society would not look kindly on Jordana or her interests if she were given freedom to pursue them.

Possibly I can find her a gentleman who would be encouraging of her passions.

Marissa had played matchmaker before with excellent results. But it would take some time to find the correct man for Jordana. One who was open-minded and would not be intimidated by her intellect or her dedication to helping women.

Jordana now had her arms stretched out and was glaring daggers at Marissa.

"My lady." Madame Fontaine came forward and looked at the pattern book in Marissa's lap. "If I may give my opinion?"

Marissa nodded. "Please."

The dressmaker flipped open the book, pointing an elegant finger stained with pencil lead to the pattern of a simply cut dress. "This one, I think. Simple, with clean lines. The design can be adjusted easily to a ballgown as well. She does not strike me as a young lady who will appreciate frills or additional embellishment. Modest necklines." Madame

Fontaine cocked her head taking in Jordana. "Her bosom is generous."

"It is?" Marissa sat up and looked at Jordana. Madame was right. She'd never taken notice with Jordana always jumping about in dresses much too girlish for her.

The modiste nodded.

"Agreed." Squinting at the pattern book in her lap, Marissa finally sighed in resignation before reaching into her reticule for a pair of reading glasses. Perching them on the end of her nose, Marissa leafed through the pages, agreeing with the suggestions or choosing something else, but staying with the same basic design Madame Fontaine had suggested. After selecting fabrics for a handful of dresses appropriate for paying calls and walking in the park, Marissa took off the glasses and set the book aside.

"I also have these." Madame Fontaine gave a sharp clap.

An assistant rushed forward to drape a lovely dress of periwinkle over a dressmaker's dummy to Marissa's left. "I will add a ribbon of darker color here," her hand ran along the neckline, "as well as the sleeves. This can be ready in a day or two." She snapped her fingers and another dress was brought out, this one the color of summer grass.

"These are the only two I have at present, my lady. But both dresses need only minor alterations to fit Miss Ives."

"Perfect, thank you."

"It is my greatest pleasure, Lady Cupps-Foster."

Madame Fontaine sauntered off and pulled another pencil from her hair. "I assume you will want new under-things for Miss Ives as well?" she said, brow raised at Jordana's slightly worn chemise. "Petticoats. Chemises." She gave another wave of her hand.

"Yes. Thank you. Everything to be sent to the home of Lord Haddon." Marissa rattled off the address.

Once the assistants had whisked away the two dresses, Madame Fontaine informed Marissa the gowns she'd ordered for herself would require one more fitting.

Marissa looked to where Jordana stood clenching her fists, waiting impatiently for her gown to be buttoned up, eager to be gone from the dressmaker's and off to Mr. Coventry's. "I think I'll return later this week." She smiled. "Miss Ives grows ever impatient."

"I concur," Madame Fontaine agreed. She bowed politely to Marissa and went to greet Lady Barton and her three daughters. "I bid you good day, Lady Cupps-Foster."

Jordana hopped off the podium, ignoring the outstretched hand of one of the girls sent to help her. Her skirts lifted, showing a great deal of ankle. "May we go to Mr. Coventry's now?"

"Dear, must you leap and jump at every turn? A lady *waits* for assistance. And yes, I did promise you a trip to Mr. Coventry's. Thank you for not biting off anyone's fingers."

"You're welcome, my lady."

"I think perhaps you should call me Marissa after all of our adventures." Regardless of her initial reluctance in taking on Jordana and the girl's difficult manner, she was enjoying herself immensely. She hadn't realized how much she missed mothering another 'duckling'.

I will miss Jordana dreadfully when Haddon's sister arrives to take charge.

"Marissa." Jordana tested the name on her tongue while taking Marissa's arm. "Thank you, Marissa." Her silver eyes, so like Haddon's, gleamed with real affection.

Marissa blinked and turned away, ashamed to find her eyes filling with tears over the prospect of losing Jordana.

"Oh, Mama." A familiar shrill voice cut the air. "I simply *must* have the dress of peacock blue to wear to Lady

Ralston's ball. Madame's assistant assures me no one else has taken the silk. I shall stand out in the crowd."

Lady Christina Sykes, stunning in a confection of peach satin and lace, came around a table on which several bolts of fabric were stacked, trailed by her mother, Lady Stanton.

"The color is a bit mature for a girl your age," Lady Stanton cautioned. "Though I agree, you would look lovely in it."

Jordana quickened her pace, towing Marissa along in a most unladylike fashion. "Please hurry, my—*Marissa*."

"Are you avoiding someone?" She cast a glance at Lady Stanton who was smiling at her daughter. "If you are, it is a foolish task. Better to confront obstacles head-on."

"I don't wish to speak to Lady Christina or Lady Stanton. I've had my fill of them both. They're always inviting me to tea or to go shopping. I don't care to renew our acquaintance."

"It is very kind of them to wish to bring you into their circle." Marissa's heart had started a slow pounding at the sight of Lady Stanton and her daughter. Knowing the pair were making efforts to ingratiate themselves with Jordana told Marissa how far things had progressed with Haddon.

"She wants to marry my father."

Marissa had an inclination to punch Lady Christina right on her perfect nose. Wouldn't that cause a scene? A longing for Haddon filled her, one she could not easily push away. "I'm sure your father has his reasons for considering her. Come. Our backs are to them. They won't notice us."

"You know the reason my father tolerates her," Jordana said, her voice soft as they exited Madame Fontaine's shop. "I *know* that you do."

Marissa's lips tightened as she shot a look of annoyance

at her charge. "I have no idea what you're speaking of, Jordana."

"You shouldn't frown," Jordana said in an airy tone. "Wrinkles."

"*Jordana*." Marissa admonished. "I am *not* frowning. I am deep in thought, considering the best way to get to Mr. Coventry's." She nodded to the footman who had been patiently standing outside.

"Don't you *dare* leave me with Christina as a stepmother. I shall never forgive you."

The words were so quiet, Marissa wasn't certain she'd heard Jordana correctly. "What, dear?"

"I said don't you dare leave Mr. Coventry's without your special order." Jordana looked straight ahead, stomping in the direction of the apothecary. "The one for—" She tipped her chin to Marissa's hair.

"I shan't. Nor do I need you to remind me." Seeing Lady Christina had rattled her, which was ridiculous since the girl was an overindulged twit. Would Haddon really marry her? Jordana seemed to think so. The very thought caused an unpleasant roll of her stomach.

I just need some tea. Perhaps a biscuit.

The night before, she'd wept as she hadn't since Reggie's death—painful sobs which had torn at her and threatened to break her heart. Over Haddon. The man she'd driven away.

I never thought you a coward, Marissa.

Marissa stiffened her shoulders and strode in the direction of Mr. Coventry's, waving furiously at the footman to keep up.

She *wasn't* a coward.

18

The visit to Mr. Coventry's apothecary shop was far lengthier than Marissa had anticipated.

Jordana had peppered the elderly man with questions, barely pausing to take a breath much less allow Mr. Coventry to speak. Marissa watched in utter horror as Jordana, a young girl from good family—and a *virgin*—asked Mr. Coventry to explain to her the various ways in which a woman could prevent a child.

Mortified, her cheeks burning, Marissa had hurriedly explained Jordana's interest in medicinals as Mr. Coventry had tried to hide his amusement. Changing the subject to something safe, namely the bottles of hair dye Marissa had ordered, she'd made the mistake of turning her back on Jordana, who had immediately begun to inquire after remedies for Marissa's frequent 'female-related' headaches.

Marissa had never been so embarrassed. She thought it would not be the last time she would feel so with Jordana.

Mr. Coventry, bless him, assured Marissa of his utter discretion.

After leaving the apothecary, Marissa and Jordana

visited several other establishments, loading their purchases into the waiting arms of the footman whose name Marissa still could not remember and, since he'd been with them all day, didn't wish to ask.

Finally reaching the coffeehouse Jordana had first seen when they had arrived on Bond Street, Marissa ushered her inside to a small table by the window. Ordering hot chocolate for Jordana and tea for herself, Marissa nodded her head at various intervals as Jordana chattered with enthusiasm over their visit to the apothecary. The chatter quickly evolved into an improper recitation of how *all* women should be educated on the benefits of preventing a child.

"Jordana," Marissa said firmly, looking into the shocked face of an older lady seated at the table next to them. "*Please* keep your voice down. While I tend to agree with you—"

"I *knew* you did." Jordana nodded, opening her mouth to continue.

"But," Marissa placed a hand on Jordana's arm, "we do *not* speak of such things in public. In a coffeehouse. Not everyone is as . . . *openminded* as I." She removed her hand and sat back, smiling at the older woman who was observing Jordana as if she were a wild animal who'd invaded Bond Street.

Jordana shut her mouth and nodded, deflating like a ruined soufflé that the entire world didn't agree with her assumptions on the care of women. "I just want to help. It is so important."

Marissa's heart went out to her. "I know it is, Jordana. But you must be careful with such talk. Promise me?"

"Yes, but—"

"I will support you whenever I can, be assured. And I am thrilled, dear, you enjoyed the visit." Marissa smiled to take the sting out of her chastisement. "We will go again. I promise."

"You'll take me? Even after Aunt Flora comes to stay?" Jordana shook her head. "She won't understand how important it is to me. But you do, don't you, Marissa?"

"Yes." And she meant it. No matter what happened with Haddon, and at the moment things didn't look promising, Marissa *refused* to leave Jordana floundering about. She couldn't.

But yet you will sacrifice Miss Higgins.

Reggie again, whispering in her ear, reminding Marissa of what she meant to do. Her hand trembled as she pushed away the half-eaten biscuit on her plate.

"Marissa?" Jordana leaned close. "You are very pale. Do you have one of your headaches?"

"No, dear. I'm only just realizing how tired I am. Shall we head home now?"

They left the coffee shop, arms linked, and walked in the direction of Marissa's waiting carriage. The footman, arms full, followed closely behind. The poor lad was loaded down with an assortment of boxes, his head barely visible over the top.

I should have sent him back to the carriage earlier. He's bound to drop something.

The hour had grown late, the day beginning to wane by the time the carriage came into sight. She had underestimated Jordana's fascination with the apothecary shop.

"I can't wait to return to visit Mr. Coventry." There was a tiny dot of chocolate above Jordana's upper lip as she grinned, blissfully happy, Marissa was sure, to have spent at least part of her day discussing the ingredients for a childbirth poultice. "You may even have to return next week for your special dye."

"Jordana, I thought we discussed the need for discretion."

"Mr. Coventry wrote down the name of a book he consults when mixing various medicinals and the like. But it's in French. I suppose I should have paid more attention to my governess." She gave Marissa a rueful look. "But truly, I'd no idea I would ever need to know French."

"Possibly you should have made more of an effort to know Madame Fontaine or one of her assistants." Marissa laughed. "As it appears now you will have use for them." She looked up as the carriage came into view. "Finally."

Spending the entire day on Bond Street had been wonderful but exhausting. She wanted nothing more than to sink into a hot bath with a glass of whisky and think of Haddon.

Marissa was at war with herself. She had no idea how to proceed.

Glancing down the street, Lady Stanton and her daughter appeared, weaving through the well-dressed ladies and the few gentlemen clogging the sidewalk. The pair paused, admiring something in a shop window before Lady Christina turned with an exclamation of surprise on her pretty face. She began to wave her gloved hands in an excited greeting to someone further down the street that Marissa couldn't quite see.

A flash of evergreen moved in the direction of Lady Christina and her mother. A gentleman, tall and lithe, appeared. There was no mistaking the magnificent bone structure of his handsome face nor the way his beautiful mouth formed a devastating smile as he greeted the pair.

Damn it.

Lady Christina giggled, placing a hand over her lips as if

suddenly shy, batting her lashes flirtatiously at the gentle-man, doing everything but leaping into his arms.

That girl needs a lesson in comportment.

Marissa had little experience with envy, so it took her a moment to recognize the twist of her heart. As the daughter of a wealthy and powerful duke, *Marissa* was envied. But seeing Haddon's attention on that little puff of a girl in peach stole the breath from her chest.

She glared at Haddon, willing him to look her way.

Her young footman struggled mightily, with the help of Marissa's driver, to secure the packages she and Jordana had accumulated today on the top of the carriage.

Jordana, oblivious to the fact Marissa was distracted and her father was just down the street, leapt into the carriage without an ounce of decorum.

How many times must I remind her that ladies do not jump?

The carriage rocked, jostling the idiot footman, who was doing his best to lash the packages to the top.

Marissa's driver jumped nimbly aside, catching one of the boxes before it could slide from the lad's hands.

Marissa stepped away, stumbling a bit, to avoid both of the men. She would need to speak to Greenhouse. The lad was clearly not ready to advance to the position of footman as evidenced by his inability to complete a simple task. She turned to admonish Jordana, who was hanging out the carriage window, watching the young footman's efforts with a dubious look on her face, when Marissa realized she couldn't lift her leg. She pulled back her skirts.

Of all the rotten luck.

Her left foot was lodged into a small hole. A wiggle of her ankle did not produce the desired result of freeing herself.

"Drat." Turning back to Haddon and the fawning Lady

Christina, Marissa struggled to free herself, unwilling to be caught in such a ridiculous predicament.

Eyes narrowing, she took in the giggling Lady Christina as she tugged at her leg. How *could* Lady Stanton allow her daughter to throw herself at Haddon in such a way? It was *shameful* behavior. Sparing a glance at her trapped foot, Marissa tried to be discreet. She didn't wish to attract attention nor distract the bumbling footman and her driver. Imagine the fun the gossips would have if Marissa's hair dye flew from the top to splatter against the cobblestones.

I should have insisted on a more seasoned footman.

The entire day was bound to end in disaster if she didn't manage to get herself out of the present situation.

Good Lord. Lady Stanton must take hold of her daughter. There is not an inch between the girl and Haddon.

"My lady!"

Marissa looked up at the footman's horrified exclamation. The stack of boxes he'd been trying to lash down burst free because he wasn't securing them correctly. Her eyes remained fixed on the box from Mr. Coventry's, praying the glass containers inside wouldn't break, shocked when it flew right at her. The rest of the boxes followed, knocking her to the ground.

Death by hair dye. I should never have listened to Adelia.

Then everything went dark.

19

"Marissa."

Haddon whispered her name as he lay next to her, naked, his large hand drawing circles against the bare skin of her stomach. He smelled so good. Like the spices her cook used when making those small cakes Marissa liked with her tea. Was it ginger?

She giggled at the thought of Haddon smelling like a cookie one had with tea.

Wanting to touch him, Marissa found it a struggle to lift even so much as her finger. Her entire body felt boneless. Sated. Haddon must have made love to her, but she couldn't remember. Not that it mattered. It was just as pleasurable having him beside her, speaking of nothing yet everything.

"She's twisted her ankle a bit, but it isn't serious and there's a small bump on her head. A little rest and her lady-ship should recover. I gave her something for the pain."

Marissa pushed aside the authoritative voice. She was stroking the side of Haddon's cheek wanting to tell him how he filled her heart. How stupid she'd been to send him away after they'd made love in her parlor. What lay between them wasn't *meaningless. She hadn't meant to hurt him. And it was exhausting pretending she didn't want him. Marissa didn't want to do it anymore. She wasn't a coward. Taking his hand, she pressed it to her breast. "You are not a dalliance."*

"I know." He didn't sound convinced.

"We are not a dalliance." It was very important he understand.

"My lady, can you open your eyes?"

No. Her eyelids were weighed down. Heavy. It would be an enormous effort to open her eyes or move at all. She was so comfortable. Warm. Almost like floating in a bath. Besides, if she opened her eyes, Haddon might disappear.

"I'm not a coward."

"I know. Wake up, Marissa." Haddon sounded very insistent.

Finally, she managed to push her eyelids open.

Marissa was in a bed, with Haddon sitting next to her, far too close for propriety's sake, and holding her hand but thankfully *not* her breast.

I was dreaming.

Haddon's silver eyes were filled with worry. What was he concerned about?

Me. "Are you worried about me?" a raspy whisper asked as her heart fluttered in her chest. She would do anything to have him keep looking at her in such a way.

"Yes." His voice sounded strained but she saw a hint of the mischievous smile he so often wore tugging at his lips.

Marissa struggled against the pillows, trying to sit up, but the pain in her temple made her fall back. "My ankle hurts." She blinked at Haddon as her fingers curled more firmly around his. "I'm thirsty."

"If you've no further need of me, my lord—"

Marissa glanced at the foot of the bed where an older

gentleman with snow-white hair stood. *Good Lord, is that Enderly?*

"Thank you, Dr. Steward, for arriving so quickly. I think my staff and I can take things from here."

Marissa blew out a puff of air relieved. *Not Enderly*. But a physician.

"Send for me if you need anything. I'll see myself out, Lord Haddon."

She tried to focus on the departing Dr. Steward, but her eyes refused to look at anything but Haddon. Her fingers tightened on his, afraid he would leave with the physician.

I don't want to run away from him anymore.

He cast a bemused look at their clasped hands but didn't try to pull away.

"Don't leave," she whispered.

"I'm not going anywhere." His voice was soft. "You've a little bump on your head and you twisted your ankle. But you'll live." A squeeze to her fingers.

Marissa squeezed back.

"I'm not certain how you managed to wedge your foot into the *only* hole on the entire street—"

"I'm sure it isn't the only one." She wanted to touch Haddon's face. Press a kiss to his brow. He looked so worried about her.

"I managed to save your shoe. Considering how attached you were to that little hat, I thought I'd do my best to salvage it. Weren't you watching where you stepped? You could have been seriously injured."

"No, I—" She bit her lip, not wishing to admit she'd been too preoccupied watching him fawn all over a girl barely out of the nursery. "I'm very thirsty."

"Ah, yes." He stood, reluctantly releasing her hand, and moved to the small side table where a carafe sat. He poured out a glass of water and returned to sit at her side; he held the glass to her lips, watching her mouth as she drank.

"Better?" He took her hand again.

She relaxed immediately, feeling the warmth of his fingers entwined around hers. "Where am I?" Her eyes ran down the hideous coverlet of the bed she lay in before turning her head ever so slightly to take in the room.

"Good God," she whispered.

A ghastly blue paisley motif with gold thread surrounded her, contributing to the pitching of her stomach. No one had used that particular design for at *least* twenty years. Even then it had not been one of Marissa's favorites. She couldn't *possibly* be in her own home. The décor was one she never would have approved.

"A guest room in my house. Your assessment of the room décor isn't flattering in the least."

When Haddon smiled at her, as he was doing now, he was so . . . *blinding* he took her breath away. The first time he'd smiled at her in such a way had been across the dinner table at Pendleton's house party during the fish course. She'd had a bit of trout drenched in an overpowering sauce on the end of her fork and was about to take a bite when she'd noticed him watching her. His silver eyes had glinted in the candlelight as he had followed the movement of her fork, watching her mouth the entire time.

I nearly dropped my fork.

She'd forgotten all about the terrible sauce and overcooked trout. At the time, she could only think about how bloody beautiful Haddon was with his dark hair and glorious cheekbones.

The bed jiggled as he moved, his fingers releasing hers.

"No," she whispered, suddenly terrified he'd leave her

alone with the atrocious paisley. Her fingers wiggled toward him.

The bed dipped as Haddon sat back down. "I'm not leaving you, Marissa. Just setting down the glass on the nightstand."

Marissa's chest tightened in the most wonderful way even though she was sure Haddon only meant he wasn't leaving her *at that moment*. Perhaps having her day's purchases knock her unconscious had been for the best, for she'd awoken with her thoughts firmly in place in regard to Haddon. An epiphany of sorts. He was the only man who'd made Marissa feel . . . *anything* in over twenty years. The next thought wasn't nearly as welcome, causing her to wince at the pain it brought to her temple, and she shut her eyes.

How can I avoid telling him what I've done to Pendleton?

He and Pendleton *were* friends though based on the comments he'd made at Lord Duckworth's, she no longer thought them close. *But still.* Haddon wouldn't want to believe Pendleton's father had committed murder. Or that Marissa's actions toward the family were justified.

"Are you in pain?"

"No. I only have a slight headache. And the curtains are not helping. I fear you weren't exaggerating when you claimed I could assist you with your decorating. I thought, Haddon, you were joking. But now," her eyes opened to see him watching her, not the least concerned she found his decorating atrocious, "I can see the situation is far more serious than you led me to believe."

"There I was on Bond Street thinking to catch up with you and Jordana—" he started in a quiet voice.

"You were?" Maybe he hadn't seen her watching him.

Haddon's lips twitched. "I was right down the street, as you well know."

Drat.

Marissa pursed her lips. "I don't know what you mean. Certainly, if I *had* seen you, I would have flagged you down to ask your assistance. In doing so, I might have avoided being hit by a flood of boxes."

"Of course." His forefinger began to stroke a line against her palm. "Saved from having your junior footman—"

"He's *aspiring* to footman. I believe he was a groom not a week ago."

"Whatever he is, my opinion is the lad should be sacked for allowing a small case holding several bottles from an apothecary shop," another smile hovered at his lips, "to fall on his employer's head.

Her hair dye. "Did any of the bottles break?" she asked cautiously, not wanting to disclose the contents.

"No. Had you been paying the least attention to your own safety, you would know that." His voice roughened. "Instead, you were too occupied watching me and Lady Christina Sykes. A girl who you find too young for me but one you are convinced will give me the heir you assume I require."

"All titled gentlemen require an heir." She tried to pull her hand away.

"And whom you claim, very firmly, you don't care if I marry. Which I think we can both agree is a lie."

She tugged at her hand and he finally let go. "I wish to go home." His observations made her sound ridiculous. Clasping her hands, she stared straight ahead, dismissing him.

"Good Lord, *really*? Not only can you *not* dismiss me in my own home, but you aren't going anywhere." He ran a hand through his hair causing the ends to stick up like spikes. "You aren't to be moved, according to Dr. Steward. At least for the night."

The night? She couldn't stay with Haddon. "Just send a note—"

"I've already sent word to your niece, Lady Malden. She declined to come and fetch you, by the way."

Well, this was mildly embarrassing.

"Spencer, then." She waved a hand. "Lord Kelso. He'll come fetch me."

"Unfortunately, he can't. He and Lady Kelso left this morning for Gray Covington. No one is coming to your rescue."

Admittedly, it was slightly *thrilling* to be held captive by Haddon, despite his sudden air of annoyance. She preferred his concerned demeanor of a moment ago. But at least he wasn't coldly furious as he'd been at the theater, thinking Nighter was her lover.

I don't want another lover.

"But I've none of my things," Marissa said tartly. Lifting the covers, she was shocked to see not the clothing she'd worn to take Jordana shopping, but a silk robe. At least she still had her chemise on. She sniffed at the silk. It smelled of Haddon.

"I appear to be wearing a man's robe."

"You are. I'm thrilled to see the little knock on your head didn't damage your eyesight."

"Does this garment belong to you?" Heat washed up her chest to her cheeks. *Good grief.* The physician had seen her wearing Haddon's robe. "What will Dr. Steward think?"

He didn't answer, but a mischievous glint entered his eyes. "You are my guest for the night until I can be assured you are well."

"How kind."

"It's the least I could do for my daughter's *elderly* chaperone."

He tried to take her hand again, and she slapped at it.

"Marissa, I'm teasing." Haddon laughed. "I don't give a fig about your age. I never have." Leaning over, he took a strand of her hair between his fingers. "And while your precious little bottles from the apothecary weren't damaged, you need not visit Mr. Coventry on my account."

"It isn't for you. How presumptuous." He needn't know she'd only visited the apothecary for the first time after returning to London.

"I prefer the silver in your hair. It's beautiful, like a slice of moonlight on a dark night. And it matches my own."

Marissa's eyes took in Haddon's full head of hair, discerning only a sprinkling of gray. She'd never noticed before; why, she wasn't sure. "You're mistaken. I didn't do it for you."

A soft chuckle came from his chest. "I must be. Forgive me." Placing his hands on either side of her head, Haddon leaned over her as if he were about to bestow a kiss.

Her lips parted, eyes falling shut as Marissa's pulse raced in anticipation.

The brush of his lips against the curve of her ear sent a slow, delicious burn down the length of her body. "Both myself and Dr. Steward were relieved," he murmured, "to find out I was not a *mere* dalliance."

Marissa's eyes snapped back open. Haddon's mouth was inches from hers; he was so close, their noses nearly touched. She pushed at him weakly with both hands.

Haddon caught her fingers, moving her hand until it lay over his chest.

His heart thudded dully beneath her palm, each beat

calling to her. "Get some rest," he said, sliding off the bed. "I'll check on you later."

Once Haddon left, Marissa stared at the closed door for the longest time. Fingers shaking, still warm and tingling from the feel of Haddon, she clasped the blanket, pulling it up to her chin, listening to the quiet sound of her own heart as it beat out the truth.

Marissa had driven Haddon away in a useless attempt to save herself and avoid the thing she feared the most. But in the end, it hadn't mattered.

I'm in love with him.

20

Marissa awoke sometime later, groggy from the medicine the doctor had given her, which, she was certain, was laudanum. She kept her eyes closed as the remnants of her dream lingered at the edges of her mind.

Reggie was sitting in his study, surrounded by rocks and fossils, digging away at a large chunk of gritstone on the table, determined to find something of value. He did so love his rocks.

When she approached him, Reggie waved her away.

"I'm working, Marissa. Go up to bed."

"But—" She started to protest.

"I've left you something on your pillow." He turned, inky black curls falling over his forehead, and smiled. "Off with you."

Marissa blew him a kiss before climbing up the stairs to their rooms at Somerton. As she moved closer to the landing at the top, the scene around her changed from the estate in the Peak District she'd lived in with Reggie, to her house in London. When she reached her chambers, Marissa threw open the door and rushed to the bed. Reggie was often absentminded, but he was good at surprises. He sometimes left her love notes, or a pretty stone he'd

*found. A small token, but one which was a reminder of how much
he loved her.*

Marissa moved closer, parting the bed curtains.

How odd. She didn't remember having bed curtains.

Haddon was in her bed, asleep. On her pillow.

A tear slipped from beneath her lashes, and she lifted a
finger to wipe it away.

Damn it, Reggie. I see your point. I'm not an idiot.

"You're awake."

Marissa opened her eyes to see Jordana curled up in a
chair at her bedside, an oversized book on her lap. Turning
her head, Marissa read the title with a grimace. *Discourses on
the Nature and Care of Wounds.*

"Why can you not read poetry? Or a lurid romantic
novel?" she said. "*Wounds,* Jordana?"

"Despite your best efforts," Jordana replied, closing the
book with a snap, "I fear I will never be a proper young lady.
But for *you*, I will try. If you don't like this book, I have one
with drawings of the human heart. Would you like me to
show you?"

"Goodness, no." The very idea would compel Marissa to
take another swallow of the medicine Doctor Steward had
left behind, and she detested laudanum. No wonder she felt
hazy.

"How are you feeling? I've checked your pupils—"

"You did what? While I was asleep?"

"I overheard Doctor Steward tell Papa what to look for.
Are you well?"

"I am, but not so recovered to allow you to read to me
from such a thing." Marissa tilted her head in the direction
of the book. "I fear I am squeamish at best."

"Only of medicinal things? I truly thought you might
have a fit of apoplexy when I asked Mr. Coventry about the

little sponges he sells. I wasn't sure how I would explain that to my father."

"You shouldn't even know of or ask about such things."

"I think you are incredibly brave, Marissa. You took me on and," she said conspiratorially, "*everyone* in London has heard of your niece."

Marissa placed a hand over her eyes. "I fear my influence has not been beneficial."

"Do not blame yourself. One moment I had settled myself in the carriage—"

"Leapt in," Marissa corrected her. "Your jumping was reminiscent of a grasshopper."

Jordana bit her lip. "I *may* have startled the footman. George is new."

"His name is George?" Marissa tucked the name away.

"Yes. And he has a nervous disposition to begin with—"

"All the more reason for him not to be my footman. How do you know his name?" Marissa narrowed her eyes. Was Jordana flirting with a footman? It seemed unlikely, but stranger things had happened.

"Greenhouse told me. George is his nephew."

Well, that explains things.

"I think he became more clumsy thinking he would displease you," Jordana finished.

"Well, I assure you, allowing my own purchases to assault me, like an attack from the heavens, did not endear him to me. Your father wants me to sack him." Marissa shot her a look. "But I won't."

"Papa was *very* upset," Jordana said in a serious tone. "*Very*."

"I'm sure Lord Haddon was only concerned for *your* safety. You'd been entrusted to my care, and after seeing what my groom and driver managed today, chances are he won't allow you out with me again."

"I doubt that." Jordana placed her elbow on the arm of the chair, propping her chin up with one hand. The silvery eyes held a hint of mirth. "I've *rarely* seen him in such a state, which is saying something as he lives with me and my horrid sisters. Yes," she leaned forward, "all the tales of us are true. Even so, Papa rarely raises his voice, not even when a slew of governesses quit or the dancing instructor he hired from London ran out of the house. But that was because Poppy stuck a frog down Mr. Monograt's trousers."

"I see."

"You wouldn't have liked Mr. Monograt," Jordana rushed to assure her.

"Possibly. Lord Haddon possesses a patient and calm demeanor." No one was more appreciative of such a character trait than Marissa.

"I would not have called him patient or calm earlier today."

Marissa plucked at the coverlet. She didn't care for the turn of this conversation. "I'm surprised he noticed us at all. But how fortuitous he was there."

The silver of Jordana's eyes shifted, making her appear much older than she was. "I've only ever seen him run so fast one other time," she said matter-of-factly. "When Martie fell from her horse while riding bareback."

"Bareback? That is hardly something a young lady should be doing."

Haddon had run to her aid? In the middle of Bond Street?

"We Ives girls are not proper young ladies." Jordana blinked innocently. "Though I suppose you will change all that."

"I don't know what you mean, Jordana," she stuttered. "I

can't imagine I'll be involved at all with your sisters, though I should like to meet them. Once your aunt arrives, I doubt she'll need my assistance though I'm happy to help her where necessary."

Jordana rolled her shoulders, a careless gesture Marissa had often seen Haddon make. "Papa wouldn't allow *anyone* else to touch you."

Oh dear.

"*Everyone* on Bond Street saw. Even horrid Lady Christina Sykes and Lady Stanton. Another gentleman rushed to your aid after watching you fall. Papa *threatened* him with bodily harm if he so much as laid one finger on your skirts. Lady Stanton was *horrified*. Lady Christina nearly burst into tears. She kept asking her mother why Lord Haddon seemed so concerned for my *chaperone*."

This was far worse than she could have imagined.

Jordana leaned forward. "Papa ordered your driver to take your packages and return home. He bent down, *in full view of everyone,* and picked you up in his arms and *carried* you down the street to his carriage. People were gawking. A small crowd may even have gathered. Papa didn't spare a glance in my direction to make sure I was following behind him."

"I see." *My God, Haddon basically abducted me from Bond Street in broad daylight.*

"Once we were settled in our carriage, I was shocked when Papa held you in his lap *all the way home*. I would go so far as to say he *cradled* you. Rather *improperly*, I might add."

Marissa swallowed. "Well, I was unconscious and could not correct him. I rarely faint but I suppose with the shock of the boxes falling atop me . . ." She stared right back at Jordana. "I shall bring him to task for creating a scene."

"I would call it more a spectacle." Jordana sat back with a look of satisfaction.

"You're enjoying this far too much." All of London was probably aware of what had occurred on Bond Street, and if not now, they surely would be this evening. Everyone would know she was at Haddon's and speculate on their relationship.

A tiny thrill ran through her.

Very much like a Viking marauder. One who saved my shoe and my hat. And now me.

"I'm fairly certain my father won't be marrying Lady Christina."

"The future is not set in stone." But Jordana was probably right. Lord Stanton would never allow his daughter to marry Haddon under the circumstances, even if Haddon wished it. And Marissa didn't think he did. "You should not sound so *pleased*, Jordana." It appeared the scandal she'd wished to avoid had found her anyway.

Although it was satisfying to know Lady Christina's hopes had been dashed by an *elderly widow*.

Marissa's stomach growled. Loudly. "Jordana, dear, did I miss supper?"

"I'm afraid you did." She stood and clasped the large book to her chest. "I'm to let Papa know the *moment* you are awake."

"I'm sure that isn't necessary." Haddon had staked his claim on Marissa in front of a large percentage of the *ton*. It was wildly inappropriate. And terribly romantic. He'd declared his intentions toward her. Publicly.

There will be no going back now.

The soft flutter started again in her chest. His presence in her life was either going to give her apoplexy or keep her heart beating. She thought the latter.

"I don't wish to bother him," Marissa said.

"It isn't any bother. I'm sure he'll be up directly. And I'll have something for you to eat sent up." She nodded to a small valise next to the bed which Marissa recognized as hers. "And a maid."

"Thank you, dear."

Jordana paused before the door. "I am grateful you weren't seriously hurt, Marissa." Her gaze fell to the floor as her toe drew a design in the rug. "Even though I've not grown used to society or London, I find I *have* grown used to *you*. You've made London bearable for me." The shy, almost tentative smile crossing her lips transformed Jordana's entire face, giving Marissa a glimpse into the striking woman Jordana would one day become.

Jordana is lovely, and best of all, she doesn't know it.

"I'll send a maid right up." Jordana shut the door softly behind her.

Both father and daughter have such a hold on my heart.

Marissa turned her eyes back to the perusal of the hideous canopy above her head, wiping another tear from her cheek.

21

A tray arrived a short time later, a bowl of hearty soup and fresh-baked bread with butter. Marissa felt immeasurably better after eating and after the arrival of a maid who brushed out her hair and helped her see to her needs. Her ankle felt much better as did the ache in her head.

"My lady," the young maid said. "Shall I help you into this?" She held up a plain cotton nightgown from the valise Marissa's own maid, Felice, had sent over.

Marissa looked down at Haddon's robe which she was *still* wearing. She'd rolled up the sleeves and belted it tightly to help hide the fact she'd discarded her chemise to wash earlier. Toying with the sash, Marissa shook her head.

A decision of sorts had been reached between her and Haddon. Unspoken, but there, all the same. Marissa had known from the second she'd awoken to Haddon at her bedside, holding her hand with no concern over Dr. Steward observing them.

The dream she'd had earlier came back to her. Reggie obviously approved.

"I believe I'll stay in the robe."

The maid only nodded and began folding up the night-gown to place back in the valise.

"My ankle is paining me," Marissa hastened to explain to the girl. "I'm much more comfortable as I am."

"Very good, my lady." The maid bobbed and left the room.

Once the girl left, Marissa's head fell back on the pillows. A delicious scent lingered on the silk as if she were enfolded in Haddon's embrace. For the first time in years, at least in recent memory, Marissa could do nothing but allow someone to take care of *her*.

It was a novel concept, one she'd never been faced with before.

Her first husband, Kelso, had been such a flagrant rake, he'd never spared a thought for her comfort or well-being. Shortly after their marriage, he'd left Marissa in charge of everything; it was Marissa who had ended up managing Kelso's holdings as well as the household.

A blessing, as it turned out. It had prepared her for the future.

Once she had given birth to Spencer, she had rarely seen her husband at all.

Reggie, bless him, *had* truly loved her, but even so, she'd always come in second to his love of rocks and minerals. When he'd disappeared, she had been suddenly left to manage the affairs of both her young sons until they could do so on their own. When her brother and his wife had died, Marissa had taken on the care of Nick and Arabella, her niece and nephew. Those years had passed in a blur of activity.

Cupps-Foster, Marissa barely remembered. Or her reasons for marrying him. He had never shown her the slightest regard once they'd wed, not that she would have welcomed it.

None of her husbands, even Reggie, would have carried her off as if she were something rare and precious, creating a scandal in the process.

Something told Marissa Haddon didn't care.

A soft knock sounded at the door.

"Come."

The object of her thoughts came through the door. His hair was ruffled, coat discarded, shirt unbuttoned to show the lightly tanned column of his throat.

Her heart skipped a beat as it did often in Haddon's presence. She was getting used to the feeling.

A decanter of amber liquid dangled by the neck from one of his hands. The other held a lone crystal glass.

Marissa pulled her eyes from that delicious triangle of exposed skin up to his face.

He kicked the door shut with a booted foot and grinned at her. "Would you like some company?" Cradling the decanter and glass, he turned back to the door and the click of the lock sounded. "I've brought whisky." He held up the decanter.

Abducting her from the street. Now locking her in. Plying her with spirits.

Her chest ached in the most delightful way. *I adore him.*

"I'm not certain you should be in my rooms so late at night," she answered primly.

"I have discreet servants." A dark brow lifted. "Reasonably discreet."

"I'm not sure it matters given *your* lack of judgement earlier today. Jordana related what occurred. You caused quite a scene."

His broad shoulders rippled with indifference. "Perhaps

I did behave a bit . . . *strongly*. My concern for your welfare was probably evident."

"You threatened another gentleman who sought to give me aid."

A scowl of displeasure crossed Haddon's lovely mouth. "He was peering up your skirts. And I didn't think you'd wish to be groped by a complete stranger."

"As opposed to being groped by you? I'm sure he only meant to assist me. There is also the matter of this robe."

"Which you've chosen to continue wearing." Satisfaction shone in the silver eyes.

"I *want* to believe one of your maids relieved me of my clothing upon my arrival in your home. That the same maid put me in this robe before the arrival of Dr. Steward."

"You may believe what you wish."

Though Marissa already knew the answer, she asked the question anyway. "Did you undress me, Haddon? And then put me in your robe?"

"I've already seen all the important parts." His eyes shifted to her breasts, lingering on the place where the robe parted. "Despite your futile attempts to hide yourself with an unlimited supply of strategically placed pillows, sheets and poorly knit blankets." Haddon nodded toward the chair his daughter had vacated a short time ago. "May I?"

"Please." Marissa took in every delicious inch of him. Her outrage at his actions was all an act and Haddon knew it. She'd never felt so . . . *cherished* by a man.

"Is the décor still giving you a headache?"

"And my stomach to sour." She nodded toward the decanter. "I'm certain some whisky would help."

He poured her a generous amount in the glass and slid to sit on the bed.

Marissa didn't object, welcoming his weight next to her.

Bringing the glass to her lips, he stopped. "You haven't taken any more of Dr. Steward's special medicine, have you?"

"No, and it's laudanum. Nothing special about it. I don't care for the stuff."

"Nor do I. I think you'll like this much better." Haddon tilted the glass.

Her eyes fluttered closed as she savored the taste and the feel of Haddon next to her. There was something so intimate about the way he liked to share a glass with her. The whisky was delicious, with a hint of smoke and caramel. "Mmm."

Opening her eyes to see Haddon watching her, Marissa's breath hitched at the look in his eyes. There was desire in his gaze, but something else as well, an emotion that sent her own heart thumping hard against her ribcage.

Haddon shifted his focus to the bed's canopy. "My mother updated things after Anne and I were married, thinking we would spend part of the year in London. But Anne hated town and this house even more. She'd no interest in updating a house she never planned to live in." He gave her a rueful look before taking a mouthful of the whisky for himself. "So you have my mother's poor taste to blame for this monstrosity."

"You've told me your wife was unwell. At Brushbriar."

"She was sickly even as a child. I brought Anne here after we married, to show her the sights, but we left after only a few weeks. She never came again. Eventually, I became tired of asking. The air bothered her lungs. And society irritated her sensibilities."

"I think that's the point of society. It offends us all."

Haddon's mouth twitched while he held the whisky to her lips again. "My late wife had many lovely character traits, but humor wasn't one of them. She wasn't anything like you if that is your question."

"You find me amusing?" Marissa pretended affront.

"You *amuse me*. There's a slight difference."

"Well, you aren't like any of my three husbands either, were you to ask the question."

Haddon chuckled, his voice low. "I assumed as much; there was no need to ask." He took a swallow of whisky. "Anne and I weren't compatible in the least which never changed over the course of our relationship. She tolerated the marriage bed only because she loved children and wanted them. She considered it her duty to endure my . . . *attentions*."

Having been the recipient of Haddon's *attentions* in the bedroom, Marissa couldn't imagine any woman merely *tolerating* him. It must have been difficult for a man of Haddon's passionate nature to have been married to a woman who most would describe as frigid. No wonder he'd come to London so often and indulged himself.

Marissa found herself irrationally angry at a dead woman.

"You were lonely." She and Haddon were kindred spirits in many ways. The bond she'd felt with him, so apparent from the first time he touched her, strengthened, pulling her tight. Marissa was finally ready to accept such bondage.

"Lonely?" The wicked little grin returned but didn't reach his eyes. "With four girls? Perish the thought."

He was making light of his marriage for her benefit, not wanting her sympathy, perhaps. She understood that better than anyone after being widowed three times. "I was lonelier in my marriages at times than I am now. It isn't unusual." Difficult to admit, but true, nonetheless. She thought

Haddon had probably tried to have a real marriage with Anne and had been rebuffed for his efforts.

"I took advantage of this house by coming to London as often as possible. I spent much of my time here, though *obviously* it never occurred to me to redecorate. I'd no idea I'd one day be judged for it." He winked at her.

"Your reputation precedes you," she said. From what she could glean from the gossips, Haddon had cut a wide but discreet swath through the ladies of the *ton*, never once maligning his wife. Most thought he'd been widowed years earlier since he rarely mentioned Anne, only his daughters.

His heat-filled gaze flitted over her, touching her skin and sending a warm tingle down between her thighs. "I have not been that man for a very long time, Marissa, if that has been your concern."

"Oh, I have experience with rakes." Another excuse she'd given herself not to become involved with Haddon. But common rogues and despoilers don't carry off notorious widows in full sight of the young lady all of London is certain they'll offer for.

Haddon was nothing if not intentional in his actions.

"More?" He filled the glass up again from the decanter.

Marissa nodded, waiting for him to bring the whisky to her lips. "You don't frighten me, Haddon."

"Good."

She took a sip of the whisky. "According to Jordana, I'm fearless. She gave me such a compliment after I watched her question the apothecary, Mr. Coventry, on the various methods a woman can use to prevent conception. She must have asked him a hundred questions alone just on *sponges*."

Two tiny spots of pink brushed against his sharp cheekbones before Haddon swallowed the remainder of the glass.

"What am I to do with her?"

"Don't be distressed."

"Learning how to mix a poultice is one thing. Please tell me she did not ask after things a gentleman might—"

"I am sorry to tell you that is *not* the case." Marissa bit her lip. She didn't think Haddon would appreciate her amusement at the moment. He looked terribly distraught. "Dissuading her won't work, Haddon. She is very determined. And please say nothing to her. Jordana trusts me to keep her secret. I do not wish to abuse that trust."

"I agree. I'll say nothing. But . . . *sponges*?"

Marissa tried not to giggle as she watched Haddon pour himself another finger of whisky. A languorous heat was spreading across her chest and through her limbs. She'd missed this, just talking to him, even more so than the physical aspect of their relationship, though that was marvelous.

"How are your quarries? Limestone, correct?"

The flicker of a shadow crossed his face, but it passed quickly. His lips turned up in his patent mischievous grin.

What a devil he must have been as a young boy.

"You *were* listening at Duckworth's. Even with Enderly salivating all over you."

"Ogling my bosom, perhaps, but I didn't notice any *drooling*."

A deep, masculine laugh echoed in the room as Haddon threw back his head in amusement.

The tiny lines around his eyes crinkled deliciously when he laughed. How could any woman find bedding him no more than a duty? He was handsome, yes, but it was the parts no one could *see* which made Haddon so *beautiful*.

Desire throbbed in a steady rhythm between her thighs. "Enderly no longer calls on me." It seemed important to relay the information.

He stopped laughing abruptly, his eyes on her darkening to pewter. "I know."

"You think you know me very well, don't you, Haddon?"

"I never meant to marry Lady Christina Sykes." He shifted off the side of the bed to set the glass of whisky on the side table, before settling next to her again. This time, he was so close her thigh brushed against his. Fingers traced the outline of her leg through the coverlet, circling her knee and trailing down her calf.

"Why haven't you discarded my robe yet?"

Marissa looked up at the paisley swirling above her head.

"I doubt you'll find the answer in the bed canopy."

"The pattern is akin to tea leaves. The answer will appear at any moment."

Another deep chuckle. "Christ, you're difficult." Haddon bent and began to remove his boots. "So stubborn. But worth the trouble."

"What are you doing?" she whispered.

"Taking off my boots." He held up one hand. "I know what you're thinking; wouldn't we be far more comfortable in *my* room? The answer is yes. The bed *is* larger and the mattress softer. There aren't any outdated swirls of paisley to give you fits. But I'd have to carry you down the hall. No telling who we'd run into. I think one scandal today is probably enough."

"Haddon, you can't possibly mean to . . ." She sputtered, eyes widening in appreciation as Haddon tossed off his shirt. A line of muscle flexed in the firelight. Oh, she'd forgotten how bloody *amazing* he looked without clothes. She shut her eyes. "Jordana is home. And I'm . . . *injured*."

"If you keep your eyes shut, Marissa, you'll miss all the best parts," he said suggestively. "Parts you rather enjoy."

Heat rose up Marissa's chest to flood her cheeks. "Are you going to ravish me?" she whispered a bit too hopefully at the sound of his trousers dropping to the floor.

"Yes." He flung the sheets aside and stretched out next to her, naked and beautiful, the heat of him bleeding through the thin silk of the robe. "If *ever,*" he paused, nuzzling one breast, "there was a woman in dire need of ravishing . . ." Haddon inhaled sharply, taking in her scent. "Adored." His teeth grazed the side of her neck. "*Savored.*" The tip of his tongue slid along the crease of her lips. "It is *you*, Marissa."

"Yes." Her fingers caught in the thick silk of his hair, tugging his mouth to hers.

Haddon's lips met hers, in a slow, lingering kiss as if he were memorizing the shape of her mouth. Tasting her. *Savoring* her as he'd promised. There was infinite patience at the press of his lips. A slow burn of exquisite longing like the warm embers of a fire that would burn for hours with very little stoking.

"You've led me on a merry chase," he said as one hand found its way into the robe to cup her breast, rolling her nipple between his thumb and forefinger. "Are you ready to let me catch you?"

"I'm not a bloody fox or a rabbit, Haddon." She *was* ready for him to catch her, Marissa just wasn't sure what being caught would mean. All the posturing and excuses she'd made about their relationship had been nothing but a waste of time, time she could have spent with Haddon. Even if he left her—*when* he left her, she corrected herself—she still couldn't bring herself to regret being with him.

"Answer the question," he said roughly, pinching the tightening peak of her nipple.

A tear ran down Marissa's cheek though she tried to stop it. "Yes."

He kissed the tear from her cheek. "Don't, Marissa."

When his mouth fell on hers this time, there was little gentleness, only the sense that Haddon would feast on her. Devour her. His tongue traced the outline of her lips until Marissa's mouth opened.

Haddon groaned, his tongue sinking between her lips to curl around hers.

Marissa arched against him, her fingers sliding up to cup his scalp, as she struggled to get closer to him. The heat from his mouth spread outward, over her chest and down across her stomach, slowly twisting into an irresistible hum of pleasure between her thighs. She rubbed herself against Haddon, begging him to ease the ache.

How in the world did I keep myself from him?

He flung back the covers, staring down at her. "No more fucking games, Marissa."

"No," she whimpered as his finger slid between her folds. "I promise."

Two large fingers sunk into her, thrusting slowly as his thumb teased around the sensitive bud demanding his attention even as he nipped at the slope of her neck.

The sting sharpened the pleasure building within her to a point, hastening the rush of sensation. His thumb moved in a torturous circle, ignoring the flesh begging for his touch. His lips moved down to her breast, sucking at the taut peak of her nipple. The hard length of him burned into her thigh.

Marissa rocked her hips up into his hand.

"We are not a dalliance." Haddon's teeth grazed the tip of her breast. "Do not ever dismiss me, or us, again."

"I won't." She was panting. "Please." He had a way of stoking her desire until Marissa became mindless with need.

"Not yet, my love."

Her heart swelled at the endearment, wanting to bask in his adoration for as long as he would give it to her. "Please, Haddon." Unsurprisingly, he'd managed to unbelt the robe and push the silk aside without her objecting. And he'd not doused the lamp.

Marissa didn't care.

Teeth nipping at her delicate skin, Haddon moved down to her stomach, while his fingers thrust gently inside her, deliberately not touching her there in any other way.

"You are a terrible man." She tried to rub herself against him, anything to relieve the tension tightening her body.

"Indeed, I can be. But I want *all* of you, Marissa. Every delicious, *elderly* matron inch." His mouth hovered just above her mound.

"Horrible." She gasped as his tongue dipped between her legs.

"There will be *no* more hiding from me." His tongue teased her, lightly touching the tiny bud, just enough to keep Marissa on the precipice until she was thrusting herself shamelessly into his mouth.

"No." Her breathing was ragged. "I promise. Only—" The rest of her words disappeared into a loud moan. He'd sucked the bit of flesh into his mouth as his fingers curled inside her.

A thousand bits of light appeared before Marissa's eyes, like the stars in the sky at night, as she arched off the bed. Her thighs tightened, and Haddon growled, pushing one of her legs over his shoulder. His mouth and fingers coaxed her through every bit of her climax, drawing out her pleasure until Marissa lay panting against the bed.

"My lord, but you're good at that."

"Does your ankle hurt? Your head pain you?" His voice was rough. *Aroused*. He wasn't close to being done with her.

"No. I feel—"

"Good." Haddon flipped her over on her stomach. His mouth trailed down the length of her spine until he reached her buttocks. "Get on your knees, my love."

Legs still shaking from her release only moments ago, Marissa did as he asked.

With no warning, Haddon grabbed her around the waist, sinking deep inside her with one hard thrust. He paused, his breath ragged against her ear, and sat back slightly, pulling her with him.

Then Haddon ravished her. Thoroughly. *Completely*.

It wasn't gentle. There was little tenderness. Marissa sensed every thrust was meant to possess her. Claim her. Haddon was always demanding in bed, but this was something different. Something primal. As if he really *was* a Viking raider who had taken her captive.

Marissa's own arousal barely had time to retreat before his fingers found her again while he whispered, in great detail, all the wicked things he meant to do with her. Every word brought her closer to the edge, but Haddon never allowed her release. When she began to beg, his thrusts became slower, more controlled.

He turned her head, taking her mouth in a slow sensuous kiss. She tasted herself and the whisky on his lips along with all the hunger this man had for her.

"Marissa." Haddon thrust once more, stroking her flesh until Marissa sobbed as the climax rushed through her body. She heard herself cry out his name over and over, feeling the rush of warmth within her as he found his own release.

Haddon fell to the side with a masculine grunt of satisfaction, pulling Marissa with him. He stayed buried within her, his heart beating madly.

Marissa gave a deep sigh of contentment. Her limbs were languid, weak, her body softening and molding itself to his. She felt *completed* in a way she never had before, resting in the circle of Haddon's arms.

"Are you still well?" he said softly, his breath fanning her cheek.

"Oh, yes."

"Those things I said, Marissa, how I mean to debauch you—"

"Yes." She held her breath.

"I meant every one."

22

The bed dipped as Haddon's warmth left her side. She'd been dozing, lulled into that wonderful place between sleep and wakefulness by the sound of his heart beneath her ear. The need to keep Haddon close caused her to stretch her fingers out, not wanting him to leave and return to his own bed.

"Shush, my love. I'm only going to stoke the fire." He tucked the blankets around her securely and pressed a kiss to her temple.

Marissa opened her eyes a slit, admiring Haddon's movements as he brought the fire back to life. He was lovely to watch, the lean muscle of his body moving gracefully as he bent to the task. Satisfied, he stood and walked back to her, the flames outlining him with a soft, amber light.

He's so bloody beautiful. And mine.

Tonight had been an exercise in demonstrating the fact.

She flapped open the blankets to allow him to slide back beside her. Curling her body next to his warmth, Marissa waited as his heat seeped deep into her skin. He'd been gone only a moment, but she'd been so cold without him.

That is what my life would be like if Haddon were gone. I would be forever chilled.

He ran a finger over her cheek, tracing the outline of her jaw. "Have we reached an understanding then, Marissa? I've caught you. I mean to keep you."

A sob stuck in her throat at his words. She'd been alone for so *bloody* long. Most of it by choice, her heart closed off. It was terrifying to realize, after all these years, that she *needed* someone. Particularly when that someone would tire of her in time and end things between them.

Or *worse*. She *had* been widowed three times.

"You worry that I will leave. Whether by dying or tiring of you."

Marissa shut her eyes. It was unsettling how well he seemed to know her, guessing at her thoughts before she herself knew them. "Is it so far-fetched? I am tragically unlucky in love." Her head fell to his chest.

"Your luck *has* changed." Haddon grinned, pleased with himself. "There are *barely* nine years between us."

"Nine years?" Marissa's mouth parted in horror. This was *terrible* news. How could Haddon smile at such a pronouncement? "Nearly a *decade*?" She would be laughed out of London. "An older woman casually taking a younger lover, like my friend Lady Waterstone, is mildly acceptable but—"

"You may dispel *casual* from your vocabulary in regard to us," he stated, his arms tightening sharply around her.

Us. She'd assumed as much. Haddon had behaved rather possessively with her from the moment they'd met, and Marissa doubted he would look kindly on any other man's interest in her.

I adore that about Haddon, but I won't tell him so.

"Can you not see, Marissa?" he said calmly, in a voice

she thought he used with his daughters when trying to explain a crucial point. "My *age* is an advantage. I am *unlikely* to die before you." Haddon gave her one of his impish grins. "That should please you. Given previous circumstances."

Marissa swatted him. "*None* of my husbands died because they were old. And we'll be the scandal of the *ton*." She'd never wanted to invite such attention again. When Kelso had ruined her, it was all London had spoken of for months.

"You are missing the most important part." He nibbled on her ear. "Don't you want to know what it is?"

"Besides your being nearly a decade younger than I?" How could he be so *blasé* about their age difference?

He cupped her face in his hands. "I won't leave you, Marissa," he whispered pressing a kiss to her lips. "Ever."

Marissa stilled, not daring to breathe at his declaration. Haddon wasn't speaking of a short-term affair. Her heart thumped in disarray for a moment. "I—"

"*I won't leave you*," he said again. He took her hand, kissing her fingertips, and placed it over his heart. "You must trust me."

When Marissa had been a child, her father, the duke, had thought to teach her to swim. He'd taken her to a cliff overlooking the sea near his estate a few miles from the Scottish border. The rocky outcropping wasn't terribly high, but to the child Marissa had been, jumping into the ocean from such a height was terrifying. Her father had grasped her hand in his larger one, pressed a kiss to her fingers, and smiled. "You must trust me, Marissa." They'd jumped together into the blue water. Her father had never let go. Not for an instant.

Haddon wasn't going to let go either.

23

I *can't seem to let go of his hand.*

A moderate look of surprise shone on Haddon's face as he stood before Marissa in the foyer of her house. After breakfasting together, *discreetly*, in the guestroom, he'd brought her home in his carriage, taking the long way through the park.

She'd no idea there were so many things one could do in a slow-moving carriage. Haddon apprised Marissa of at least *two*.

It had been Marissa who insisted Haddon walk her inside, even knowing all of her neighbors had likely seen the gossip in the papers by now or had heard the rumors at whatever social gathering they'd attended the night before. They were probably peering at her from behind the curtains of their parlors.

Marissa lifted her chin high and marched up the steps.

Greenhouse, for his part, appeared somewhat outraged at the appearance of Lord Haddon in Marissa's foyer, especially so early in the morning and behaving in such an informal manner toward his employer.

Her butler was a prig. She'd have to do something about that.

"Marissa, are you sure you are all right?" The dark tendrils of his hair were blown about his ears from the wind outside, and his eyes shone like pewter. "Jordana has told me that sometimes when a person is hit in the head—"

"I'm fine. And it was only a small case of hair dye and a hatbox or two." Marissa's heart threatened to come out of her chest just looking at him. "It isn't as if I was stomped on by a horse."

"Even so," the right side of his mouth tipped up, "you should rest."

No, what she *should* do was attempt to dispel the rumors making their way around London about her and Haddon, even though it was likely a wasted effort. She was lucky, she supposed, that her nephew, the duke, wasn't standing on her doorstep, and Spencer was at Gray Covington with Elizabeth else Marissa might fear for Haddon's life. Adelia would probably arrive at some point today to crow over Marissa's tarnished reputation.

It was all very distressing.

But worse was this terrible dread at the thought of Haddon leaving her.

Her fingers wrapped more firmly around his.

"I'm not tired," she insisted, trying to push away the rising panic. She and Haddon, over tea for her and coffee for him, had agreed to an *understanding*. She didn't fear he'd change his mind. That wasn't the source of her mounting anxiety. It was perfectly normal for Haddon to return home. He had his own affairs to see to, and Jordana wanted to go to Thrumbadge's.

Goodness, she'd lived forty-nine years without Haddon in her life. Nevertheless, her fingers tightened around his forearm like a steel band, clinging to Haddon as if she wouldn't survive a moment without him.

Marissa had never been a woman who *clung* to a gentleman. It was *unseemly*.

There is a first time for everything.

"I'm sorry," she whispered as Haddon gently disengaged her fingers.

"Everything will be all right, my love." He kissed her forehead. "I promise."

My love. A tremor ran through Marissa at the brush of his lips. No one had called her that in a very long time, not since Reggie. If Haddon didn't leave, she might embarrass herself further by sobbing into his coat like some nitwit.

"Curl up in your delightful parlor and nap, why don't you? We have an understanding, do we not?" he whispered against her ear.

"I suppose we do."

"I'll expect you to dream about me." He pinched her bottom, grinning when she squeaked in outrage.

Greenhouse gave a gasp of horror at their antics before composing himself.

"How in God's name did you end up with such a prude for a butler?" Haddon smiled into her hair, his body shaking as he tried not to laugh out loud. "And we most certainly *do* have an understanding. That will *not* change. I'll send you a note later."

Marissa nodded as he pulled away from her.

"You're acting very odd, Marissa." He leaned down, peering at her in concern. "Do you want me to stay? Jordana will understand."

"No. And she will *not* understand." Marissa was being ridiculous. *Needy*. The behavior reminded her of the way she'd dissolved into a puddle of grief when Reggie had disappeared. She had promised never to conduct herself in such a way again. It was unbecoming. Haddon would find it appalling and rescind their understanding before it had even begun. And she wouldn't blame him.

"I do have a small headache."

"All the more reason to rest." Haddon strode to the door and winked at her before making his way outside.

She stood in the middle of her foyer, waiting until she heard Haddon's carriage pull away before making her way up the stairs. Her ankle did hurt. Just a bit.

Felice rushed to Marissa, taking her arm.

"My lady, we were so worried for you."

"Just a small bump on the head and a twist of my ankle. My shoe is in worse shape." Marissa gestured to her foot. The shoe looked as if a large dog had been gnawing at it. "But I am in need of a bath, I think." Maybe a nice soak and a nap would help set Marissa to rights and keep this feeling of dread at bay. She already missed Haddon. How much worse would she feel when he actually *did* leave her?

Maybe he won't, her heart murmured. *He said he wouldn't. Ever.*

Marissa was sure Haddon meant the sentiment. *Now*. But she was realistic; after having three husbands, one had to be. He would eventually remarry to produce an heir. No matter the attachment between them.

Her foot faltered on the step.

This was why she'd avoided romantic entanglements for the better part of twenty years.

I'm not very good at them.

"My lady." Greenhouse came up the stairs. "This arrived for you a short time ago. My apologies. With all the—"

"Thank you." She interrupted him, taking the note, her annoyance with her butler clear. The writing was Tomkin's.

Her latest report on the state of the ruination of Pendleton as well as Nighter's efforts in regard to Miss Higgins.

Remorse filled her at the thought of Miss Higgins.

Shaking off Felice, she clutched the note in her hand.

"A bath, Felice. See to it at once. Greenhouse, tea please, in my room. Also, send one of the footmen to the flower market. I'm sure no one has been there yet today as nothing in this house smells *fresh*."

As her maid and butler rushed to do her bidding, Marissa flopped onto her bed, Tomkin's note falling to the coverlet.

She would read it in due time.

24

T rent regarded his eldest daughter from across the carriage, taking joy in her happiness. And Jordana was absolutely, *blissfully* happy.

It was amazing what could be accomplished with the promise of new books and a trip to Thrumbadge's. Jordana's fingers traced the outline of each book's spine, fluttering over the brown paper and twine in which the tomes were wrapped with obvious anticipation. She could hardly contain herself; Trent was sure she would run upstairs with her treasure as soon as they arrived home.

Which was what Trent had intended. He wasn't ready to answer his daughter's questions about Marissa. Books were a perfect distraction.

Jordana was far from stupid. He thought she'd probably ascertained how he felt about Marissa. If she hadn't, the whispers that had followed him about Thrumbadge's would have informed her.

The moment he had stepped inside the booksellers a low hum had started up, though Thrumbadge's was far from crowded. Trent ignored the curious looks sent in his direction. The conversations that ended as soon as he turned a corner. He imagined Lady Stanton was even now sitting in her drawing room, besieged by callers who all wanted to express their horror at yesterday's events with a pitying glance at Lady Christina.

Until now, Trent had forgotten how much he detested the way society gossiped.

Marissa hadn't been exaggerating about the scandal. He'd kept the papers from her as he drizzled honey over her toast, but she'd probably seen them by now.

The rescue of a certain older lady by a much younger gentleman set London on its collective ear yesterday. One wonders if our thrice-widowed Lady C.F. is doing more than performing chaperone duties for Lord H. Our sympathies to Lady C. S.

Yesterday, when he'd seen the packages topple from the carriage and she had fallen to the ground, Trent had thought of nothing but getting to Marissa. He'd shocked Lady Stanton speechless and blatantly ignored Lady Christina, shaking her fingers from his arm. His temper had flared out of control, stoked by his worry over her well-being, when another man had also rushed to her side.

I suppose no one thinks her merely Jordana's chaperone any longer.

Truthfully, Trent had been committed to Marissa since their night together at Brushbriar, she just hadn't realized it. He knew she still assumed their understanding to be little more than an affair, one which may well last years but would eventually end. She was still holding onto the absurd notion that he needed an heir, assuming Trent would one day toss her aside in favor of a younger woman. One whom he wouldn't *love*, all to procure an heir he didn't *need*.

At least she's made peace with our age difference.

Trent pressed a finger to his lips and looked out the window. *Not exactly*. Her absolute horror at the exact amount of years between them had been hard to mistake. She was so dismayed over those nine years, Marissa hadn't even asked how he knew her age.

But Lady Waterstone had been very forthcoming.

Christ, I hope the papers don't set her off.

She *had* agreed to an understanding with Trent.

He intended she agree to a great deal more.

"Papa?" Jordana said as the carriage rolled to a stop in front of his house. "You have a visitor."

Trent recognized the black carriage with matched bays. He didn't need to see the crest on the door. *What does Pendleton want? He's already taken every penny I have.*

"It would appear so."

If Pendleton thought to guilt Trent into giving him another cent, his distant relation would be sorely disappointed. He didn't want to see the man until Pendleton walked down the aisle with Miss Higgins. It would be worth attending the wedding to ensure he did so.

As he and Jordana left the carriage and climbed the steps, his butler flung open the door in greeting.

"I see we have a guest," Trent said, handing over his hat and gloves.

"Yes, my lord. I've placed *Lady* Pendleton in the drawing room and brought her tea." He took Trent's coat. "She's been here the better part of an hour."

Jordana was already skipping up the stairs to her room unconcerned with who was visiting when she had a stack of new books to pore over.

Lydia was here? Why in God's name would she visit me?

"Very good." Trent made his way to the drawing room, dreading having to make small talk with his guest. This couldn't be a social call. He opened the door and tried to form his lips into some semblance of a polite greeting.

Lydia had positioned herself in the middle of the sofa so she would be the first thing Trent saw as he opened the door. A pot of tea, steam still curling from the lid, sat before her on a low table, along with an assortment of biscuits which he knew Lydia wouldn't deign to touch.

Her upper lip curled slightly, pleased at the discomfort her visit caused him.

"Lady Pendleton." He bowed to her. "To what do I owe the pleasure of your visit?" he stated bluntly.

"Lydia, please." Her dark eyes were smug. "We're *family*, after all."

Trent flinched. He didn't care for the reminder of their relationship. Going directly to the sidebar for a glass of whisky, he caught a whiff of brandy as he passed Lydia. He poured out three fingers of whisky and took a sip before turning.

"It's a trifle early for spirits, don't you think, Trent?"

Nothing good could come of her visit, as evidenced by her use of his given name.

"Is it? The hour doesn't seem to have stopped you, Lydia." He nodded at the cup of tea sitting before her. Lydia had always enjoyed her brandy. Probably more so now with Pendleton's financial situation so precarious.

Yes, but I've taken care of that, haven't I?

Lydia's upper lip rippled into her patent sneer. He recognized it as the same one she used to turn on his wife, Anne, when they'd crossed paths in Castleton. There was a slight tremble in her gloved hand poised over the handle of the teacup she held. Lines of dissipation colored her once smooth cheeks.

Trent wished with all his heart he'd never accepted a farthing from Lydia's husband.

"Is there something I can help you with, Lydia?" The longer she stayed in his house, the more his irritation grew. "I'm sure you're not here merely to avail yourself of tea and pleasant conversation. I'd appreciate it if you'd get to the point."

"Your manners have undergone a transformation, Trent. But then, considering the company you've been keeping, it's no wonder. I understand you've taken up with Marissa Tremaine." Lydia's face grew ugly. "Isn't she a little too long in the tooth for you? My word, she's nearly the same age as I am."

Trent swished the whisky around in his mouth, letting the taste soak into his gums. *Bitch*. "Is there a point to this discussion? My personal life is truly none of your concern."

"May I be direct?" Her fingers fluttered delicately over the teacup.

"Please do. I'd like this visit to be as short as possible," Trent replied smoothly. Would Pendleton miss Lydia if Trent lost his temper and just snapped her neck? He thought not.

"My, how things have changed. You used to be much more *cordial*. But you wanted money then, which we gave you."

Trent drained the remainder of his glass. "That was a long time ago."

"Marissa Tremaine. I find it easier to call her by the name she was born with than the multitude of names she's carried since then. I'm almost embarrassed for you, Trent. You've made such a fool out of yourself over her in public. All of London is twittering about the scandal brewing. Pretending she was your daughter's chaperone." Lydia shook her head. "I fear Lord Stanton will never give you his daughter now, not when you've made such an ass out of yourself."

"Fortunate, because I never had any intention of offering for her." He strolled back to the sideboard. "I'd ask if you'd like some brandy, Lydia, but I can already smell that you've helped yourself. I hope you're enjoying it."

Lydia's ghastly white complexion paled further. Her left eye twitched. The teacup rattled against the saucer.

Trent really didn't want the added scandal of Lydia dropping dead in his drawing room. She didn't look well.

"I *would* thank you for finally repaying the great favor my husband bestowed on you so many years ago when you were so desperate—"

"As I recall, Lydia, you advised John *not* to help me. Anne relayed how you raged about your parlor insisting he might as well have set the money on fire than give it to me. I believe you told your husband I'd be impoverished in a fortnight."

"John was far too sympathetic when Anne came begging. He always had a soft spot for her, sickly, weak kitten that she was." She glared at Trent. "The point is you owe my family a debt."

"Which I've repaid. Pendleton has the funds to pay off his markers." Trent swallowed a mouthful of whisky.

"A truly honorable man wouldn't expect his money to be returned."

A slow burn of anger caused Trent's fingertips to flutter against his thigh. So that was why she was here; she expected Trent to forgive the loan to Pendleton, even though the sum he'd advanced him was far more than what John had given Trent years ago to save the quarry.

"An honorable man wouldn't have such a sum in dozens of markers all over London."

Lydia's cheeks turned a blotchy red. It wasn't a becoming look. Hard to believe she'd once been considered a great beauty.

"Did you know Marissa is trying to take the Blue John mine from us?"

The words startled Trent. "Why would she do such a thing?" he said, confused at Lydia's declaration. "Perhaps you've had too much brandy."

Lydia's lips pursed into a tiny hill, as if reluctant to speak, which he doubted, or she wouldn't be here. Brandy fumes filled the air as she opened her mouth.

"Her late husband is reason enough. Reggie was jealous of our luck in finding Blue John on our land. He came to my husband with some fairy tale," Lydia waved her hand around, "that the mine was actually on *his* property. Shortly before he disappeared, Reggie even approached John, insisting he'd found a survey, of all things." Lydia chuckled as if it were the most insane thought in the world. "It was *obviously* a forgery. A poor forgery, at that, which only fed Reggie's jealousy and delusions. Reggie was always a little addled. He and John argued. Then Reggie disappeared."

Trent's eyes narrowed on Lydia, watching her twitch about like a drunken squirrel as she sipped her tea. "I'm not as well-versed as I should be in the law in regard to such things, but if the survey is such an obvious forgery, how is it possible Marissa could challenge you for the mine? Surely a forgery would be thrown out of court. And Reggie has been dead for years. What would be the point of doing such a thing now?"

Lydia jerked again. "Marissa has her powerful family and the Duke of Dunbar's solicitors behind her. Forgery or not."

"Again, I have to ask, why in the world would she be

interested in doing such a thing?" Marissa's family was so wealthy, a Blue John mine would be no more than a pittance to them.

"She blames us for Reggie's death. The truth has become twisted in her mind. Madness does run in her family." Lydia was warming to her topic. "She's even gone so far as to accuse John of murder. Can you imagine my husband guilty of committing such a crime?"

Trent could. The previous Lord Pendleton had been a greedy man.

"Until Reggie's bones were discovered, we all thought he'd run off with some gypsy and left Marissa. I'm still not sure that isn't what happened."

Trent kept his face carefully composed, refusing to give away his thoughts. Marissa was the furthest thing from being mad. "I'm still not sure why—"

"She wishes to *punish* us." Lydia's voice raised an octave. "Though we aren't to blame for Reggie's death. I came here to warn you, Haddon. Marissa is capable of great treachery. She might even be dangerous to you and your daughters."

"I seriously doubt that." The very thought was ridiculous.

"Did you know she deliberately ruined Catherine's engagement to Mr. Kendicott?"

"Kendicott and Catherine?" The very idea boggled the mind. Kendicott was a crude, often foul-mouthed son of a pig farmer who'd inherited a fortune from his late wife. "Even if you are correct, how in the world would Marissa accomplish such a thing? You're assigning her a great amount of deviousness of which you've no proof."

"Poor Catherine was broken-hearted." Lydia sniffed.

Trent thought Catherine was more likely dismayed at losing Kendicott's fortune rather than the man himself.

"You don't know her at all."

"I still fail to see how I am involved in your quarrel with Marissa. If there is a survey or a dispute about the Blue John mine it isn't any of my affair and should be handled by the courts." Trent set down his glass. He wanted the coiled snake drinking brandy out of his mother's china teacup to depart the premises. He needed time to sort out Lydia's words. "I'll see you out."

"I fear you are *deeply* involved, dear boy." Lydia pierced him with a brutal look, not bothering to move from the sofa even though Trent was showing her the door. "As I told you, Marissa had no reservations about ruining my daughter's courtship with Mr. Kendicott, and she would have no compunction about doing the same to my son."

"Her son fell in love with Petra Grantly. I doubt she orchestrated—"

"I'm not talking about that little tart," Lydia spat out. "Morwick is welcome to her. Yesterday as I rode through the park, I spied Miss Higgins, my son's *new* betrothed, sitting on a bench and conversing with a handsome gentleman who, after making inquiries, I'm told is Captain Ross Nighter."

Trent turned at the mention of the name. Nighter was the gentleman Marissa had been conversing with at the theater. The one he'd accused her of having a tryst with. Lady Waterstone had assured Trent when he'd called on her that wasn't the case.

An odd choking sound came from Lydia. It took a moment for Trent to realize the horrible noise was laughter. "I see you know the name, Trent. Nighter is a flagrant womanizer. A dishonorable man, though he served his country. He is also engaged in a torrid affair with Lady

Waterstone, Marissa's closest friend. I am not comfortable with the coincidence."

"I think you are drawing conclusions where there ought to be none."

"Captain Nighter is a problem for us both, Trent. If you think for one moment Nighter striking up a friendship with Miss Higgins who is betrothed to my son is mere *coincidence*, then you are a bigger fool than I originally thought. I see Marissa's hand in this *accidental friendship* and unless you implore her to *stop this nonsense* immediately, we will all end up begging in the streets. She'll attempt to ruin the girl publicly, in front of as much of the *ton* as possible." Lydia put a finger to her lips. "Lady Ralston's ball, I think. Everyone in London is invited to hear Lord and Lady Ralston announce the engagement of their daughter."

Trent said nothing, wishing he could simply toss Lydia out the window. Perhaps start the day over and avoid her visit altogether.

"You must implore her to cease these attempts to punish me and my son when we've done *nothing* wrong." Lydia's eyes gleamed with righteous indignation.

Trent doubted that was completely true. She watched him far too closely, obviously greedy in her desire for him to believe every word she spoke. Trent's mind was already connecting the threads of her wild tale, picking out the pieces which held a ring of truth.

Marissa's absolute hatred of Pendleton on full display at Duckworth's.

"What makes you believe it is Marissa who is behind all your problems, Lydia?" But Trent's gut told him even before she answered. Hadn't he sensed a hint of her father, the 'Old Spider', dwelling inside Marissa?

A brittle laugh bubbled up her throat along with the fumes of the brandy in her tea. "Don't be foolish, *Trent*. Who do you think bought up all of my son's markers to begin with?"

SEVERAL DAYS AFTER LYDIA'S VISIT, TRENT WALKED INTO Marissa's private parlor where a small table had been set for an intimate dinner. A fire burned and popped in the hearth, casting a cozy glow over the entire room and the woman waiting for him.

His heart thumped hard twice in a row, as it always did at the sight of Marissa. At times, he felt like a youth in the throes of his first crush, except this was no youthful infatuation. Nor was his feeling for her simple lust. It had gone far, far beyond an uncomplicated physical relationship.

Trent was *madly* and *completely* in love with her.

His passion for Marissa flowed over him, imbuing his entire being. She made him *whole* even though Trent had never thought his soul lacking in any way. Looking down into her eyes, glowing like the rarest sapphires, he saw the hint of the hardness glittering in the depths of blue. He was not so foolish to think Marissa was not her father's daughter. Trent was attracted to the ruthless determination he sensed inside her as much as the generous and giving heart beating in her chest.

Trent just hadn't thought he'd witness her bloodthirsty nature firsthand.

Despite Lydia's depiction of Marissa as a deranged woman whose grief over her late husband had unhinged her, Trent knew the truth was far more complicated. He'd heard the stories of how Marissa mourned, wearing black for years, suffering the rumors that Reggie had run off with a gypsy or fled to America with his mistress. But there were two sides to every story. Sometimes three. He'd thought to write to Morwick, Marissa's son, for the truth. But getting a letter to Morwick would take far too long. So he went to the only other person in London who might be able to give him the truth.

Pendleton.

Christ, he wished he hadn't.

"Roasted chicken," Marissa announced with a smile. "A favorite of yours, I think."

A smile tugged at his lips. "Jordana told you, I suppose?" None of what Pendleton had confessed to Trent changed his feelings for Marissa. He was pleased she'd worn her hair loose tonight, streaming down her back, the streaks of silver shining in the firelight. Something else Marissa had done for him. No more visiting Mr. Coventry for bottles of hair dye.

It was a subtle, yet firm announcement of her commitment to him.

"Possibly," she said. Standing on her tiptoes, Marissa wrapped her arms around his neck and kissed him full on the mouth with enthusiasm. There was no overt seduction in her manner, only joy at his presence.

"You missed me, I think," he whispered against her cheek, hugging her tightly to his chest.

"I did." Her fingers trailed down his jaw. "Very much, though I saw you only two days ago." A light blush infused her cheeks at having to admit how much she longed for him, as he did for her.

Trent's chest squeezed painfully as he looked down into her lovely features, still struggling to accept the truth of Marissa.

Pendleton had given up everything when Trent had

appeared on his doorstep, with little reluctance. It was almost as if the burden was too much for him to carry any longer. Much of the viscount's usual smug behavior had been wiped from his features as he'd relayed his tale.

Trent had been so hoping the death of Marissa's late husband had been accidental.

The previous Lord Pendleton, John, had indeed murdered his best friend in cold blood. While John had pulled the trigger, it had been Lydia who'd planned everything, right down to the cave where John would hide the body. It had also been Lydia who'd had the foresight to spread the rumors Reggie had run off with another woman so the search for him would eventually end.

Lydia had done all of that while visiting Marissa daily to offer her comfort. Holding Marissa's hand while Marissa had wept on her shoulder.

Evil, spiteful bitch.

A fierce, almost violent wave of protectiveness for Marissa rolled over him.

My poor love.

Trent tucked a dark curl of Marissa's hair behind one ear. "I missed you as well. I adore roasted chicken. And you."

The survey *was* real, not a fake, the relief at finally telling the truth evident on Pendleton's face. Lydia, in one of her brandy-fueled stupors, had told her son everything, but by then, Pendleton was already on his way up the political ladder and he'd grown accustomed to the wealth the Blue John mine provided to his family. Still, the guilt had eaten away at him. Pendleton was stealing from his neighbor and had been for years. His parents were murderers.

Lydia insisted her son keep his mouth shut. Opening it would only result in the loss of his brilliant career.

"I did warn my mother, Haddon. Marissa surely knew the

truth after her husband's remains were discovered. Her entire family would be coming for ours. I told Mother I feared I would awake one night to find myself being strangled by Kelso or worse, the Duke of Dunbar. I have connections at the Ministry. I know what both of those gentlemen are capable of. The things they've done. Marissa wasn't going to allow such an insult to stand. She'd want revenge. Mother laughed and told me I was weak. Well, she isn't laughing now."

"Are you hungry?" Marissa took his hand.

"Yes." He bent down and pressed an open-mouthed kiss to the juncture of her neck and shoulder, inhaling the warm vanilla scent. "But I think my appetite is for something besides chicken. Elderly widow, perhaps."

It had been all Trent could do to stay a moment longer with Pendleton, listening to his fears and regret. Still, he had the presence of mind to make the same request of Trent that Lydia had: implore Marissa to cease in her attack. After all, if Pendleton didn't marry Miss Higgins, Trent would become impoverished as well. Didn't he care about his daughters? Did he wish to spend the rest of his life digging in the dirt just to put food on the table?

She arched against him, her fingers moving beneath his coat to slide it off his shoulders.

"Marissa bought up all my markers. The legal fees to defend our ownership of the mine are only adding to my debt. She owns me, Haddon. I fear she means to put me in debtor's prison. Or worse."

They undressed each other slowly while their dinner grew cold. Trent's fingers traced every curve and hollow, memorizing the feel and scent of her. The way she tasted beneath his tongue. Those beautiful creases at the corners of her eyes.

If she were threatened or hurt, what would Trent do?

More importantly, what would he do *now*?

He'd spent several sleepless nights trying to answer those questions.

She was laughing, pulling him in the direction of the sofa before falling against the worn cushions, her arms held out to him.

"Should I put out the fire? The lamp? Plunge us into total darkness?" he teased. "Perhaps cover you with the blanket and use only these strategically placed holes?" Trent held up the poorly knit blanket her niece had made her so long ago.

"No."

Marissa's shyness had dissipated, at least for now, secure in the promise he'd made to her. She was no longer hiding from him, at least not in this.

Trent's heart contracted sharply. Would she have ever told him of Pendleton?

Marissa giggled but her eyes on Trent were serious. "We have an understanding," she whispered.

"We do." He pulled her on top of him, entering her with exquisite care, groaning with pleasure at the way her body clasped his. The dark curtain of her hair fell around them until all he could see was Marissa as they moved together in unison. As they always had. The two halves of their hearts seeking to find each other and be whole.

Trent willed for this moment to last forever.

"I love you," he whispered, looking into her eyes as his release shattered through him. "I love you."

25

"I'm glad to see you've recovered completely. Unfortunately, your reputation hasn't." Arabella sauntered into Marissa's parlor.

Putting aside her book, Marissa discarded the spectacles on her nose, somewhat relieved for the interruption. She'd read the same page at least a half-dozen times, far too absorbed in Haddon to be able to concentrate on anything other than him.

He loves me.

Looking up at her niece she said, "So Adelia tells me, much to her delight." Haddon had fed her cold chicken as they shared whisky from a single glass after making love on this very sofa. He'd held her for hours afterward, stroking her hair as she dozed and watched the fire.

I love him.

"You seem unconcerned about the gossip swirling about you, Aunt," Arabella said primly. "It isn't like you to invite scandal."

She raised a brow. "You didn't exactly rush to my aid.

Didn't Haddon ask you to come and retrieve me from his home?"

Arabella shrugged. "I didn't wish to move you lest I cause you more injury."

"Haddon and I have reached an understanding." Marissa patted the space on the sofa next to her. "Come sit."

Arabella walked past the sofa, ignoring Marissa's invitation to roam about the parlor. "You are happy." Her niece's hand twitched against the folds of her skirts, a sure sign Arabella was distressed about something. "The flowers are lovely." Her niece waved her hand to the enormous vase of roses covering a small side table. "You adore roses. I'm sure they're from him."

"They are." Marissa frowned. "Arabella, sit. What is wrong?" If Lily, Arabella's infant daughter was ill, she wouldn't have left her daughter's side to visit Marissa but would have instead sent word.

Arabella stopped her perusal of the roses. "I told Greenhouse we would want tea. You may wish for something stronger. I've come with news."

Before Marissa could ask, a knock on the door announced a servant bearing a tray with tea and an assortment of small biscuits. Once the servant bowed and left, Arabella sat down across from Marissa and poured out two cups of the steaming liquid.

"Milk or sugar?"

Her niece knew very well she took neither. Arabella was stalling. "Out with it." Marissa brought the teacup to her lips. "I've not the patience this morning."

Arabella didn't touch her tea; instead, she clasped her hands together and forced them into a twisting mass on her lap. "Pendleton's debt has been paid."

Marissa sat back as the air left her lungs, shocked at her niece's words. "Impossible."

The sum was enormous. She'd only just called them due and Pendleton had no way to get a hold of such an amount in a short time. He hadn't rushed Miss Higgins to Gretna Green in order to access the girl's dowry. She had Tomkin watching the house and the Higgins's home, just in case.

"It's true, Aunt Maisy." Arabella's hand flipped in her lap though she tried to still it.

"How?" A choking sensation started in her throat. How had he managed to get his hands on such a large sum? Marissa had taken away Pendleton's only other source of income—the mine. Miss Higgins was the only way to save himself. "Brushbriar has been stripped bare. Tomkin's man in place at the estate has assured me of such. All of Lydia's precious Blue John has been sold along with most of her expensive furnishings. My solicitors persuaded the court to put all profits from the mine into a trust while ownership is being contested. He can't touch one single pound. I've destroyed his sister's chance of marrying Kendicott, which Catherine may thank me for later. Imagine." A laugh escaped her. "Catherine married to the son of a pig farmer."

"I can't," Arabella agreed.

"And Pendleton would *never* go to any of his friends in Parliament. Begging money from the likes of Enderly or Duckworth would only tarnish his pristine reputation and lead to questions on the Blue John mine and how it came to be in his family's possession, which would raise questions about Reggie's murder. So where did he get the funds?"

Arabella's hand flopped again, harder this time. She bit her lip.

"Did Higgins advance him the sum from his daughter's dowry? It would be highly unusual, but I suppose . . . I should have ruined his courtship to Miss Higgins long before now. Their betrothal—"

"It wasn't Higgins," Arabella said so quietly Marissa barely heard her.

Marissa set down her cup and saucer with a loud clatter, not caring if the delicate china shattered against the table. Standing abruptly, she stood and went to the sideboard, pouring out a generous glass of whisky. Taking a mouthful, she swallowed the amber liquid, allowing the burn to settle in her stomach. "Even if his debt has been paid, Simon is *still* broke. *Impoverished.* He won't be able to survive without the mine's income *unless* he weds Miss Higgins. Which I'm not about to let him do."

Marissa had suffered no small amount of guilt over Miss Higgins. Destroying the poor girl because her parents had the misfortune to betroth her to the wrong gentleman hardly seemed fair. She'd considered changing her mind. It wasn't too late. Nighter had done nothing but discreetly befriend the girl, though Miss Higgins was falling in love.

I've no choice but to ruin her now. It's the only way to stop the marriage to Simon.

"Well, who was it?" She turned to face her niece. "I'll destroy them too." Marissa was ready for this to be over. Her life had taken a wonderful, unexpected turn, and she wanted to spend as much of it as possible with Haddon.

Arabella stared down at her untouched tea as if studying the contents. "It was Haddon, Aunt Maisy."

Marissa went completely still, her vision narrowing and darkening at the corners. She swayed, fingers biting into the sideboard to keep herself steady. Surely, Arabella was mistaken. "I don't think I heard you correctly, Arabella. It sounded as if—"

"It was *Haddon.*" Arabella looked up from her tea to

Marissa. Her niece rarely expressed sympathy; seeing it now on her face caused a sob to catch in Marissa's throat. "I didn't want to be the one to tell you, but . . ." Her eyes fell to the beautiful display of roses. "Pendleton's solicitor has drawn up a loan repayment for the *exact* sum, payable to *Haddon* but not until *after* Pendleton weds Miss Higgins."

There was no point in asking if Arabella was certain. Marissa could see she was. Arabella had her own network of individuals for information, something that came in handy during instances such as this.

Marissa's chest felt as if she'd been punched or fallen from her horse. "He wouldn't." She shook her head.

"And yet, he has."

"It makes no sense, Arabella. I think Haddon admires Pendleton's work in Parliament, the reforms he seeks, but not enough to beggar himself. They are friends of a sort," Marissa said. Haddon was well off but paying Pendleton's debt would cripple him financially. "I can't imagine he'd risk so much. Not with his daughters to consider."

"Two large quarries in the Peak District were recently mortgaged to raise capital. I saw the report on Rowan's desk." She waved a hand. "He's always looking at properties where the owner has done something stupid and put said properties at risk." She shot Marissa an apologetic look. "Rowan finds stone and such to be a solid industry and one worth investing in."

"Yes. The stone for fine houses, roads, and walls must come from somewhere," she said, remembering the words Haddon had spoken to her at Lord Duckworth's. "Haddon's quarries."

Arabella nodded. "Is there any chance Pendleton suspected you of buying his markers?"

"Lydia," Marissa said quietly, thinking of the conversation she'd had with the woman at the Chenwith Society function. "I may have expressed my dismay that Catherine wouldn't be marrying Kendicott. I fear that is why Pendleton hurried to secure Miss Higgins. As discreet as you were in having the markers purchased, she must have surmised it was me, and frankly, I didn't care. I assumed there wasn't anyone else Pendleton could go to for such a sum."

"You were mistaken. As to why Haddon did such a thing, I'm not certain. But his doing so speaks of a much closer relationship than he led you to believe. He's never questioned you about Pendleton? Could he know or be helping him?"

"No, I—he was only here last night." Marissa went over their evening together, bit by bit. They'd made love. Laughed. Talked about their children. But Marissa *had* sensed a sadness in Haddon, putting it down to him missing his three younger daughters. He'd told her he loved her.

"He said nothing." A trickle of unease slid down Marissa's spine. Had Lydia or Pendleton voiced their suspicions to Haddon, and he related to them he'd seen Marissa with Nighter? "Perhaps Lydia begged Haddon's help, but if that were true, why wouldn't he confront me? Especially given that if Pendleton doesn't marry Miss Higgins, Haddon would be—"

"Ruined," Arabella finished. "Maybe we are wrong, and he doesn't know."

The more she considered it, Marissa was certain Haddon did know. "Lydia would never miss an opportunity to disparage me to Haddon, especially since our attachment to each other was made quite public."

Marissa thought she might well be ill. *Oh, Trent. You fool. What have you done?*

"Will you end this now, Aunt Maisy? I confess I have

never been able to reconcile myself to the damage a man like Nighter will do to Miss Higgins's reputation. I've gotten to know the girl quite well from her visits with Lady Higgins. She doesn't speak of Pendleton with affection if she even mentions him at all. Instead, she sips her tea with a starry look in her eyes. Nighter's influence, no doubt. Can you not—"

"No. Do not dare ask me such a thing." Haddon's betrayal was throbbing like a spoiled bit of pudding in her stomach.

"Aunt Maisy," Arabella started calmly. "I know Pendleton kept his parent's secrets and knowingly stole from Brendan, but putting him in the poorhouse is more than *enough* punishment for him, don't you think? You've taken back the mine, Aunt. Or at least you will. They will *never* profit from Reggie's death again. Even with the dowry Miss Higgins brings, the family will remain in genteel poverty. Lydia was forced to sell *all* of her precious Blue John. Catherine will not marry the wealthy son of a pig farmer. You've *won*, Aunt."

Marissa clutched the glass of whisky harder, frustrated her careful planning had been upended. And by *Haddon*. She forced herself to think of poor Reggie, left alone to bleed to death in a cave. Shot by his closest friend. All so Lydia could be wealthy. Stealing from Brendan all these years while treating her youngest child with contempt.

"Lydia and her pompous prig of a son need to pay for what they've done. I won't be happy until I see Pendleton so tainted by poverty, he will never be thought a brilliant star of Parliament. I want Lydia on the street, begging for money to buy her precious brandy." Marissa took a deep gulp of air ignoring the squeeze of pain. "It is my duty to Reggie."

Trent, how could you?

Arabella nodded slowly and stood. "And what, Aunt Maisy, is your duty to Haddon?"

Marissa turned away, not willing to meet Arabella's eyes.

"You love him. Any fool can see it."

She didn't bother to deny it. *Never* had she imagined this would be the way her affair with Haddon would end. And it *would*, because surely after Miss Higgins was ruined with Haddon not far behind, he wouldn't even be able to look at Marissa again.

He told me he loved me.

Perhaps he did. Or maybe those beautiful words were only an attempt to get her to stop the destruction of all things Pendleton. Guilt her into ceasing the revenge she was inflicting. Could he possibly be in league with Lydia?

Another dull, painful ache went through her. The very idea sickened her.

"I'll take my leave as I sense you need to be alone for a time." Arabella paused before the door. "How ironic, Aunt Maisy, that you now find yourself in the same situation both Nick and I have faced. Revenge or the desire of your heart." She said nothing for a moment though Marissa sensed her hovering in the doorway.

"I don't envy you, Aunt. It is a difficult choice."

26

Marissa pulled her cloak tighter as the carriage rolled up the drive to deposit her at Lady Ralston's doorstep. It was a crisp, cool night. There were even stars twinkling in the darkness if she peered out the windows of her sleek carriage.

"They will never profit from Reggie's death again. Even with the dowry Miss Higgins brings, the family will remain impoverished."

At least Lydia wouldn't benefit any longer. Marissa had received the news last night from Tomkin that Lady Pendleton, after drinking a substantial amount of brandy, had tripped in her son's drawing room while sitting in her chair before the fire. Lydia hadn't fallen into the roaring flames on the hearth, which would have been a fitting end. Witches *are* often burned to death.

Instead, she'd hit her head on a portion of the mantel which, ironically, was made of *Blue John*.

Marissa breathed on the glass of the window, seeing it fog immediately from the cold outside.

According to Tomkin's report, the physician summoned had declared Lady Pendleton had likely suffered a fit of some sort before hitting her head. Lydia couldn't speak. Or walk. She would be bedridden for the remainder of her life. Simon was, even now, making plans to have her removed to Brushbriar where Catherine could care for her.

Marissa felt a rush of pity for Simon's beautiful, wanton sister. Catherine would now be trapped playing nursemaid to the incapacitated Lydia in the hollowed-out husk of Brushbriar.

"You've won, Aunt."

Marissa should be gloating over Lydia's unfortunate but timely accident; instead, it was the loss of Haddon which was foremost in her thoughts. Nearly a fortnight had gone by since she'd seen him. Not since the evening before Arabella had visited with her unwelcome news.

He'd been telling me goodbye.

There was no question any longer that Haddon knew of Marissa's revenge against Pendleton. Shortly after her niece's disturbing visit, Marissa had fortified herself with another glass of whisky. There had to be a logical reason why Haddon would beggar himself for Pendleton, Marissa just didn't know what it was. Unable to wait a moment longer to confront her lover, she'd dashed off a note to Haddon, requesting he call upon her directly to discuss something of import.

There was no immediate reply. In fact, Marissa didn't receive a response until well after tea. Business, Haddon had written, would keep him from calling on her. He expressed his deepest apologies for the inconvenience but gave no indication of when he *would* call. Or if he meant to.

More unsettling, Jordana declined to visit Marissa for tea the following day, claiming she was feeling ill.

Marissa pressed her fingers into her stomach as Lady Ralston's mansion came into view. The sickening dread, the same darkness she'd felt since Haddon had left her after promising he *never* would, filled the carriage, threatening to strangle her.

Two more days had gone by with no word from Haddon, so Marissa had tried again, this time asking him to join her for dinner.

An immediate reply came from Haddon's secretary. Lord Haddon, the missive read, had left London for a few days on personal business. There was no indication of his return.

Her heart had lurched painfully at thinking of Haddon, and Marissa bent, her palm on her chest, trying to stop the anguish she felt. Only the knowledge that Haddon hadn't closed his house and fled back to his estate in Derbyshire gave her hope.

There was absolutely no doubt in her mind Haddon knew exactly what she'd done thus far and what she meant to do to Miss Higgins. Worse, he'd made no effort to ask her to stop. There was no ugly confrontation in which Marissa could explain herself. No Haddon at her door, pleading mercy for himself or Pendleton. She didn't see him in the park. Or at the theater. Nor at the few events she halfheartedly attended with Spencer and Elizabeth.

Haddon was very deliberately avoiding her. Jordana, as well.

Nighter informed Marissa, through Tomkin, that Miss Higgins was enamored of him. She'd even written him a love poem and assumed her affection was returned by the ex-soldier. He assured Tomkin that Miss Higgins would do whatever he asked of her.

Including agreeing to leave her future husband's side to indulge in an indiscretion with Nighter at Lady Ralston's ball tonight. The girl thought Nighter meant to marry her. The entire breadth of London society was in attendance this evening. Pendleton wouldn't dare wed Miss Higgins after such a public disgrace, not if he wanted to hold on to the tiniest shred of dignity. Sir Richard would certainly not expect him to.

The scandal would completely eclipse Haddon's rescue of Marissa on Bond Street.

Marissa pressed her palm harder against her chest as if attempting to stop a wound from bleeding.

The carriage crawled up Lady Ralston's congested drive at a painfully slow pace. Finally reaching the entrance, Marissa stepped out, automatically smoothing her deep sapphire skirts. She'd wanted Haddon to see her in this gown, a gorgeous confection she'd ordered from Madame Fontaine. He would appreciate the low, heart-shaped neckline skimming the top of her breasts and the way the gown bared her shoulders before tightening at the waist. Tiny bits of jet decorated the bodice and skirts, which sparkled in the light when she walked.

A perfect gown to witness a ruination in.

As Marissa entered the crush of bodies, the smell of pomade assailed her. Pasting a smile on her lips and telling her nose not to wrinkle at the scent, she dove into the crowd, spotting Adelia immediately. Her friend's red hair was brighter than usual tonight, more copper than dark auburn.

"Marissa," Adelia cooed as she came forward, ivory skirts swirling about her slippered feet.

"Adelia." Marissa leaned over, brushing her lips to her friend's cheek in greeting. "I can see your *nipples*." Two half-moons of pink were visible through the froth of lace lining Adelia's bodice. The neckline of her friend's gown made Marissa's seem positively *matronly* in comparison.

"Oh good, darling." Adelia didn't so much as blush. "That's rather the point. Nighter's interest has strayed a tiny bit so I wanted to do something to grab his attention."

"And that of half the gentlemen in the ballroom. I think you must be mistaken, Adelia. I saw his attentiveness to you at the theater. At any rate, your display of bosom this evening is surely enough to keep him in line. It is exceptional."

Adelia preened before leaning forward. "I caught him walking in the park with Miss Higgins. Miss *Clare* Higgins. The future Lady Pendleton."

"*Caught* him? Dear, I understood your relationship to be of a casual nature. You aren't following him about, are you? That would be very unbecoming for a lady such as yourself. Even so, I can't believe for a second Nighter is interested in Miss Higgins."

Adelia's lips pursed. "True. The girl is a *complete* milk-sop. I expected her engagement to Pendleton to be announced, perhaps even spoken about tonight, but his mother," she whispered to Marissa, "had an unfortunate accident. My understanding is Lady Pendleton is a complete sot."

"So I'm given to understand, poor dear." Marissa managed to sound sincere.

"At any rate, I confronted Nighter the moment I saw him enter the ballroom this evening, but the brute declined to give me an explanation for his attentions to Miss Higgins. He did promise we would *speak* later. Tonight."

"Adelia, do you have an assignation at Lady Ralston's ball?"

"I do." She gave a half-smile. "Oh, I know I'm being ridiculous. I've no future with Nighter. But I'm not ready for things to end yet." She shrugged and her nipples raised so dramatically Marissa had to restrain herself from pulling up her friend's bodice.

"He's a soldier and used to scouting hostile terrain," Adelia pointed out. "So he's found an appropriate meeting place," she said with a tilt of copper curls. "A quiet corner for him to *explain* himself to me in due time." She glanced up at the clock. "I think he'll appreciate the dress for our . . . *discussion*."

"I don't doubt it," Marissa assured her.

Nighter hadn't deviated from the plan in the least, which didn't surprise Marissa. He was a soldier, albeit a very tortured one.

Miss Higgins stood across the room with her parents, Sir Richard and Lady Higgins, eyes firmly fixed on the crowd filling the ballroom. Viscount Pendleton stood just to her left, surrounded by pandering supporters, as he often was. Simon ignored Miss Higgins, barely sparing her a glance while holding court, his handsome features flushed with his own self-importance. It wouldn't be difficult for Nighter to coax Miss Higgins down one of the darkened hallways to her ruination. The girl would probably sprint into Nighter's arms.

Once Miss Higgins was ensconced with Nighter, *someone* had to walk in on them. And that person needed to be a recognized member of the *ton*. One who would be outraged, draw attention, and immediately go to Higgins and his wife. Who better than Lady Waterstone, a woman already engaged in a sordid affair with Nighter?

Miss Higgins's betrothal to Viscount Pendleton would be dead within the hour.

"I've seen your Lord Haddon," Adelia said from beside her, drawing Marissa's attention from her perusal of Miss Higgins and Simon. "That atrocious girl's sister, *another* Miss

Higgins, is clinging to his arm. Lady Christina Sykes has been glaring at them nearly all evening. It's the only amusement I've had thus far tonight."

"Haddon is here?"

"Yes, *everyone* is. I was disappointed to see him arrive alone because I thought you two had come to some sort of understanding after his"—she paused dramatically —"*abduction* of you on Bond Street. Carrying you off in his arms." Adelia fanned herself. "My goodness, I wish Nighter would do something like that for me."

Haddon was here. Somewhere in this seething mass of pomade, talc, and an overuse of perfume, the man she loved was wandering about, waiting for her to ruin his life. What had made him come tonight?

"What in the world did you do to Haddon to warn him off?" Adelia's eyes grew concerned. "The way he looked at you—well, I found myself quite jealous, I admit. Especially after we got to know each other when he called on me."

Marissa immediately tensed. "Haddon called on you?"

"Now, don't be jealous, Marissa. We only had tea. I didn't give away all of your secrets. Only some of them. He just wished to know your favorite flowers and what type of whisky you liked best."

At least now I know how he discovered my age.

"I didn't try to seduce him if that's your fear," Adelia continued. "He's in love with you; it's so plain I can't believe you tried to pass him off as a dalliance."

He's not a dalliance.

"We had a disagreement. A rather terrible one." Her glance landed on a broad pair of shoulders marching through the crowd with military precision, a path which would take him directly behind Miss Higgins. Nighter's hair shone like a newly minted guinea as his chin dipped just slightly in Miss Higgins's direction.

Marissa's gaze shifted to Miss Higgins, who flushed immediately when Nighter glanced her way. Her parents didn't notice when she drifted off toward the path Nighter had taken. Simon didn't either.

She held her breath, the noise in the ballroom fading as she focused on the disappearing Nighter and Miss Higgins, her gaze drifting over the crowd.

Don't do this, my love, Reggie whispered. *You won't be able to live with yourself.*

"I do adore your gown, Marissa. Is that a design of Madame Fontaine's?"

Marissa barely heard Adelia. She'd caught sight of Haddon standing near the refreshment table. He'd been watching her, for how long, Marissa didn't know. He'd certainly seen Nighter. And Miss Higgins. Still, he did not take a step in Marissa's direction.

She inhaled sharply.

He's not going to stop me.

It wasn't until that moment Marissa realized how much she'd been *counting* on Haddon stopping her.

Adelia placed a hand on Marissa's arm. "Are you well, darling? You're so pale."

"I'm fine, Adelia. You might want to freshen up a bit before your assignation." Marissa finally tore her eyes from Haddon's. "Perhaps a little color for your lips."

Adelia winked. "I'll find you later, darling. And let you know if my discussion with Nighter was productive."

Marissa watched the fluttering ivory skirts of her friend disappear as Adelia departed, in search of a mirror, no doubt, for some last-minute preening.

Her heart thudded loudly, the sound echoing in her

ears. She smoothed her skirts, shocked to see her fingers trembling against the silk.

Oh God.

"I don't want to do this," she whispered under her breath. "Reggie, you're right."

27

M arissa hurried to the right side of the ballroom, toward the hall Nighter and Miss Higgins had disappeared down. She *had* to stop this. *Immediately.* Nodding politely, Marissa started through the choking crush, desperate to get to Nighter before Adelia found him with Miss Higgins. She glanced in the direction of her friend who had been stopped and was now caught up in a discussion with, of all people, Enderly. Adelia was trying to be polite but her skirt was puffed out at one side as she tapped her foot impatiently. Enderly could be terribly long-winded.

I don't have much time.

Marissa took off through the mass of silks and satins. How could she ever have thought this a good idea? Destroying Catherine's chances of marrying Kendicott was one thing; Simon's sister was a slut. But hurting a young girl and possibly destroying that girl's chances of *ever* making a decent match was quite another. Miss Higgins was innocent of Lydia's sins.

A portion of Marissa, the part which had been groomed

by her father, screamed she *must* take her vengeance. It was so *bloody* close. Miss Higgins was, regrettably, collateral damage.

I can't. I just can't.

Panicked now, worried she couldn't stop the series of events she'd set in motion, Marissa quickened her steps. She startled two elderly matrons who were deep in conversation, bumping into one with a mumbled apology. A fan snapped at her in disapproval.

Marissa ignored them. Lady Venworth was a sour old thing anyway.

Hurrying down the hall, she was dismayed to feel the toe of her slipper catch in her skirts.

"Good Lord. What *am* I paying Felice for?" Her maid was in dire need of a discussion on the maintenance of her employer's clothing.

Slowing her pace lest she trip, Marissa sped as quickly as she could down the hall, praying Enderly would bore Adelia for at least a few more minutes. Pausing every few steps before a closed door, Marissa crooked her ear, listening for sounds of ruination.

I have to stop them.

The music faded as her journey took her further away from the ballroom. A muted giggle met her ears.

A low, raspy murmur replied.

Finally.

She looked behind her, but the hallway was thankfully deserted. For now. Marissa took a deep breath, assured of the way forward. Flinging open the door with no warning, she stepped inside to a small, private, *well-lit* sitting room.

Nighter was *exceedingly* thorough.

Miss Higgins gasped in surprise, jumping back from Nighter as if she'd been seared by a flame. Marissa couldn't find fault with the girl's affection for Nighter, misplaced though it was. Few young ladies would be able to refuse the ex-soldier, fewer still would wish to. Even Marissa had to admit, he *was* rather spectacular looking.

But Nighter didn't possess magnificent bone structure nor have eyes like aged pewter. Both of which Marissa was fond of.

More than fond. Love.

Miss Higgins, thankfully, *blessedly*, was fully and completely clothed. Her breasts were in their proper place, tucked safely inside her very modest bodice. No curls had escaped her coiffure. Her lips weren't even swollen from a clandestine kiss.

I'm just in time.

Nighter's eyes widened slightly at the sight of Marissa before one side of his mouth tilted up in a half-smile. "Lady Cupps-Foster. Good evening."

"Lady Cupps-Foster," Miss Higgins repeated in a horrified whisper. Her mouth trembled at Marissa's pointed stare, uncurling her fingers from Nighter's lapels with reluctance. She looked up at Nighter. "Ross?"

Nighter said nothing, but his chin dipped in Marissa's direction, waiting for her to speak.

"I saw Lord Pendleton searching the ballroom for you, Miss Higgins," Marissa said in her most matronly tone.

Nighter's lips twitched at Marissa's lie. They both knew Simon didn't give a fig where Miss Higgins was. Only her dowry.

"Lord Pendleton," Marissa admonished. "Your betrothed, Miss Higgins. Have you forgotten?" She put her hands on her hips and peered at the girl as if scandalized at her behavior.

Miss Higgins lifted her chin. "I don't wish to marry Lord

Pendleton. I'm going to run off with Ross." She beamed adoringly at Nighter. "Not that it is any of your affair, Lady Cupps-Foster."

Brave little thing. Perhaps there was hope for Miss Higgins yet. Marissa made a mental note to search the girl out when all the dust had settled and befriend her.

Nighter looked at Marissa then back at Miss Higgins. "Clare, Lady Cupps-Foster is right. I should not have encouraged you to sneak off with me. Think of your reputation."

"I don't give a fig for my reputation," Miss Higgins declared in a passionate voice, her hand taking Nighter's.

"Yes, but *I* do," he said gallantly. Bringing her hand to his lips, he pressed a kiss to her knuckles. "Please." He leaned over and whispered something in her ear.

Miss Higgins nodded. "I understand." She looked up at Nighter with absolute adoration.

"We would beg your discretion," Nighter said. "For her sake."

He sounded so bloody sincere, except for the icy, empty look in his eyes. How did Miss Higgins not notice? Marissa had the urge to applaud his performance but now was not the time.

"I would speak to you in private, Captain Nighter." Marissa pointed at Miss Higgins. "Return to your parents immediately lest I drag you out of here and to them myself."

"Please do not." Miss Higgins let go of Nighter's fingers, appropriately terrified of Marissa. "I'll go. Your discretion, Lady Cupps-Foster, would be appreciated. I *assure* you nothing has occurred." She gave one final lingering glance at Nighter before gliding out the door.

Once the sound of the girl's footsteps had faded, Marissa went to the door and shut it. Not only did she not want

Nighter to be discovered with Miss Higgins, *she* didn't wish to be found with him either. Adelia would never speak to her again.

Not to mention Haddon.

"Your presence here," Nighter started in a dark, raspy tone, "instead of Adelia, leads me to the assumption you wish to . . . *end* this affair."

"I do," Marissa said. "Miss Higgins's reputation is to stay intact. Her marriage to Viscount Pendleton will go forward as planned."

A frosty smile met her words. "Clare detests him, you know. Says he's a cold fish with little warmth."

"Yet she found you more appealing?" Marissa hissed before she could think better of it.

The briefest bit of anger flashed across his beautiful features before the icy, aloof mask fell back into place. "I can be human when it is warranted."

"I'll make note of it should we meet in the future. Your friendship with Miss Higgins is at an end. Do not approach her again. A large sum of money has been deposited in the account you designated. Our brief association, Captain Nighter, is over."

The pale blue frost of his eyes lingered over Marissa while she spoke. "It doesn't have to be, my lady."

"Yet, I'm fairly certain." The coldly furious words came from the doorway. "It does."

28

Nighter and Marissa both turned to face the gentleman now standing at the entrance to the parlor.

Haddon.

"What are you doing here?" Marissa whispered as her eyes lovingly traced every inch of him.

"I thought you eschewed scandal, Marissa. Yet here you are inviting it again. And so soon after the last one." Haddon stalked into the room. "You've been dismissed," he said pointedly. "Good evening, Captain Nighter."

A smirk crossed Nighter's lips before he bowed to Marissa. "A pleasure, Lady Cupps-Foster, doing business with you. Should you ever have need of me again—"

"She won't," Haddon snarled. "Get out."

Nighter inclined his head and left the room, shutting the door behind him.

Haddon moved to stand before her. Two tiny spots of pink stood out against his magnificent cheekbones as he struggled to regain control of his emotions.

She'd never seen him in such a state. Despite the circumstances, Marissa found it rather thrilling.

"Have you concluded your business with Nighter?" Haddon stalked toward her.

"What business do you imagine I have with him?"

"We have a fucking understanding, Marissa," he growled.

"Language, my lord. Do we?" She moved to the other side of the room. Haddon was so bloody handsome, especially when he was angry. "An understanding would require you to call upon me, which you have refused to do."

The color on his cheekbones deepened. "Have I?"

"I haven't seen you in weeks, Haddon. Nor received word from you except some note from your secretary informing me you weren't in London."

"A fortnight. I had business. I cannot always be at your beck and call, Marissa," he snapped.

Beck and—"Let us *not* beat around the bush, Haddon. You have been avoiding me as if I were diseased." She hated the way her voice broke, the pain of being apart from him bleeding into her words. "And you know very well what I was discussing with Nighter. You know about Pendleton."

Why wouldn't he confront her? Rail at her?

"Marissa—"

"You'll be *ruined*, Trent. *By me.* Your quarries gone as well as your daughters' dowries. All to help Pendleton, a man not worth saving. *Why* aren't you trying to stop me?" Her voice had gone up an octave, mad at him for being so *bloody* obstinate. "I am doing something *so* terrible that even my son Kelso is appalled. But you? *Nothing.* Not a word."

Haddon turned away from her for a moment, his fingers stretching down his thighs. When he finally faced her, anguish clouded his features. "You want to know why I'm not trying to keep you from what you want. Is that what you're asking?" The broken words echoed in the room.

"Yes," she whispered, wanting nothing more than to pull Haddon into her arms. "I do."

He paced before her, his lean body so taut she could see the lines of his muscles stretching beneath the fabric of his coat. Stopping abruptly, he glared at her, agony etched across his face. "*You,* Marissa Tremaine," his voice resonated with pain, "are the *only* woman I have *ever* loved. I've wanted nothing in my life as much as you. *Ever.* If someone had hurt you, what lengths would *I* go to?"

"Trent—"

"There is nothing I would not do for you. *Nothing.*" His eyes shut for a moment, the dark lashes fanning across his cheeks, before opening them again. "If I must be *ruined* in order to prove the depth of my love for you, then I humbly agree."

Marissa stepped back, wrapping her arms around her waist.

No. He couldn't mean that.

"Miss Higgins will no doubt be better off *not* married to Pendleton. *Christ*, anyone would be. I could chase Nighter down right now. Warn Pendleton. *But I won't.*" His face was savage. Determined. "If, in ruining Pendleton, you finally find some measure of peace"—his voice thickened with emotion—"so that *we* may be together and be happy, then do it. *Ruin us both.*"

Marissa stared at him, mouth open, unable to speak. Then she promptly burst into tears, which turned into horrible gut-wrenching sobs.

"*Jesus.* Marissa, come here." His arms were around her in an instant, rocking her back and forth, whispering to her it was all right, comforting her as if she were a child. He didn't mind being impoverished, he assured her. *He loved her*. All would be well.

My God, how could I ever have doubted him?

She sobbed harder, clinging to him and shoving her nose into his coat. Her head flopped to his chest, her tears dampening the fabric of his evening clothes.

Haddon's arms didn't loosen as he gently moved her to the loveseat in the center of the room.

Marissa wept for what seemed like hours. She cried for Reggie and the life he hadn't gotten to live. For the years she'd been alone. And Haddon. The man who loved her so unconditionally he was willing to lose *everything* to have her. She didn't deserve Haddon or his love, but Marissa would take it and him, for as long as he would stay with her.

She squeezed him tight, feeling whole for the first time in years. Maybe in forever.

Finally, with her eyes swollen, hiccuping as her sobs faded, Haddon produced a handkerchief which Marissa gratefully accepted.

"I love you," she said to the heart beating beneath her cheek.

"I know." His fingers slid through her hair, destroying her coiffure.

The last thing Marissa cared about at the moment was her hair. "I didn't," she said in a quiet voice. "Why do you smell like spices? Ginger?"

"Didn't what, my love?" He pushed a loose tendril from her forehead, pressing a kiss to the spot. "And you adore ginger cookies. I have it on good authority."

He'd found that out from Adelia too. "Ruin Miss Higgins. I wasn't giving Nighter instructions for the evening, I was telling him to *stop*."

"I see." Haddon's lips brushed her temple again.

"I know you think I'm terribly . . . bloodthirsty."

He said nothing for a moment, only stroked her hair. "Yes. You would have made a good pirate or highwayman."

Another sob left her. "But—"

"Pendleton told me what his parents did to Reggie. What they stole from Morwick. I wanted to kill him myself."

"He confessed?" At Haddon's nod, she said, "Reggie was a kind and thoughtful man. He would never have approved of my methods. Nor would he have sought revenge. I could never have lived with myself had I harmed Miss Higgins." She plucked at his coat. "And I *could not* hurt you. Doing so would have destroyed me. I love you." Marissa looked up at Haddon, tears still clouding her eyes as she thought of the dream of Reggie leaving Haddon on her pillow. "Even if you are only a dalliance."

Amusement rumbled low in his chest. "Are you done with revenge then, my love?"

She was. Her father may not have approved of leaving Pendleton still standing, but Marissa was not the 'Old Spider'. Only his daughter.

"Yes. And *you* won't be impoverished, Haddon." Marissa curled into him, as close as the mountain of silk of her gown would allow. Safe and comforted by the steady beat of his heart. This was where she always wished to be. With Haddon.

A deep, resigned sigh moved his chest. "It's just as well I won't be poor because I've finally decided to take your suggestion."

Marissa turned her head to look up at him. "You have?"

"Yes. I've decided to take a wife."

29

"Now tell me *why* you helped Pendleton. You don't even like him. Not really."

"No. I don't."

She and Haddon lay in Marissa's bed, Haddon's long legs entwined with hers and the sheets tangled around their bodies.

After becoming a watering pot for the better part of an hour, they'd finally been interrupted by Adelia, who immediately rolled her eyes at them and left, muttering she had the wrong room. There was no telling how many assignations Adelia had interrupted during Lady Ralston's ball in her pursuit of Nighter.

After concluding they couldn't very well spend the night in an obscure parlor of Lady Ralston's, primarily because there was no whisky to be had, Haddon had taken her hand and led her through the gardens and up the street to her carriage. Cradling her close to his chest, he had stroked her head, his fingers sifting through her hair. "I won't leave you, Marissa."

Marissa had clung to him, blinking back tears.

Greenhouse, lips thinning at their arrival, had given a small sound of disapproval as Marissa took Haddon's hand and led him up the stairs, but nonetheless recovered himself. "Shall I fetch your son's robe for Lord Haddon?"

"No," Haddon had answered before she could. "I don't think I'll need it tonight. Perhaps you can bring the robe to me in the morning?"

The butler had turned an alarming shade of purple. It had been very gratifying.

"I would like an answer first to my earlier inquiry." Haddon's dark hair fanned over her breasts as his tongue tasted the tip of her nipple.

"Mmm." Her back arched, bringing her breast closer to his mouth. "I didn't realize you'd asked me a question. Only stated what you planned to do, Haddon. Which is very like you. Why did you help Pendleton?"

"Correct on both counts. In regard to Pendleton and myself, we're related by marriage. *Distantly*. Through my late wife."

Marissa sat up abruptly, shocked at his words, the sheet falling from her breasts before she grabbed at the linen.

Haddon growled in frustration. "My mouth has been on every inch of you." His gaze fell to her breasts. "Especially your magnificent bosom. I thought we had dispensed with your need to constantly cover yourself."

"How is that possible?"

"Because I'm an admirer of your breasts. I started on one side and—"

"No." She swatted at him but dropped the sheet, drawing his gaze. "I mean, how can you *possibly* be related to Pendleton?"

"Well, I'm not, exactly. My wife was the late Lord Pendle-

ton's great-niece. They weren't close. Lydia barely acknowledged the connection when Anne was alive."

Marissa mulled over the information in her mind. "But
when I bankrupted her son, she did."

Haddon traced the outline of her ribs, sending flutters
back down between her legs. "It was Lydia who sent
Pendleton to me, demanding my help and reminding me of
the favor I owed his father."

"A favor? And I'm not surprised at all. Lydia never
forgets any small kindness she might have bestowed. She
enjoys having we lesser mortals in her debt."

"The year I turned twenty-four there was a terrible accident at the quarry. I won't go into details but suffice it to say
without a large infusion of funds, I couldn't save the quarry
or the village, which depended on the quarry's employment,
let alone my small family. My sister was about to be married.
My younger brother had just gone back to Harrow—"

"Wait. You have a brother? You've never mentioned
him."

Haddon's brows drew together, and his fingers stopped
their movement across her skin. "I'm certain I have. Perhaps
you weren't listening? Your mind does wander."

Marissa tugged at his hair. "Haddon," she warned.

"His name is Randall." His fingers were gliding back and
forth over her thigh. "His eldest son, also Randall, is my
heir."

Haddon already had an heir. No wonder he was so
nonchalant about the need to procure one. "You could have
told me about him sooner."

His fingers dipped lower between her thighs, chuckling
softly when she gasped. "I did. You weren't listening. Money
was tight. I had a sickly wife. One child, another on the way.

A hundred or so villagers depending on me as well as my brother and sister."

Marissa was losing her focus. Haddon's fingers were incredibly wicked, just like the rest of him. His thumb did the most amazing things. "That murdering bastard John," her breath hitched as he found a sensitive spot, "gave you the money, didn't he?"

"As a gift to Anne. If I'd known he'd gotten rich by murder I never would have taken his money. I would have found another way."

Very sweet of Haddon to say so, though impractical.

His thumb pressed against her. "*Just return the favor one day,* John said. When Pendleton came begging and reminding me of my honor, I couldn't refuse though I dearly wished to."

Haddon would never have refused, something Lydia had counted on. He *was* far too honorable.

"Now I must have your answer." He pressed a kiss to her stomach.

"I feel compelled to remind you again, Lord Haddon, that you did *not* ask me a question. Only told me what you've decided." She toyed with the swirls of hair on his chest thinking how determined Haddon always was. Marissa loved that about him. "I can't believe you're serious, Trent."

His eyes softened at the sound of his given name. "I've never been more serious about anything in my life. It is a lot to ask—"

"I must point out again you haven't actually asked me anything."

He ignored her. "I *know* I come with four bits of baggage—"

"You do. All in dire need of mothering, guidance, and encouragement. Fortunately, I excel at all three."

A smile hovered at his lips. "You do. Jordana already loves you, and she is the *second* most difficult daughter. And do not dare bring up your age."

"No. The *ton* will do so enough for both of us. And who is the most difficult?" Marissa couldn't imagine another girl more stubborn than Jordana, save Arabella.

"Poppy." His lips brushed hers.

"Trent, are you sure?" The last word dissolved into a moan as his mouth moved lower. "I am . . . terribly unlucky in marital affairs, as you know. What if I'm cursed? If anything were to happen to you—"

"Don't be ridiculous. Nothing will happen. Don't you love me?"

"So much." Marissa looked down, her eyes running over his beloved face. "I just never thought I would find love again." Her voice broke. "So late in life."

Taking her hand, he pressed a kiss to her wrist. "Not so late."

The challenge of four daughters would be *daunting*, but Marissa was no stranger to adversity when dealing with young girls. Her work with Arabella and Jordana spoke for itself.

Her finger traced the line of his cheek. "Are you descended from Vikings, Haddon?"

"Possibly. Stop stalling." He rolled on top of her. "I need to hear you say it."

"I love you, Trent." Her fingers trailed down his jaw. "Desperately. I agree."

"Then it is settled." He kissed the tip of her nose. "Lady Haddon."

30

M arissa snuggled deeper beneath the covers, seeking out Haddon's warmth. He'd been sleeping at her house most nights since sending Jordana to his sister. Marissa and Haddon meant to fetch all the girls back to London in time for the holidays. After Marissa became acquainted with Martie, Poppy, and Delphine, Haddon meant to tell them he and Marissa were getting married.

Another group of ducklings to mother.

Adelia thought Marissa had lost her mind.

"Why must you wed him?" Adelia had said in a horrified voice. *"I grant you, Haddon is delicious. But you could just have an understanding. Some couples do so for years and never marry."*

Marissa tried to explain to Adelia that it was *important* to Haddon he be able to call her his wife. And truthfully, she wanted to be Lady Haddon. Her friend's dramatics over Marissa's future were probably due more to the fact that Nighter had left London *and* Adelia after Lady Ralston's ball.

Spencer and Brendan didn't know yet that Marissa and

Haddon planned to marry. Nor did her nephew, Nick. Only Arabella had been apprised of her plans with Haddon. And her niece had been sworn to secrecy. She hoped they would all be happy for her.

A loud snore came from the man next to her. He lay atop the sheets, completely naked. As he often did. Marissa poked him with a finger, and Haddon turned over and ceased making noise. She settled back against him with a contented sigh.

Miss Higgins and Simon had been married quietly a week ago. Haddon's money would be repaid in time, but he need not ever worry over losing the quarries. Rowan had seen to the loan repayment on Marissa's behalf. She didn't trust Pendleton to honor the terms of the agreement he'd made with Haddon despite the official documents Pendleton's solicitor had drawn up.

She hadn't yet informed Haddon. He was bound to be both relieved, but also annoyed. The news could wait.

Lydia was back at Brushbriar, her once fine home now stripped of the precious Blue John she'd loved. She'd lost everything. Now that she was no longer busy ruining Simon, Marissa had instructed her solicitors to settle the case. The court declared the survey to be valid and the mine the property of the Earl of Morwick. Simon had chosen not to contest the decision further. Very wise on his part.

A door slammed below, followed by the murmur of voices.

Greenhouse sounded confused and then deferential. But he often did.

Good Lord. Who could be calling on her at this hour? Well, Greenhouse could just explain she wasn't receiving callers so early.

"Mother! We're here!" A curse sounded. "I don't care if

she's *indisposed*." The deep baritone growled in irritation at Greenhouse. "I'm her *son*. She'll want to see me." A heavy tread thumped up the stairs.

Marissa sat straight up in bed, eyes popping open. He was *at least* a week early and bounding up the stairs like an overgrown toddler. A tiny squeeze of her heart followed. She'd missed Brendan so much.

Haddon rolled over with a grunt.

Oh dear.

"Haddon." Marissa placed a hand on his shoulder. "*Trent*. Wake up this instant." When he didn't move, she shook him harder.

He turned his head, and one eye opened a slit. "For the love of God, Marissa, let me sleep. You're insatiable for an elderly widow. I'm exhausted." The eye shut again.

The heavy footfalls stomped down the hall in the direction of her room. Had she locked the door? She couldn't remember. Her servants would never enter her rooms without permission.

Brendan had no such boundary.

Oh, this is very bad. I meant to break the news to him gently.

"Trent," she whispered again in a panicked voice, throwing the coverlet over his naked body. "You must get up."

He turned and tossed the heavy damask back off. "I know you're always cold, Marissa. But I'm *not*." His armed snaked out, fingers grabbing at her hip. "Come here. I'll warm you."

"No." She slapped his hand away. The coverlet was flung over his naked body again. "Brendan is *here*. Now. Climbing up the stairs. You must get up and . . . put a robe on or something."

"I don't have a robe. And I will stop you now," both eyes

opened to regard her, "from suggesting I hide under the bed. I suppose I could conceal myself behind those draperies, but I don't have the inclination to do so. Besides, haven't we already—"

The door swung open. "Mother! Where did you find such a stuffy butler? Says you're still abed. Are you ill? You never—" A vile curse erupted from Brendan's lips as he caught sight of Haddon, who thankfully, had the lower part of his body covered.

"You've got to be joking."

Marissa gave Brendan a weak smile. "Hello, dearest." She looked to the lovely blonde standing behind her son. "Petra, I'm so happy to see you."

Haddon smiled. At least he didn't kick off the blanket. "Morning, Morwick."

I HOPE YOU ENJOYED **WICKED AGAIN.** I THINK EVERYONE deserves a happy ending especially a thrice-married widow like Marissa. If you liked the book I hope you'll consider leaving a review.

Join my readers group on Facebook!

https://www.facebook.com/groups/historicallyhotkathleenayers

Or subscribe to my newsletter at www.kathleenayers.com and be the first to learn about new releases, cover reveals and more.

https://www.facebook.com/kayersauthor/

https://www.bookbub.com/authors/kathleen-ayers

https://www.instagram.com/kayersauthor/

NOTES FROM THE AUTHOR

I've taken some artistic liberties (as my readers in the U.K. will probably notice).

Blue John, the source of the Pendleton wealth is a semi-precious mineral and a form of fluorite discovered by the Romans. In Britain, it can be found in one of only two places; Blue John Cavern and Treak Cliff Cavern, both outside of Castleton in Derbyshire.

The Blue John mine which is the cause of Reggie's death is purely fictional.

ALSO BY KATHLEEN AYERS

The Wickeds

Wicked's Scandal

Devil of a Duke

My Wicked Earl

Wickedly Yours

Tall Dark & Wicked

Still Wicked

The Beautiful Barringtons

The Study of a Rake (Prequel - coming soon)

The Theory of Earls

.

Printed in Great Britain
by Amazon